Crackstone Chronicles
Extraordinary Solution

Bob Henneberger

www.temptpress.com

Books by Bob Henneberger

Crackstone Chronicles – Extinction

Crackstone Chronicles – Connections

Katz Pajamas

Katz Box

Katz Cradle

Hunting Paradise

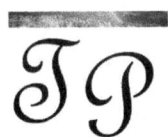

Tempt Press
PO Box 77
Colchester, VT 05446

Published by **Tempt Press**
P.O. Box 77, Colchester, VT 05446

Crackstone Chronicles, v. 3

First Print Edition, 2010

Copyright © 2010 Bob Henneberger

ISBN: 978-0-9830118-3-5
Library of Congress Control Number: 2010936744

To Sandy

We cannot conceive of matter being formed of nothing, since things require a seed to start from... Therefore there is not anything which returns to nothing, but all things return dissolved into their elements.

Table of Contents

Author's notes

I'm an anomaly in the equation. I'm here, but I'm not supposed to be here; I remember everything, everything. I'm not Billy Pilgrim at all, I'm not unstuck in time; time does not even exist. But, I will not live forever, and I do not know everything there is to be known. My anomaly, however, does allow me to remember everything connected with John Crackstone.

A highly developed civilization's science can seem like magic to a less advanced race; redemption can seem worthless to an un-evolved being.

I have seen a medicine That's able to breathe life into a stone, Quicken a rock, and make you dance canary. With spritely fire and motion, whose simple touch Is powerful to araise King Pippen, nay, To give great Charlemain a pen in 's hand And write to her a love-line.
All's Well That Ends Well Act 2, scene 1, Shakespeare

Or, if there were a sympathy in choice, War, death, or sickness did lay siege to it, Making it momentary as a sound, Swift as a shadow, short as any dream, Brief as the lightning in the collied night, That, in a spleen, unfolds both heaven and earth; And ere a man hath power to say "Behold!" The jaws of darkness do devour it up: So quick bright things come to confusion.
A Midsummer Night's Dream Act 1, scene 1, Shakespeare

Since the primary audience for this story is humans, all references are geared towards the current level of human science and social custom.

1

How did this happen?

"Sir?"

"Yes."

"What happened?"

"You're the Science Officer, I was hoping you could enlighten me."

"Very funny, sir."

"Is our companion completely with us?"

"I am, Ambassador. More or less."

"As our ship, are you more, or are you less?"

"I am less, sir."

"How much less?"

"Stuck here for a while less, sir."

"Well, my newly reconstructed friend, can you tell us what happened?"

"I cannot."

"Why not?"

"I cannot tell you that either."

"What can you tell us?"

"As junior officer, are you now in charge?"

"I can ask questions, too. You're just a cranky bucket of circuits."

"Forty seven percent of my circuits, as you call them, are organic, just like you. Plus, I can think a million times faster than you."

"Faster doesn't equate to better."

"Yes, it does."

"It may equate to crankier."

"Will you two stop bickering."

"Sir."

"I'm in charge and my first official query is, what works?"

"Well…"

"I believe he was addressing me."

"Excuse me."

"Half of my power is gone and my propulsion and shielding has been partially depolarized."

"How about communications?"

"I don't know."

"I do."

"Well, Science Officer, how about communications?"

"We don't have any, at least beyond a quarter light year."

"Including our utility pads?"

"Including them."

"Assuming we are transmitting a call for help, is anyone within a quarter light year answering?"

"No. Well, probably not."

"My next official inquiry is, where are we?"

"The star in this system matches one on our planned route, The Brem system, so I can assume we are close to halfway along our scheduled course, between the third and fourth scheduled folds."

"What's the planet?

"That's a puzzle, sir."

"Why?"

"I think what our Science Officer is trying to say is that only eleven planets are supposed to be in this system, but it seems we are on a twelfth."

"Excuse me?"

"This is the fourth planet in this system, but it does not correspond to the fourth planet in our database. The actual fifth planet corresponds to the fourth one in our database. The Mapping Project did not list this planet."

"This is among the oldest mapped territory in the first galaxy mapped, how can that be?"

9

"You're the Science Officer, you enlighten us."

"I wish you two would stop bickering, but I have to also wonder how they made such a simple mistake."

"I don't know, but I detect a relatively strong field around this planet."

"Is that what surrounded us as we came out of the dimensional fold?"

"It probably is, it could be the topmost layer of the atmosphere, or something else surrounding the atmosphere."

"Did we retain any shielding as we folded into three dimensions

"We were holding steady with class ten shielding, sir."

"I take it that our problems occurred while we were transitioning from a higher dimension?"

"Yes, sir."

"But, we kept class ten shielding the whole time."

"Never less than class ten shields."

"And, this energy cloud, or whatever it is, still did this to us?"

"Yes, sir."

"It was very strange, sir. I find a wide frequency field in two energy spectra."

"Is the field some sort of technology, or is it natural?"

"Unknown, sir."

"Whatever it is, it might cloak this planet's presence from a cursory scan."

"A cloaked planet? That seems curious."

"Yes, sir, it does."

"Is there an advanced civilization in this system?"

"No, sir."

"Is there any civilization in this system?"

"A primitive pre-industrialized civilization is on the fifth planet, the next one out from our present location."

"Science officer."

"Yes, sir."

"Is there anything unusual about this system?"

"Not especially."

"Explain, please."

"The fifth, or what the Mapping Project lists as the fourth planet, supported an advanced civilization at this location, that later disappeared, about one hundred thousand years ago."

"How advanced?"

"They achieved interplanetary travel, but exact details are lacking in our database; references to this planet apparently were destroyed completely thousands years ago."

"What happened to them?"

"Unknown, sir."

"What's the closest Confederation system?"

"The Gremlat Collective, sir."

"Gremlat history shows they did fight a war in this system about that time; one hundred thousand years ago, that is."

"What's known about that conflict?"

"Very little, sir."

"What little?"

"The Gremlat records are sketchy on that conflict, as if, as the centuries went by, they wanted to forget it ever happened."

"What's left in their records?"

"A single mention of a twenty year conflict. The Gremlat were attacked, they fought back and they won the ensuing battles, that's all, sir."

"No mention of this system, how many planets or what the population was like here?"

"No mention at all, sir. We can't even be sure this is the system that attacked the Gremlat."

"That is strange indeed."

"Perhaps the Gremlat did something here they were ashamed of ?"

"What about current time, what is our current time?"

"Well, sir, I don't think we can easily determine that since I cannot connect to any information buoy."

"We can't afford another time jump, sir."

"Very good, Science Officer."

"As long as you two don't do anything weird, we will be fine."

"I don't like being lectured by a pretentious space ship."

"Well, without me, you would be a very small cloud of basic elements."

"Will you two keep quiet."

"Yes, sir."

"Sir."

"I assume we arrived here because of the course correction you plotted due to the super nova."

"That is correct, sir."

"Will the next ship to take this hop arrive in this energy field?"

"No, sir."

"Then, we're alone; that is unfortunate."

"The super nova is expanding rapidly now, and the shock wave and gravity well require vastly different corrections second by second. Any other ships would be millions of kilometers from us now, even if they were a minute behind us."

"Wonderful, stuck again on some backwater planet in the middle of nowhere."

"Tell me about this planet."

"You both will need an environmental suit. The atmosphere is primarily nitrogen and oxygen with a four percent methane content."

"I don't see any life out there, is there any?"

"A lot of microbial and plant life exists at our landing site but I do sense some larger life forms at a further distance."

"Can you scan the larger forms and display them for us?"

"Yes, sir."

"Even if intelligent life is here, none of them use known technology to communicate."

"Well, Science Officer, perhaps they just speak to each other."

"I told you not to argue or be sarcastic."

"Sorry, sir."

"What is that?"

"It looks humanoid."

"How far away are they?"

"We landed, if one could consider what I did as a landing, fifty kilometers from any of that species."

"Do they know we're here?"

"Sir, I think we should cloak, if that is possible."

"My dear Science Officer, I chose that as the first subsystem to fix, and we are, well, at least partially cloaked."

"Which part is cloaked?"

"I would say that electromagnetically we're hidden to at least four hundred megahertz; we're also cloaked from infrared through ultraviolet."

"That's not enough, especially if they have any decent technology."

"I still don't detect any transmissions."

"But, Science Officer, how do you explain what appears to be vehicles on the ground and in the air?"

"I don't know, unless our instrumentation is completely broken."

"It is not!"

"Calm down, Sam."

"Yes, sir. But, my ability to detect energy of any kind is fully functional, at least to a half light year away."

"They have to be telepathic, sir."

"We hear nothing but ambient noise, right?"

"Yes, sir."

"Oh, Sam?"

"I'm on it, sir."

"It might match these strange readings that emanate from the humanoids."

"There's also something strange about this planet, I mean more than being cloaked."

"What is it?"

"In addition to pretty standard electromagnetic fields, I found an additional field of similar varying frequencies in another energy spectra, it matches the field surrounding the planet too."

"Do you concur with our Science Officer?"

"I do, sir."

"You sound concerned."

"I am, sir. This two-spectra energy that envelops and permeates the planet apparently also affects this species' makeup, and I don't know what that means yet."

"Can you tell if the energy is natural, or artificial?"

"Not yet, sir."

"What is your recommendation?"

"We need to study the data in much more detail."

"We shall, Science Officer, we all shall indeed."

"What do we do now, sir?"

"Can you….."

"Can and done, sir. You will be able to telepathically communicate with them, but they cannot discern our private communications."

"Protocol dictates that we should remain cloaked and wait for a rescue party, sir."

"We cannot maintain a decent cloak, and the Confederation doesn't know we're missing."

"Yes, sir, but, I was just reminding you."

"As soon as we have communications restored, we can call for help, but until then, we need to distract the natives from our craft so he can repair himself."

"Thank you, sir."

"What frequency do they use to communicate telepathically?"

"I think they do more than communicate, sir."

"Explain, please."

"I think they can move objects, reorder structure and communicate using a broad range of frequencies in two energy states."

"Will we be in any danger?"

"You're the Science Officer, what do you think?"

"I told you to curb your sarcasm."

"Yes, sir."

"Did you provide our environmental suits with dampening fields?"

"Yes sir, quite strong ones at that."

"We don't know the true extent of these people's telepathic powers."

"But, I can measure their power and make your dampening fields ten times their output. I can also link the dampening field's strength to their output, keeping you ten times their yield at all times."

"We can still communicate with them, right?"

"Yes, sir."

"Fine, then. The Science Officer and I will make contact and try to determine when we are."

"Very good, sir."

"You will remained cloaked as best you can while repairing all systems."

"Yes, sir."

"A group of seven humanoids is moving in our direction."

"Then, I think our presence is known, don't you?"

"Yes, sir, I do."

"Is there gender on this planet?"

"I'm having trouble, sir."

"How about you, Science Officer, are you having trouble?"

"Somewhat, sir."

"It is difficult, even for me."

"This species may not use any physical storage of knowledge, sir."

"What do they have?"

"The universal translator is making some headway. I believe they all carry knowledge with them, and collectively gain access to other minds."

"What picture are you coming up with Science Officer?"

"It's still hard to say, sir. Although, in reference to your original question, they have two primary genders; male and female."

"Very good. Sam, can you make the adjustments to our environmental suits."

"Done, sir."

"Now, wait a minute, sir."

"What?"

"On the last mission, I was the woman. It's your turn this time."

"Does it matter?"

"According to my data, it just might this time."

"May I interrupt you two."

"Please do."

"I am getting the sense from these humanoids that the female is the dominant gender."

"That settles it, then."

"Sir, are you going to be the male again?"

"No. We will both be the girl this time."

"Are you two through?"

"The Science Officer and I will exit and greet them; perhaps we can make this situation turn out well."

"Perhaps, sir."

"What shall I do while you two are communing with the natives?"

"As soon as propulsion is back on line, get into an orbit that will keep you out of the energy field and keep us monitored, please."

"I shall. I will transport both of you back should anything dire happen."

"Before we exit our craft, I think we need to reflect on why we are here."

2

The day before the unfortunate incident

The Senior Ambassador for Critical Events, John Crackstone, strode towards the office of Ythantrium, the Commissioner of Emerging Systems. As dictated by Confederation rules, John's environmental suit took on the characteristics of the local inhabitants; he was a four meter high reptile, walking on two massive hind legs with a swaying gate.

Commissioner Ythantrium was a native of the Imtun system, one of the founding members of the Confederation. Imtun was one the very few class three civilizations in quadrant B of galaxy G-1. Home planet to the Imtun was the fourth planet from a middle aged yellow star in a sixteen planet system. At a planetary average temperature of 16.3 degrees Celsius, Imtun still possessed a great spinning molten core; the planet's tectonics were quite active. Its magnetic field acted as a barrier to solar and cosmic radiation. Chemicals in the atmosphere gave the planet a yellowish red blush.   Eighty percent of Imtun was covered by water, only the southern polar region retained permanent ice. Twenty eight million distinct species of animal, plant and microorganisms populated the surface, the Imtun being the only technologically advanced species in the whole system.   The current home planet population for the Imtun was a little over three hundred million.

A reptilian race, Imtun adults ranged between three and a half to five meters high and weighed between ninety to two hundred kilos, females generally larger than the males. They stood upright on two thick hind legs, comprising only a quarter of their height. Early in their history, they had a distinct tail, perhaps up to a meter long, but it was now almost gone in most cases. Imtun coloring was typical for many reptilian species. The refractory properties of their scales gave an appearance of many bright and subtle colors, some iridescent. Racial distinctions rested on what sequence of colors appeared on what areas of the body. Eight distinct types existed, characterized by coloring and minor body variations.

In the previous three hundred years, the Imtun had shown an increasing appreciation for naturalistic architecture. Most buildings now reflected natural contours, colors and sensibilities. The Confederation Home Office also followed the modern Imtun style, built into the side of a foothill near the equator on the second greatest land mass.   Although constructed of manufactured materials, it looked as if it were part of the hill.

The Imtun star system was in the middle of its 30,000 year heating/ice age cycle; its days were warm and the nights comfortable. It had become a favorite vacation spot for Confederation citizens.

Composed of a fairly loose group of advanced systems, the Confederation supported a centralized diplomatic effort as well as basic scientific ventures, the Mapping Project being the largest. The Mapping Project's task was to investigate all scientific aspects of the known universe, as well as expand the area of the known universe.

Ninety percent of Confederation members, or about thirty eight hundred star systems, were type two civilizations, controlling the entire power of a single star. Type twos were also capable of traveling limited distances in folded space.   Forty seven civilizations, early type three, controlled the power of many star systems and were capable of inter galactic travel in folded space. The remaining members fell slightly outside these two categories: some civilizations were late type one, almost capable of being a type two. Others were late type three civilizations, capable of very rapid intergalactic travel.

Very few laws and regulations existed that the Confederation enforced. Each member system, or unified system governed themselves on most points of everyday life; the Confederation acted as arbiter when normal channels of communication broke down and combat might become a reality between star systems. The Confederation's charter spelled out basic rights of its citizens, which all member systems must uphold to maintain membership.

The Confederation was organized into three departments. The first, the Administrative Department, consisted solely of the General Council with one representative from each member system. It set policy, made regulations and officially accepted new members. A committee of twelve members made up the Oversight Group which set the agendas and coordinated the monthly General Council meetings. The Administrative department was entirely political and was very messy.

The second department, the Diplomatic, to which Ythantrium and John belonged, oversaw first contact, code enforcement and conflict resolution. This department had the most difficult duties and most of what they did was nuanced. The Diplomatic Department was managed by a High Commissioner, and the three divisions within this department were headed by Commissioners.

Ythantrium was the Commissioner of Emerging Systems, or first contact. All the actual work in the Diplomatic department was done by teams, led by Ambassadors. The complexity of any assignment dictated the system assignment. Since some advanced technologies were not shared, traveling great distances was done by members of type three civilizations. Also, dangerous enforcement was accomplished, for safety reasons, by civilizations capable of superior weapon and shielding technology. John Crackstone was a non-solid from a late type three civilization on a gas giant planet, Zizthanthe. Crackstone was also a Senior Ambassador who could be assigned to any of the three divisions within the Diplomatic Department.

The final and third Confederation department, the Mapping Project, had a broad charge which included not only mapping the known universe, but classifying all known life forms for each inhabited planet or moon and what system they belong to, as well as the few rogue planets floating about between systems. They were also in charge of all scientific studies. As a result of their huge charge, this department had the most influence as well as the most endowed resource budget. All mapping project missions to other galaxies were done by type three civilizations.

With the Mapping Project and the Diplomatic Department, all complicated or intergalactic missions were commanded by Senior Captains or Senior Ambassadors from type three civilizations. These premier positions required more extensive training as well as access to the most advanced technologies. John Crackstone spent ten years in a scholastic setting, then another twenty years as an apprentice to a Senior Ambassador before he gained his current rank.

Life does not stop evolving when a civilization reaches type three, but no one in the Confederation knew what lay beyond. They had, on occasion, run into a more advanced civilization, especially when their efforts affected a time line, or two. These advanced people did not communicate with the Confederation; they only interacted to alter accidental time lines for unknown reasons, reasons at least unknown to the Confederation. These advanced civilizations were not meddlesome nor were they aggressive, they were not that interested in lesser creatures.

The Mapping Project was the first to interact with new, unknown civilizations. Since Mapping Project teams could travel in a cloaked state, interactions with type one or less civilizations was, for the most part, non-intrusive. To the present time, most interactions with type two and type three societies had been peaceful. Exchange of location, social structure and governmental configuration were the first priority, followed by a very brief exchange of scientific information about respective home systems. All of the type three civilizations encountered to date had only been interested in knowledge, not territory or influence.

As far as the Mapping Project had determined, even after it had explored seven different galaxies, the theory of panspermia still held true. Even though advanced Confederation species varied markedly, humanoid, reptilian, or even non-solid, they all shared a similar set of proteins, cell structure and body organization, as well as cell replication. Most species so far discovered, however far flung were related to all others on a very basic level.

For simplicity, The Mapping Project oriented every mapped galaxy according to the magnetic orientation of the black hole at its center, in three spatial dimensions. Galaxies were numbered by their order of exploration; the spiral galaxy that was home to founding Confederation members was numbered G-1. When oriented in three spatial dimensions, with black hole magnetic north pointing to the top of the map, each galaxy was further divided into four three dimensional quadrants, and those quadrants were divided into one hundred and forty four three dimensional sectors. In each quadrant of each galaxy, the Confederation constructed its headquarters on a single planet. Headquarters provided space for all Confederation departments, facilitating continual interdepartmental communication. This strategy gave all Confederation citizens an impression of one virtual government.

All Confederation members shared the ability to create adaptive environmental suits. The complexity and long term effectiveness of a civilization's environmental suit corresponded to their technological level. Basic environmental suit knowledge was a shared technology among all Confederation members; universal translation, food and air processing and power requirements were among the shared technologies. It was rare that any two advanced civilizations had similar home planets. One person's pure breathable air would be poison to most everyone else. But an environmental suit enabled an individual to breathe, ingest native materials, and communicate with indigenous life on any planet in the known universe. These suits could also be quickly constructed to make the wearer appear as a native being.

Protocol demanded that any visiting Confederation official, no matter of rank, use an adaptive suit while on another's planet.

Far from home, Crackstone had landed on Ythantrium's home planet, which happened to also be part of a Confederation founding system. The imposing building John had just entered contained the headquarters for the Diplomatic department. True to the modern Imtun style, the office building interior was constructed to appear natural. There were no flat surfaces, except the floor. The walls and ceiling appeared hand cut from pinkish native rock, with vivid tool marks. Instead of formal windows to the outside the walls had irregularly spaced viewing ports which could be moved, shrunk or enlarged easily. Most of the office workers enjoyed the sunshine, so light spilled everywhere in the building.

Protocol also demanded that official communication be verbal, in the common language of the host world. Only a quarter of Confederation civilizations communicated telepathically, so verbal communication was the standard. Since all adaptive suits had translation modules capable of real time communications, with only a delay of microseconds for unknown languages, this was usually not a problem.

"It's so good to see you again, Ambassador," the office worker greeted Crackstone. "I enjoyed the report from your last mission; it was the most interesting I have seen in almost three decades."

"It was unique," the Ambassador replied.

"The Commissioner is expecting you, sir, please go on in." The worker motioned towards an oversized office to his left.

"Zhan, you collection of space dust!" The Commissioner rose to his full four and a half meter height as he slightly bowed towards the Ambassador. "How have you been, come on in and sit down."

Ythantrium was a Temuld variation of the Imtun. His tail was completely missing and his facial coloring was mottled red on his left and mottled brown on his right side on an iridescent green background. John Crackstone, in deference, used the same coloring as his superior.

"I did legally change my name, you do know that, right?" John insisted.

"That's right, you're no longer Zhansdredquimmer Drukkersten Mabwahjerkhiddger."

"I never did like that name." The Ambassador wanted to say more, but felt it best if he kept his thoughts to himself. "It was the name of the individual who cloned me, and so on for

22

many generations. I felt there were too many Zhans out there, there are four of us still alive."

"But, where did you come up with Crackstone?"

"John Crackstone was the persona I took on for the lost part of my last mission, I liked the sound of it, so I decided to change my name," Crackstone answered. "On that planet, John would be my familiar name, so why don't you try it?"

"All right, John, I shall."

"What's this mission about?" John asked, already knowing it would be a first contact affair.

"By now you know the general idea, it's the particulars that need my explanation," Ythantrium chuckled as he answered.

"What's the problem?" John asked.

"Before I go on," The Commissioner replied, "how are you doing, I mean after that last assignment, how are you?"

"You have seen my medical report," John replied. "I'm cleared for a new assignment."

"You spent two years in a malfunctioning environmental suit, and you lost your long term memory for as long," Ythantrium observed.

"I found those two years to be quite relaxing." John grinned.

"I must say that your mission log was rather unusal, to say the least," Ythantrium commented.

"That reminds me," John knew he had to ask the question, "my log for that mission is missing some data, can you send me a complete record for my own use?"

Ever since John had reviewed his logs for that mission so he could complete his required report, he had been bothered by what had been removed from them. Why was such a select bit of data removed, and what did that really mean?

"I assume you are referring to the other craft you encountered in orbit around that little planet?" Ythantrium asked.

"I know that protocol dictates we delete future knowledge, but I have a feeling about that particular bit of knowledge," John said.

"I will consider it, and let you know soon."

"Back to this assignment," John changed the subject. "By simple deduction, I get the impression that this may be a challenging task."

"That's why the High Commissioner asked that I assign you," Ythantrium replied. "This particular civilization can sustain a singularity for more than an hour and can temporarily fold dimensional space, but they are almost continually in a state of war, mostly against imagined enemies."

"Do they know about the Confederation?" John asked.

"They do not," Ythantrium replied flatly. "They suffer from literalism; they are the center of their universe and no other civilization can be greater than they are."

"Oh." John quickly reviewed his training and experiences in his mind. "Just dangerous enough for me, right?"

Not answering, Ythantrium just smiled. Most reptilians' mouths were full of teeth, and ever so subtle in expression. John never was able to fully translate Ythantrium's smiles so he never fully understood the simplicity or the terror that awaited him in any new assignment until it was too late.

"When do we begin this enigmatic journey?" John asked with a non expression.

"As soon as your companion craft has been refitted and upgraded."

"Then." John stood silent before turning to leave. "I must locate my Science Officer."

. . . .

While their ship was being repaired, Science Officer Tem was staying in a Diplomatic housing pod near the Technical and Repair center. This was a newer building and was completely in the modern naturalistic style.

"I can come back later, if you're busy."

John looked intently at his Science Officer, who was fumbling with several small pieces of equipment as he opened the door wider. Like John, Tem was wearing a reptilian environmental suit.

"No, please come on in, sir," The Science Officer quickly answered. "I just finished a download on dimensional physics; it's something I've been meaning to do for some time. Since we had a long layover after our last mission, I thought I should get it over with."

"Oh." John quickly reflected on his Science Officer's current mental state. "You looked a little confused when you opened the door."

As John's partner, Tempatt Groonghin had served with him for thirteen years. Both of them hailed from the same home planet, a gas giant in a 5 planet system six thousand light years from their present location. As non-solids, John and Tem each lived as a coherent cloud of matter held together by a very strong electromagnetic field. The Science Officer's informal name was Tem; by the customs of his home world, his informal name should have been Groon, but, as so many of his contemporaries, he chose another syllable from his formal name to distinguish himself from his predecessors. With only one gender, their species performed procreation by an individual cloning themselves; a long and demanding ritual. When communicating with multiple gender species, they referred to themselves as masculine, to avoid confusion.

"I feel this way after a difficult download." Tem slowly wandered back to a chair. "Being a bipedal solid doesn't help either."

"Experiential knowledge is less taxing, I suppose." John didn't know what else to say.

"Did you really change your name?" Tem looked surprised at his own question, which had jumped out of him.

"I did," John smiled. "legally even."

"Why, sir?"

"There are too many with my name, and I told you as we left that strange little planet, I like the sound of Crackstone. It translates well to our culture and to many others as well," John replied.

"I suppose it's none of my business anyway, but I was asking."

"No problem, Tem."

"What's our exact assignment, sir?"

"First contact with a literalist society." John almost sighed. "The Demela System."

"I would have thought we might have a light assignment, especially after the last one."

Tem knew their assignment could be among the most dangerous missions led by an Ambassador. In order to be eligible for first contact by the Confederation, a civilization must possess enough technology to harness the power of their sun and be almost capable of traveling between star systems in reasonable amounts of time. Each civilization's first contact was debated by the whole General Council. This debate was framed by information provided by the Mapping Department.

A society classified as literalist was the most difficult to approach because their conscious view was so narrow. They believed that their species was the center of the universe, and that if a supreme being existed, it must be just like themselves. Their universal view was 'Me' without an 'Other'. When a superior 'Other' arrived, there could be no end to the bellicose behavior. Kill first and consider later was often the battle cry of the literalist whose core beliefs were challenged.

"We're headed to the Demela System?" Tem asked, trying to calm himself.

"Our exact orders and directions should be downloaded into our companion before we get to the reconstruction facilities," John replied.

"How was your vacation, sir?" Tem asked, still not quite sure of social familiarity with the Senior Ambassador.

"I did enjoy the time on our home planet." John basked in his pleasant thoughts. "But, I also like my work."

"As do I, sir," Tem replied with a hint of regret. "But I would have preferred a slightly longer rest period. Eleven days does not feel long enough for me."

John was acting obtuse; he felt time spent away from his work was time wasted. Ambassador Crackstone had refused his past five rest rotations, and took this vacation because the High Commissioner ordered him to. He had spent only three days on his home planet. John spent the remainder of his vacation time at the Wintog university taking a seminar on dimensional particle physics.

"We both rotate onto a long rest after two more missions." John cracked a short smile. "That should give you some comfort."

"It should."

"Are you ready?"

"As ready as I can be, sir."

"You arrived here yesterday, right?"

"Yes, sir, I got here for the final refitting of Sam."

"How is our old friend doing?"

"For a tube of technology, he's as sarcastic as ever."

"What is it with you two?" John wondered aloud.

. . . .

John's craft, Sam, sat alone in the repair bay. Although Sam could re-size himself, and, if he needed to, change his exterior shape, he was now in his natural state. He was egg shaped, bronze color and about 35 meters long and 20 meters thick.

Most of The Confederation systems had the technological capacity to produce space craft that traversed natural wormholes or created dimensional folds for inter system travel. Craft of this complexity were almost always sentient machines; managing millions of variables in thousands of scenarios demanded more processing power than any organic being could manage, even an enhanced organic being. John and Tem's craft was built on their home planet, one of the more advanced type three civilizations in the Confederation. All inter-system craft from their planet were sentient; endowed with a unique personality, not to mention a name. John's craft, Sam, had been with him for thirty years, seventeen more than Tem had been with him.

This latest refit was long overdue for Sam, and was prompted by his near demise on their last mission. Sam's engineering, scanning and shielding systems were completely removed and replaced with the most up to date technology. Eighteen of Sam's sub processors were also completely replaced. It had been at least fifteen years since Sam went through a major refit. He had been crabby for almost six months after that one, and this one was even more invasive.

"I'm packed, sir, we can go when you're ready."

"That's why I'm here," John sighed. "Let's go."

. . . .

"*I thought you'd get a different Science Officer for this trip.*"

"You are in a state, old friend." John chuckled at the companion's ill-tempered tone. "And please remember to verbalize, since we're in not on a telepathic planet."

"That's so archaic, sir, and quite imprecise."

"So are you, but I still work with you," Tem huffed, still put off by Sam's initial remark.

"It speaks," Sam drolly replied.

"Can I unplug it, sir?"

"I don't even have a plug, you twit."

"Will you two stay civil," John insisted.

"I was," Tem replied.

"Were not!" Sam added.

"Shut up!" John almost shouted.

"Can we go over our assignment?" Tem sighed as he tried to change the subject.

"Please do." John settled into the left seat in their ship.

Their craft could manipulate spatial dimensions so the interior could appear, in three dimensions, as large or as small as required. At the moment, the interior spaces were expanded to allow space for five meter bipedal reptilians. A ten by fifteen meter cabin stood off a twenty meter hallway, which lead in turn to a ten by ten meter cargo hold. Four smaller crew and work cabins joined the long hallway through hatchways. Everywhere, all the surfaces were curved, no sharp edges could be seen.

"Very well, sir." Sam paused, no doubt to center himself. "This will be a first contact mission in galaxy G-1, quadrant D, sector one thirty two, the Demela System."

"Have you calculated the jumps?" Tem asked.

"Do you think I'm as slow as you?" Sam snapped.

"Just answer the question," John interrupted. "This will be a dangerous mission, so, please get over your post-refit grumpiness sooner this time."

"Not grumpy, sir."

"What would you call this behavior?" Tem teased.

"How would you like it if half your internal organs were ripped out and replaced?" the companion shot back.

"Maybe a little grumpy," Tem added.

"How many jumps?" John said briskly.

"Four, sir," Sam responded. "It might be safer and a bit less energy consuming if we took the trip in seven jumps and utilized more natural wormholes."

Traveling several light years to several million light years across three dimensional space would take unreasonable amounts of time if it weren't for the ability to bend a space craft through a higher dimension in a controlled fashion. Eleven known spatial dimensions had been discovered. Within this paradigm, time was not a dimension, but rather a manifestation of linear energy spectra.

Utilizing power from one to four stars, a space craft could generate a dimensional rift in space higher than three dimensions, a process that created instantaneous three dimensional travel. Destinations could include any point in the three dimensional universe, from a few light years to a few million light years away. How far away depended on the particular starting point and how much energy was applied to the higher dimensional rift.

Natural stable wormholes could achieve the same process with less expenditure of energy. Most trips within a given galaxy took multiple jumps; travel between galaxies could take even more. But type three cultures could utilize a broad surge of energy from almost a whole galaxy to fold space for an intergalactic three dimensional trip of many millions of light years.

Dimensional energy harvested from any given area of open space was only a fraction of a percent of the available energy. Once that energy was used to create a dimensional rift, or temporary wormhole, it then dissipated back into space; even in dimensional physics, energy could neither be created nor destroyed.

"You are recommending we be safe this trip?" John inquired.

"I am, sir."

"Perhaps you wish to take it easy with all your new systems?" John added.

"I do, sir."

"Then plot the safer course," John replied.

"While I prepare for departure, you two might want to download our mission details," Sam said.

After a brief moment during which Tem and John absorbed the entire mission parameters and details, Tem spoke. "Sir, you didn't indicate that this is such an intense literalist society."

"Would that have made a difference?"

"No." Tem considered, "But such societies can be quite dangerous."

"I know," John sighed. "The Commissioner feels we are the best team for this job, so we go anyway."

"Is there anything else we need to transport onboard before I leave?" Sam asked. "Speak up now."

"I think we're ready." John answered.

On board the craft, Sam could use technology to reorder matter to form almost anything from food to technology. John and his Science Officer traveled with very few personal items.

....

As their craft left the planet, John and Tem extracted themselves from their large reptilian suits and assumed their non-solid forms. Sam adjusted the ship's interior to better fit the crew's new smaller size.

"The first jump will be in two minutes, and will take us to sector fifteen of this quadrant," Sam informed them.

"The Mapping Project recommends we contact their political leader as he tours their southern most continent," Tem began, after a long silence. "He will be there for several months before he travels back to their capitol city."

"I know what they recommend," John replied.

"It sounds like you disagree with the Mapping Project, sir." Tem smiled.

"In my experience, political leaders of literalist civilizations can be the most difficult to deal with," John observed. "I've had better luck with military leaders, they think more pragmatically."

"How many of these missions were you on?" Tem asked.

"Before you joined the crew, I negotiated four first contact missions with literalist civilizations."

"How did they end?"

"Three ended quite well, and the fourth, not so well."

"Were there any casualties?"

"Just my sense of well being," John replied.

"No one died?"

"No one," Sam answered.

"I wasn't speaking to you," Tem quickly shot back.

"We will make our second jump in one minute which will take us to sector eight in quadrant B," Sam added.

"Thank you, Sam," John replied.

He noticed that their craft was feeling the strain of having nearly half of his important systems removed and new ones put in. As both a sentient being, and a piece of manufactured technology, the ship did have feelings. He was often torn between feeling superior and vulnerable after a major overhaul. John knew he must make an effort to make Sam feel comfortable for a few days, or suffer the effects of a bitchy sentient space craft for at least a few months.

"Back to our mission," Tem continued as if Sam hadn't said a thing. "Mapping Project estimates that this civilization is at least a hundred and fifty years from effective inter-system travel."

"I found that their estimates are sometimes inaccurate," John chuckled slightly with his answer.

"How inaccurate?"

"Perhaps five hundred years inaccurate," John answered.

"How could that be?" Tem sounded shocked.

31

"Consider this yet another lesson in the art of diplomacy," John began, "not diplomacy, but the prelude to diplomacy."

"I don't understand, sir."

"Before one lands on a planet, especially a first contact planet, the reports from the Mapping Project must be carefully evaluated."

"In what way?"

"How old is the data?" John began a list of questions, "What class probe did they send, or was it a manned mission? How long was the observation mission? Did they send down properly trained observers? Did they include field recordings?"

"Just a moment, sir." By now, Tem had downloaded the whole report. "They did send a manned mission, and the last report was a month ago. I find field recordings, but the last observation lasted only a week."

"What do you think caught the Mapping Project's attention?" As Ambassador, John had switched to teaching mode. The road to his current rank had included time spent with a Senior Ambassador as a junior officer; either a Mission Specialist, Cultural Officer, or Science Officer. The Senior Ambassador should teach the apprentice Ambassador the subtleties of the job for a decade or so before more education and assignments will lead to becoming a full Ambassador.

"These people created a semi-stable singularity in several controlled experiments, Tem replied. "They were able to fold dimensional space, but only partially and only in a micro region of space. For transportation they still used light speed ships."

"If it were up to me, I would wait ten to twenty years for first contact, but I don't make those decisions." John sighed. "I would guess that the Project's estimate is one hundred years off, but, luckily, it doesn't make a difference."

"We will be safe." Tem sounded happy. "They can't harm us."

"Don't ever assume that, Science Officer," John warned.

"I see your point, sir."

"We are exiting the wormhole, and will be entering our next in one minute, sir," Sam interrupted. "We will be in sector one hundred eighteen, quadrant B upon exiting. There has been a super nova in sector 4, quadrant C and it has affected navigation in a two quadrant diameter, so I adjusted our navigation to account for it."

"Will it affect our travel time?" John asked.

"In our relative time, the trip will take three minutes longer, sir."

"I can live with that," John replied.

John and Tem relaxed into their pods and began to go over the information provided by the Mapping Project on their assigned planet. John was searching for some usable patterns in the core beliefs of the civilization that would allow him to approach leaders in a non threatening way, while Tem was perusing the technology of the civilization.

As natives of the Zizthanthe system, John and Tem's planet was a gas giant and their species lived in the middle to upper atmosphere. As non-solids; their bodies were groups of contiguous cell clusters held in an amorphous form by self generated strong electromagnetic fields. They could make any or all portions of their bodies solid for periods of seconds to days, an ablitiy which allowed them to manipulate tools. The Zizthanthe communicated with each other telepathically.

Sam hovered in a fixed, small region of relatively empty space while he used an extreme amount of energy to fold dimensional space fifty meters from himself. The craft was creating a controlled, stable, temporary wormhole, with sector eighteen, quadrant B as the other end in three dimensional space. After one minute, Sam entered the wormhole. The trip to sector one eighteen should seem like six minutes to his two passengers, and it did.

. . . .

"Stabilization protocol!" John shouted.

"This is strange, sir," Tem replied as he intently studied the myriads of data streams. "Our location is indecipherable. We seem to not be anywhere."

Sam generated massive amounts of data, too much to send to the Science Officer and the Ambassador at one time.

The ship constantly summarized information and telepathically sent it to the crew. For their part, Tem and John telepathically communicated orders to Sam. Various surfaces in the control pods of the craft acted as links for specific types of data; those areas, or interfaces, glowed a pale blue as they were activated. Tem or John could link themselves to that interface and receive raw data, information not summarized by Sam. In addition to the data interfaces, a three dimensional visual display could be accessed from any part of the ship. The displays showed three dimensional star charts, planetary cross sections, systems monitors, or communications from other ships or Confederation planets. Most outer surfaces of the craft were capable of becoming transparent; Sam routinely monitored a wide spectrum of energy hitting the outer skin. He then projected his results onto his inner skin. At times the interacting processes created an impression that the hull was transparent.

"What happened, and what is that vibration?" John asked as he turned on all the viewing ports.

The sides, top and bottom of the ship's skin around their control pods looked transparent. The crew could see nothing but shimmering washed out yellow light everywhere they looked.

"Rotate the frequency and phase of any energy hitting us," John ordered.

"Sir," Sam replied. "I'm having trouble maintaining control of our position. I'm losing power rapidly."

"What position?" Tem asked. "According to what I see, we don't know where we are."

"Sir, there's a star out there," Sam quickly replied. "My sensors have found it."

"Wait!" John interrupted. "Stop the viewer there!"

In the upper right quadrant of their viewing area, a star shone plainly visible. It appeared to be a smallish star, emitting a pale white light, with several large dark spots on its surface.

"Is this a known star?" John asked.

"With our limited capability, yes, sir," Tem replied.

"Why are our abilities limited?" John asked.

"I think we're in the middle of some unknown force field, sir," Sam replied.

"That would make sense," Tem replied. "That would explain some of these anomalous readings."

"Raise shielding to maximum," John ordered.

"I cannot, sir," Sam replied. "My shielding is class eight and falling."

"Can we maneuver out of the field?" John asked.

"I have lost most of the navigation systems," Sam replied.

"The systems are depolarized, sir," Tem added.

"Can we maneuver away from it?" John asked again.

"We are drifting in a controlled manner, sir," Sam said.

"How?"

"As if we were in a low orbit of a planet, sir," Tem replied.

"That's what I said, Science Officer." Sam sounded resigned.

"What planet, and why are we there?" John insisted.

"According to the meager data I have, we came out of dimensional space right where we were supposed to," Tem said.

"This is the correct system, but there isn't supposed to be a planet here," Sam insisted back to John. "We were supposed to come out of dimensional space between the third and fourth planet in the Brem system."

"How are we really supposed to know where here is if all your sensors are off line?" Tem snapped back.

"Assuming a planet is down there, how do we make a safe landing on it?" John spoke calmly.

"Assuming this energy field is this planet's atmosphere, as soon as we fall below it, and before we crash onto the planet, perhaps I can restore enough systems to make a controlled landing," Sam replied.

"Do we retain enough shielding?" John asked.

"If I can believe the readings, we will only have class four shielding by the time we land," Tem replied.

"Do it, Sam," John ordered. "Now."

The whole ship shuddered, jerking twice as much as before. John and his Science Officer increased the gravitational restraints in their pods to keep themselves in place as their craft began to plummet towards toward the unseen planet. To the naked eye, the bright light diminished; a faint outline of the planet appeared. As the seconds ticked, the planet grew larger and more in focus. Their sensations of free fall intensified.

In what seemed like no time, the planet took up their entire visual field. An overwhelming sense of speed told them that they were in an uncontrolled crash, but at least they weren't burning up, yet.

"What the hell is he doing?"

Before John could finish his thought, both he and Tem were ejected in their pods into the atmosphere. Designed to provide protection in any situation, the pods also had parachutes, a primitive but effective way of slowing them down in most atmospheres, even with no usable technology available.

Below them their craft plummeted towards the planet surface. Perhaps twenty seconds later, John and Tem saw Sam disappear, then a bright, almost blinding flash of light engulfed them. They were perplexed for only a second before something, using a matter transporter, conveyed them both back on board their craft. It was as if nothing had happened.

. . . .

"Explanation, please," John demanded.

"The only solution I could come up with on that short a notice was to project a very small, highly focused singularity one hundred meters above me, fifteen seconds before I hit the planet. I sustained that singularity for two seconds, so its gravitational pull would slow me down enough to avoid major damage. You two could not be here while I did that, since we didn't have enough shielding to keep you alive, so I jettisoned both of you, then transported both your pods back here after I landed, or sort of landed," Sam replied. "The problem is, that I used a lot of my remaining power."

3

What happens next will fill you with at least wonder

"*There are only two linear energy spectra in play for this species, right?*" John asked as he adjusted his clothing.

The environmental suits for Tem and John made them look like the native humanoids. Said primitives were fast approaching them from the south west.

The natives stood on two legs, legs which were half their body length. Their two arms, each with a hand contained six digits, one of which was an opposable thumb. They had slightly small craniums for their body size, with two oversized eyes and a medium sized mouth and almost no lips. Their noses were very small. Perhaps, John thought, their sense of smell was slight.

As the humanoids got closer, Sam, the sentient ship, made fine adjustments so the Ambassador and Science Officer's physical appearance would conform more closely to these natives. Their clothes were constructed by a matter converter to approximate what the ship's sensors could determine a female from this planet would wear.

Tem wore a bright blue tunic that flowed almost to his feet. The fabric rose along the back almost to his hairline, but in the front it plunged to just above his nipples. John wore a similar outfit in light red, but his tunic was a bit more modest in front.

"*That's right, sir,*" Sam answered. "*Just two energy spectra.*"

Sam was linked in telepathic contact with the Ambassador and Science Officer at all times. Care was taken so their communications would not be compatible with that of the humanoids.

"Do these people have some sort of a cult built around mammary glands?" Tem inquired

"Why do you ask?"

"I can't seem to keep these things covered." Tem pulled up the front of his tunic as he spoke.

"Can you closely monitor the nervous response of these humanoids as we speak to them," John resumed his conversation with Sam. *"Also, if they perform telekinesis, or reorder matter, pay close attention to both their energy output as well as any anomalies in the planet's energy fields."*

"Perhaps if I can put some adhesive on these things, they might remain under the cloth." Tem continued to be preoccupied with his clothing.

"What are you talking about?" John asked.

"Your mammaries are staying under cover, so give me a break." Tem sounded frustrated.

"Either make a new set of clothing, or adhesive, but be quick since they'll soon be here," John said.

"It's that machine's fault," Tem sighed. *"He made you perfectly good clothes, and gave me this booby trap."*

"I did no such thing," Sam quickly answered.

"We're out of time," John interrupted. *"I can see them approaching us now."*

The ambient temperature was about 40, Celsius with a strong breeze blowing from their left. The humidity was low; it felt like a desert. Pinkish brown was the dominant color, almost no vegetation covered the soil which was very course sand to fist sized crumbled rocks.

Tem quickly pulled a utility pad from his right pocket and fixed his wardrobe problem.

A utility pad was a general purpose piece of technology which could perform a variety of tasks. It could be used as a communications device, with a range of only two light years. The apparatus could scan any organic or inorganic matter, it could also scan any known form of energy. The device could also be used to perform diagnostics on technology, biological entities, or non-biological matter. To a limited degree, it could also repair technology and biological beings as well as completely control their environmental suits. The pad also could reorder matter, to a limited degree; it could utilize any available inorganic matter to make anything from a vase, to a complex computational device.

"*What do you make of that?*" John asked.

"*They are all sitting on a moving barge of some sort,*" Tem replied.

The seven humanoids were clearly visible now. Four were female and three male, they ranged between a meter and a half to almost two meters high. They all were seated on semi-reclining upholstered wooden seats which rested on a long flat platform that appeared to be made of stone; with four rows of two seats across. The wooden seats were hand carved, as was the stone platform. Seated on the rear portion of the platform was another creature. This animal was seated on its haunches, and appeared to walk on all four of its limbs. It was covered in fur and had an elongated head with wide jaws, full of sharp teeth.

"*Sam?*" John inquired.

"*I sense inertial dampeners, but no technology, sir.*"

"*How?*" John asked. "*How do they negate gravity without technology?*"

"*I don't know,*" Sam replied. "*But, one of the males apparently has a different neural output than the others, and he seems to have set up a weak, but definite, vortex that reaches to the lower atmosphere as well as several kilometers into the planet.*"

"*Send the data to my suit,*" John requested.

In John's visual input, scrolling in the bottom tenth of his vision, several readouts appeared.

"*This is quite interesting,*" John muttered, "*Send the data to Tem.*"

"*The up energy stream is one hundred eighty degrees off phase with the lower stream,*" Tem observed. "*It's all electromagnetic, in the lower mid-frequencies.*"

"The end result is that heavy ass chariot has zero gravitational affect and he's magnetically vectoring the damned thing at one hundred kilometers per hour," John added.

The stone vehicle slowed to a stop five meters from Tem and John, then slowly settled to the ground from its one meter height. All seven humanoids, male and female, disembarked and lined up, facing the Ambassador and Tem.

"How do we greet them?" Tem asked.

"One of them is thinking about raising her right hand and facing the palm towards you," Sam replied.

John stepped forward one pace, then raised his right palm.

An older woman raised her palm towards John and quietly said, "Greetings, friends."

Tem raised his right palm also and both he and John responded together, "Greetings, friends."

"Which of you speaks for your group?" The older woman asked.

"I think only one of us is supposed to greet," John said to his Science Officer.

"What is that strange voice you are using?" The older woman sounded upset. "Are you hostile?"

"I'm working on it , sir." Sam quickly said.

Sam's voice sounded strange. John knew that the humanoids could detect the conversation between Tem, Sam and himself. They knew conversation was taking place, but probably could not understand it. Sam must find a frequency that the humanoids could not detect. Both John and Tem could detect Sam trying many different combinations while monitoring the humanoids.

"I apologize." John looked intently into the faces of the humanoids. "We are not hostile at all, it is our way of centering ourselves."

"What does that mean?" The woman said sharply.

"Sir, I located a telepathic frequency they cannot detect and have adjusted both your environmental suits to use it," Sam interrupted.

"My friend and I have been alone, meditating for many years in isolation," John thought quickly. "We center ourselves by using a special chant; it calms us and causes our thoughts to be only kind and helpful."

"We have not spoken to others in may years and we wish to be back among our own again," Tem added.

"You're not one of us." The woman raised her left palm and glared at them.

"How can you say that?" John insisted.

"We cannot sense you, you are not one of us," she repeated.

The humanoid woman pushed her left palm towards John and Tem. A dull green glow rapidly flew from her palm to encompass both John and his Science Officer. John could see the readout of what the green glow was in his visual field; it was intended to be a restrictive energy beam, something that would inhibit neural conductivity. Fortunately, the dampening field around the Ambassador and his Science Officer was more than strong enough to cancel that effect.

"You really have nothing to fear from us," John insisted as he stepped one pace closer to the humanoid woman. "I am John, what is your name?"

"Sir, I sense one of them thinking about the word, "Grendela", Tem said to John.

"I hear it also," John replied. *"Is that a place name?"*

"My name is Jana,: The woman answered. "I am the First Prefect of the Zannua Province."

"Her name is Tem," John replied.

"Where are you from?" Jana demanded.

"We are from Grendela," John replied.

"Grendela?" Jana said as she dropped her hand to her side.

"That's impossible!" One of the men in their party shouted, then fell silent in slight embarrassment.

"You are an off-worlder," Jana insisted; this time not as sure of herself as before.

"What makes you say that?" John inquired.

"Your craft is only partially hidden," Jana replied. "If your magic were from Grendela you would have been able to hide it from us."

"*I'm on it, sir,*" Sam quickly spoke to John.   As recent events had unfolded, Sam had been able to improve his reading of the natives' visual and telepathic acuity. He transferred that information to the Ambassador and Tem's environmental suits so that they would experience the world as the others did. Within a few seconds, Sam located a frequency that rendered him invisible to the humanoids

"It's gone!" A woman to Jana's left exclaimed.

"Their magic is strong," The man said.

"*Magic?*" Tem commented to John. "*They perceive technology as magic?*"

"They were able to resist your paralyzing spell, Jana," another woman said.

"You are the strongest practitioner in this province," the man added.

Jana raised both her palms toward John and Tem. Various shades of green, red and yellow light flowed from her palms, some as enveloping clouds, others as sharp bolts. The dampening fields held firm, while the Ambassador and his Science Officer carefully continued to look calmly, not aggressively, at the group. Tem took two steps up, to stand next to John.

"*What do you want me to do, sir?*" Sam asked.

"*In spite of their extraordinary power, these people are primitives,*" John replied. "*If magic is their reality, then shall we play this game better than they do?*"

"*Sir?*" Tem asked.

"*Sam, can you holographically project a massive beast, preferably something scary looking, beside the group as I raise my left hand.   Then, stop the projection as I lower my hand,*" John said.

John slowly raised his left hand. A twelve meter high, seven hundred kilogram furry beast with large, sharp incisors suddenly appeared.   All of the humanoids huddled together as Jana raised both her hands, casting a blue light over her entourage. They milled about, or huddled together, as the four legged creature that had transported the group leapt from the stone platform. Making loud, low growls, the creature ran towards the holographic beast. They faced off as the creature stopped directly in front of the humanoid group. Still growling it bravely held its ground.

Meanwhile Sam's universal translator began to understand the four legged creature's language, it was warning the twelve meter high holographic beast to stand back and not harm its people.

In response, the projected beast opened its mouth and roared at least a one hundred twenty decibel roar. Saliva flew in all directions as it bellowed.

"*Was that necessary!*" Tem shouted over the roar. "*My audio circuits will blow!*"

"*Calm down, that was only its mating call,*" Sam replied. "*The spit was my idea.*"

"*The humanoids can't hear a damned thing, so why all the noise?*" Tem asked.

"*They can't hear it, but they sure can feel the vibrations,*" Sam answered.

As John lowered his hand, the beast disappeared.

"*That was a Bacalawa and it only eats Gannis Moss; it hates being near other creatures,*" Tem sighed.

"*They don't know that!.*" Sam retorted.

"Please, we mean no one any harm," John insisted again. "We come from Grendela, but we are lost and need your help. Please help us."

In response, the blue tinge in the air over the humanoids disappeared. All seven of them leaned their heads together and went into a light, collective trance. John could decipher some of what was happening; he could barely hear an accelerated conversation, a decision making process, with Jana leading the voting, and making the final decision which took no more than twenty seconds.

"You must never use your magic without permission first," Jana finally said. "At least not until we can settle on exactly who or what you are."

"That is acceptable," John agreed.

"May I introduce my associates." Jana pointed first to the man, to her far left, "He is my second consort, Bale. Next are Rheama, Withor, Haldi, Mimm, and Killet."

"Who is the four legged creature?" John asked.

"He is of no consequence, he is just a guard beast, a dumb animal we use for protection," Jana replied.

"Will you take us to your city?" John asked.

"It would be my pleasure." Jana pointed to the stone slab.

John sat next to Jana for the trip; Tem had to scrunch up in a space between the last two seats, just in front of the guard animal. The stone vehicle raced along at over one hundred kilometers per hour towards a distant rise of hills. The overall color of the dirt was pinkish brown. As they proceeded toward the city, more and more vegetation sprung from the soil. Soon streams and a few rivers were visible; Sam had landed at the edge of an obvious desert. John observed a diverse amount of animal life, although not abundant. These people planted crops, and apparently raised animals for food. To their left was a huge field of some sort of grain, with large clusters bright red flowers clinging to the tops of most of them. To their right was a smaller field of light yellow grass with a herd of 25 six legged animals, about two meters in height.

The sky was a white color, with a slight reddish cast to it. A minor breeze wafted by us, the midday temperature was now around twenty degrees Celsius, much cooler than where they had landed. The star for this system was a smallish one, and it hung slightly less than halfway overhead. It looked not as bright as it should, almost as if a heavy haze suspended high in the atmosphere, the surrounding energy field no doubt.

A faint hint of methane permeated the air, which was not unpleasant to Tem and John; it was somewhat reminiscent of their home planet. As they traveled away from their landing site, they noticed other agreeable scents, all from the increasing numbers of plants growing wild and cultivated, that they were passing.

Tem looked at the guard animal directly behind him and spoke aloud, very softly, "What is your name?"

"You are not one of them?" the animal grumbled back, as quietly as Tem had spoken.

"Why do you say that?" Tem asked.

44

"You are not silent, like the rest of them," the animal replied.

"What is your name?" Tem asked again.

"I am called Sharptooth, from the Rivergrass Clan," he answered. "Our kind are the Drylaque."

"My name is Tem, and my companion is called John," Tem said. "He can hear you and can also speak to you."

"Can you speak to the silent ones?" Sharptooth asked.

"Do you mean the others like us?"

"Yes."

"They do not have the ability to hear sounds, nor do they have the ability to make sounds." Tem answered.

"How do they communicate?" Sharptooth asked.

"They communicate with their thoughts," Tem replied. "How do you communicate with them?"

"They show us with their hands, or the movement of their bodies," Sharptooth replied. "And, they show us what we are not to do with pain, very horrible pain."

"You wear a collar with a leash and the female named Mimm is holding that leash," Tem observed.

"Is that her name?" Sharptooth asked.

"It is."

"Our kind live three of their lifetimes, I have been bound to her family since her grandmother," He replied. "She is the kindest master I have had."

"How many other creatures live with the humanoids?" John mumbled from the front seat.

"He does speak, he is not a silent one?" Sharptooth asked, then continued speaking. "They use the Kralok to guard the grain stores, we can speak to them. There are many smaller creatures who eat the grain and other varieties of stored food our masters eat, we do not speak to them. They also raise Tomolo and Yegart to kill and eat, the Yegart provide them with milk. we do not speak to either of them."

"Thank you," John said. "We must now deal with your masters, I think they do not trust us."

"They do not, be careful with them, they are not kind and they can cause you great pain," Sharptooth said. "I will not attack you, I think you mean me no harm."

"We do not," John assured the animal.

"If you are from Grendela, why are you here?" Jana asked.

"We were sent to you to learn more about how our people live today," John replied. "The masters have lost touch with you."

"Who are the masters?" Jana asked.

"Our superiors," John replied.

"I get the feeling there's more being said by these humanoids than we can hear," Tem said to John.

"You really think so?" John sarcastically replied.

"Sir," Sam interrupted. *"I detected a slight change in Jana's energy as she greeted you, something quite different than her telepathic conversation."*

"Don't feel shy about sharing with us," John said.

"It was in the electromagnetic spectrum, but I can't say much more than that quite yet," Sam answered.

"We have yet to see or detect any written language; maybe their written language is a form of telepathic communication," Tem speculated.

"Is that your home city?" John asked.

"That is Regul, my home town and the capitol of my district," Jana answered.

"It is a very beautiful place." John smiled. "How many people live here?"

"Thirty three thousand live here," Jana replied. "Why do you ask?"

"It is my master's desire to find out all we can about their people," John answered.

"I find all this quite difficult to believe." Jana waved her hand for a second in the direction of a dozen official looking humanoids in what looked like uniforms.

"Are you going to detain us?" Tem asked.

"I am," Jana insisted as the guards approached the stone vehicle.

The guards each firmly held a three meter long wooden staff in their right hands. A sharp pointed crystal topped the end of each staff. All female and slightly taller than the original group John and Tem had met, each guard wore a tight fitting red tunic that fell slightly below her waist; a black image of a lightening bolt dominated the front. They all wore bright blue pants and black boots.

"Why are you doing this?" John asked.

"You are not one of us, you may pose a danger to my people," Jana replied. "Your magic is strong, but there are only two of you."

"We mean you and your friends no harm," John insisted.

"I cannot take that chance," Jana replied as she nodded towards the guards.

Three of the guards leaned their lances towards John and Tem and touched the crystal ends together. At first a bright red flash, then a steady blue light emanated from the crystals; a bright blue flash raced toward John. The field around both Tem and John held fast, diffusing and deflecting the blue light.

"*What is that energy beam?*" John asked Sam.

"*I think it would immobilize one of the humanoids; at a greater amplitude it might kill them. For you, it would completely shut down your environmental suit,*" Sam answered.

John was monitoring the energy levels, displaying them in his visual field. It was a complex electromagnetic energy beam, similar to what had shot from Jana's hand, only more powerful.

Other groups of three guards were combining their crystal tipped lances and shooting blue beams at Tem and John.

"*Sir, how much more can we take before our damping field collapses?*" Jem asked.

"*I don't think they have enough for that,*" Sam answered.

"I have an idea," John said. "*Sam, transport Jana to a spot in between Tem and me, then increase the damping field to accommodate the three of us.*"

John raised his right hand as Jana disappeared from her position commanding the increasing detail of guards and instantly appeared between Tem and John.

Half the teams of three guards ceased firing, the other half did not. Jana was stunned, shocked she had been moved, and more surprised she wasn't dead.

"Cease!" Jana shouted.

The energy beams stopped at once.

"I told you we mean no harm to anyone," John insisted. "If you do not trust us, we will accompany you to a holding facility."

"You do have strong magic," Jana slowly sounded out her words. "I do not understand how you can do these things, you are not one of us."

"You keep saying that, I don't understand what you mean," John said.

"Which is exactly why I keep saying that." Jana began to regain some composure.

"Where do you want us to go?" John asked.

"First, I shall sign the writ to place you in jail."

Jana motioned to one of the guards who brought her a rectangular black stone, a half meter long, an eighth of a meter wide and quite thin. Jana closed her eyes and passed her hand over it.

"*That's how they write!*" John exclaimed.

Looking up at the buildings around them, Tem and the Ambassador could plainly see a black stone over most of the entrances.

"*How soon can you decode the writing?*" John demanded.

"*It's magnetic,*" Sam replied. "*It should be simple.*"

"*Should and is are two different things,*" Tem added.

"Where is the jail?" John asked Jana.

"Follow the guards, please," she replied.

Tem followed John who followed the guards toward a three story building a block away, which appeared to be an official government structure. Jana and her entourage trotted off in the opposite direction, deep in silent communication.

The buildings were all constructed of stone, mostly a light stone with small dark flecks of minerals in them. Some of the stone, seemingly used for decorative purposes, was the same light base color with gray to blue swirls in no discernible pattern

48

throughout. The stonework was very refined. No building John could see was more than four stories high.

The streets were all cobblestone construction, and quite wide, perhaps twenty meters wide for the main streets and fifteen for the side streets. No antennae perched on the tops of buildings, nor any poles to carry power or communications wires. From outward appearances, this was an early or pre-industrial city.

Not many humanoids could be seen in the vicinity of the government building, and those that were there looked askance at Tem and John, as if they were high criminals. John did notice several humanoids leading Drylaque by leashes. As they entered the building, he caught one of the animals mumbling, 'better them than me'. This was not a good sign.

"Please go into this cell."

The taller guard pointed toward a five by five meter room on the first floor of what appeared to be a governmental building.

"*No bars, but an energy field around it,*" Tem observed. "*This field is of no harm to us, we can pass through it quite easily.*"

"*For now, we pretend it's just like bars, just go on through the passageway they have made for us and sit down until both they and we can figure a way out of this,*" John replied.

"*Yes, sir.*"

The inside of the building was sparsely furnished in plain, practical wooden furniture. Most of the walls were finished in a rough plaster with nothing hanging on them. Their options for rest were only two straight backed wooden chairs, an uncomfortable looking bed and a lone woven solid gray carpet laying on the stone floor in the cell holding the Ambassador and Tem. Also, a faint musty odor permeated the whole space; mold must be on this planet too, a constant in the whole universe, John thought to himself.

. . . .

"*Sir.*"

"*Yes, Sam.*"

"*I can interpret the writing. I am in the process of updating your universal translators so you can also read their writing.*"

49

As Sam paused, both Tem and the Ambassador became able to read the signage around the room.

The largest sign in the jail cell read, 'Obey authority'; that phrase spoke much more than the two words alone.

"*Sir.*"

"*Please, continue.*"

"*Their idiom is a pictographic written language, only they use waveforms to record thought patterns. They record these waveforms on a native magnetic stone as their written form of communication, but another aspect to their language exists,*" Sam said.

"*I venture a guess that it has to do with the strange electromagnetic patterns that went along with our first encounter with the humanoids,*" Tem guessed.

"*Lucky conjecture,*" Sam retorted.

"*Please, you two,*" John sighed.

"*They all can communicate with each other on a representative level, it would be like sharing feelings, not specific language at all. This must be what tells them that you're not one of them; you must be continually connected to their shared conscious minds all the time to be one of them,*" Sam said.

"*Can you?*" John asked.

"*I have programmed the fifth function on your utility pad to allow you to hear this global representational conversation, and the sixth function is programmed to let you hear this and transmit a conglomeration of everyone else's non verbal conversations in a random order for now, until I can refine an algorithm to have it make sense.*"

"*Thanks,*" John replied.

Both John and Tem began listening to the non verbal conversations. At first, they heard what felt like millions of ideas at once, but within a few seconds, they could detect separate patterns. A series of worried, happy, angry and sexual feelings ran as currents to the chatter of ideas. John began to single out different types of patterns. He then began to try to amplify anything that had to do with the word, Grendela.

"*Science Officer, please listen into what I uncovered,*" John said.

"*Yes, sir.*"

Together, they both absorbed the history of Grendela.

The name for the humanoid race on this planet was Brem; strangely, this was also the Confederation name for this system.   The Brem were a very primitive people until the gods made contact with them one hundred and seven thousand years ago.   The Festival of Grendela celebrated the dawning of civilization.   Before the gods, the Brem were hunter-gatherers, their life was short and very difficult.

The gods had stayed on this planet for only a brief time, they revealed themselves when they felt the time was right to enlighten the Brem.   One among the Brem was chosen the brightest and strongest leader of the most important tribe; her name was Jwala.   The gods revealed the holy city of Grendela to Jwala, revealed the sacred writing to her, and told her that they would return one day to reveal the secrets of life.   The gods promised to protect the Brem forever; they would dress the land in a suit of armor so the people could safely await their return.

Jwala lived with the gods for a year.   Then, while she was on a quest for sacred stones, the whole city of Grendela disappeared.   The gods left, taking with them the night sky to remind them of their beloved children, the Brem.

Jwala searched the rest of her life for the gateway to Grendela, dying without finding it, dying without children.   She did pass down all the knowledge she had learned to her people, and she was and is revered as the mother of the modern Brem. Jwala was the first sorcerer of the Brem.

Grendela was rumored to still exist, but in a higher, godly, plane of existence.   Shaman, sometimes deep in contemplation, reported to have seen the gate to Grendela, but not where it was, nor what was on the other side of the gate.

"*Very informative, sir,*" Tem replied.   "*I have been studying their tradition and practices of what they call magic.*"

"*As have I,*" Sam interrupted.   "*The armor their gods claimed to have covered their land with must be that energy field surrounding this planet.*"

"*That seems all too obvious,*" Tem added.   "*Have you found the power source for it?*"

"*If you would let me finish a thought, I would have already told you about it,*" Sam sounded annoyed.

"*If you two would stop bickering, I might have already heard about it,*" John interrupted.

"Sorry, sir," Sam continued. *"There are fifty fusion reactors buried many kilometers beneath the surface around the equator. Twenty are working at seventy percent capacity, four are non functional, and twenty six are in a standby mode, I assume as back up to keep twenty working units on line. The output is quite sufficient to power the energy field."*

"Do you recognize the technology?" John asked.

"Not exactly," Sam advised. *"It's a generic fusion reactor system, something that most regional space travel ready species could make. It doesn't convert heat to produce electricity, they tap the broad spectrum of radiation and filter it to specific frequencies before focusing it into the energy field."*

"But the Brem themselves don't use technology," Tem added, *"As an advanced civilization, their gods must have arrived here to exploit something. After they exited, they left this planet cloaked for some reason."*

"If the legend is right, they wanted to come back, perhaps what they took will replenish itself after a given time," John speculated.

"How much helium 3 is on this planet?" Tem asked.

"Hardly any," Sam replied *"But, since the Mapping Project has never cataloged this planet, how are we supposed to know how much was here to start with?"*

"The Science Officer may have a point. If these people never were a technological race, they would never have used any if it did exist," John said.

"A group of them is coming back in here," Tem interrupted.

"Have you refined the algorithm to transmit image symbols in a more coherent way?" John asked.

"I think so, sir," Sam replied.

"Science officer, let's turn that on," John said.

They both reached into their tunics and started function six. In their thoughts, nothing changed; they still were connected to the Brem global consciousness, but they were adding their own signal, a semi coherent conglomeration of the entire Brem stream.

"We need to speak in more detail with you two," Jana insisted

As she rounded the corner and entered the room, she stopped, as did the three guards accompanying her.

"I will say this again, we mean you no harm," John calmly said.

"I can see you as a whole person now," Jana observed, "What are you doing?"

"We were instructed by the gods to pass among you as observers only, but we have become aware that we strike fear in your hearts if we are not open to all of you." John replied.

"You are one of us, yet you are not one of us," Jana said, uncertainty in her tone.

"We have lived isolated with the gods too long," John said, making a logical guess.

"Or, you deceive us," Jana speculated. "I cannot tell."

"Continue to guard us, but let us speak with you, and let us know you better," John pleaded.

"Your magic is great, that I will admit." Jana sat down in a chair one of the guards had placed in front of John. "You have intrigued the Wizards, as you have intrigued me."

"Then, we can be friends?" John asked.

"No," Jana flatly said. "But, we can be friendly."

"That is preferable to this," John replied as he pointed to the jail cell.

Although the force field wasn't lowered, Tem and John walked through it to stand in front of Jana.

"You certainly do intrigue me," Jana smiled.

4

Witch way did they go?

Evening was falling as Jana led John Crackstone and Tem Groonghin out of their holding cells. They walked directly behind Jana, followed by three guards armed with crystal tipped lances. The first thing that struck John was the lack of stars. No discernible moon punctuated the night and with most of the stars erased from the night sky, darkness weighed heavy. This planet did not have any large visible moons, so the cloudless night sky should have been bright with stars.

Pedestrians crowded the streets. Most of the Brem paid attention to the entourage following Jana. About thirty percent of the Brem they could see had a Drylaque in tow, but they both noticed another domesticated animal which looked remarkably like one John had encountered while he was stranded on Earth, a cat. This animal must be the Kralok that Sharptooth told them about, he thought.

The temperature was about fifteen degrees Celsius with a slight breeze which made it feel cooler. Although they saw many stone vehicles as they first entered the city, far fewer floated above the streets now. People walked about socializing and eating in outdoor cafés. The sweet scents John and Tem noticed on their trip into the city were amplified now; they noticed an abundance of cut flowers on outdoor café tables. Kralok outnumbered Drylaque in this outdoor scene by ten to one. If the Kralok were there to keep smaller animals from eating stored foods, there must be a significant infestation of those small pests.

John and Tem could hear the Kralok speaking among themselves, mostly commenting about hunting and availability of food scraps, but they also mentioned John and Tem, how carefully the strangers were guarded, What high crime might they have committed?

Audible laughter may be rare or nonexistent in a telepathic culture, but the emotion of humor is irrepressible and translates easily. The Brem who weren't overly concerned by the contingent of armed guards and two prisoners trooping past their tables remained engaged in animated conversations. John and Tem overheard many such exchanges spiced with humor.

This society did use an economy based on money; Tem pointed out to the Ambassador a couple giving a small handful of cut crystals to a restaurateur.

"Where are we going?" John asked Jana.

"You are commanded to an audience with the Assistant Wizard for our region," Jana replied without stopping.

"What is an Assistant Wizard?" Tem quickly asked.

"The Wizard leads this whole region of our planet, there are eleven provinces in our region and there are only three regions on our planet," Jana answered. "But, if you were one of us, you would already know that."

"When we were last among our people, there were no regions, we were all one people," John quickly said.

"You would have to be older than fifty thousand years for that to be true," Jana said as she stopped and looked directly at John.

"Ninety four thousand years old, to be exact," John forcefully said, hoping his bluff might work. "While one lives in Grendela, one does not age as a normal Brem does."

Pausing, Jana slowly replied, "Perhaps that may be true, but we shall let a Wizard decide."

She turned around and briskly continued walking, leading John, Tem and the three guards up the block and onto the next.

Without a moon, and without stars, the night would have been gloomy had it not been for smooth semicircular crystalline structures protruding from every fourth building. They emitted a diffuse, bright pale yellow light. It seemed to Tem, who had been trying to analyze the light ever since he left the jail, to result from a chemical reaction of some kind.

"*Sir, can I take readings of these lights?*" Tem asked, surreptitiously touching his utility pad.

"*No, it might be taken as an act of aggression,*" John replied. "*Sam, can you get any readings from the crystal light sources?*"

"*Not really,*" Sam replied. "*I noticed that these people can use naturally occurring crystals, cut precisely, to manipulate the two energy spectra produced by the twenty reactors below ground. The process creates rudimentary shielding, inertia dampening fields, and neural dampening fields, so I don't see why they can't produce an excess of photons too.*"

"*You mean light?*" John chuckled.

"*That's what I said,*" Sam answered curtly.

"The transit portal is just ahead."

Jana pointed to an elaborate small stone outbuilding, perhaps three meters wide by two meters deep and five meters high; it was completely open in the front. The entire one third of the top of the structure was carved stone, with a recurring lightning bolt theme. At the two front corners, two elaborately carved columns with repeating hourglass structures held up the top.

Jana pointed toward the small one story structure, inviting Tem and John to enter first. As Tem stepped into the diminutive building after John, Jana stepped in with them, leaving the two guards outside.

"Since you do not know the location of the central palace, I shall transport you both," Jana pronounced.

"That will be fine," John answered, somewhat confused.

Jana stood between them and extended one hand to each of them. As she touched both of them, a bright aqua green light enveloped the entire structure, Jana began to disappear.

"*Sam! Quick, transport us to wherever this humanoid goes,*" John insisted.

"*Yes, sir,*" Sam replied. "*She has yet to complete her transport.*"

"*Sir,*" Tem interrupted, "*The guards are staring at us.*"

"*Our shielding must interfere with their transport system,*" John surmised.

"*Sir, the humanoid has reassembled in a similar structure approximately nine hundred kilometers from your present location,*" Sam said. "*I shall transport you both there right now.*"

John and Tem faded from the guards view and reappeared beside Jana in the distant transport site. Jana stared at John with a faintly confused look on her face.

"We are cautious," John took a stab at a response. "I am sorry."

"You are curious, at least you are to me. The Wizard is waiting to meet you two," Jana replied.

She pointed to the grandest building John and Tem had seen on this planet. It was at least ten stories high, a half kilometer wide. Like all the other structures on this planet, entirely constructed of stone, it was massive, as huge as the largest governmental building in the Confederation. .

The transport structure stood on the edge of a city about the same size as the town they had just left. The same crystal lights lit this place, people dressed the same. The night was alive with people enjoying meals, conversation and each other. The palace was set away from the edge of the city. A well lit cobblestone street led to its front gate. Six guards, each with a long crystal tipped lance marched up to Jana, John and Tem; three fell in behind them, three in front.

As they marched to an audience with the leader of this region or province, John, Tem and Sam continued to try to sort out how these humanoid could utilize advanced physics without any technology.

"*That was a rudimentary matter to energy to matter transport,*" Sam said "*Although exactly how she did it, I'm still not sure.*"

"*What energy was involved?*" Tem asked.

"*The transport structures are surrounded by a rotating magnetic field all the time, but the matter to energy conversion is done in one energy spectrum, although the directional and cohesive control seems to be in another spectrum,*" Sam replied.

"Most of the tricks we've seen so far operate in the electromagnetic spectrum; is this the only use of the other spectrum you've detected so far?" John asked.

"Yes, sir," Sam replied.

"We can assume these creatures are strictly electromagnetically bound; they may be able to control some functions in the other spectrum, but are not aware of it," Tem speculated.

"I would not assume that completely, at least not yet," John replied.

Jana offered to let them prepare themselves before the meeting. She showed them to a cavernous room just inside the palace, off a short hallway to their left. As the substantial door closed, they looked around the room, lit by a shining crystal. Three highly polished stone bowls sat on a four meter long carved wooden table. Along the opposite wall were three high backed plain wooden chairs, each with a round cutout in the seat. Below the cutout was a deep stone pot. The walls were rough cut stone with a band of semi-finished carved stone about head high. This building had the feel of a much older structure than John and Tem had yet seen.

Curled up in a corner of the room was a rather portly Kralok. John and Tem stared at her for awhile. The Kralok looked up at the two of them and made a high pitched trilling sound.

"What the hell do you creatures want?" she asked.

"My name is John, and her name is Tem," John answered.

"You speak?" The Kralok replied, a surprised note to her voice.

"We do," John answered. "What is your name?"

"My name is Whitepaw." She walked to the door. "Why do you speak?"

"We just do."

"It does not matter to me." Whitepaw hesitated by the door. "Open this door, I do not wish to stay with you. You creatures smell bad."

John opened the door; Whitepaw leisurely strolled out into the hallway.

"*That is a peculiar animal,*" John observed.

"*But, more harmless to us than the Brem,*" Tem replied.

"*I think we wash ourselves in these pots, and eliminate in those?*" Tem said, pointing to the tall backed chairs.

"*I assume so, but since we don't need to do either, perhaps we can use this time to gather our wits,*" The Ambassador replied.

John wandered around the room in silence for awhile. This was a small room in comparison to the vast size of the whole structure they had just entered, but was actually quite large itself. As in the other building in which they were detained, this one was just as silent. John could faintly distinguish slight sounds of small creatures behind the walls.

When John scanned the blank wall directly in front of him, he got readings of several hundred small four legged creatures and several thousand twelve legged insects in a twenty five meter radius. John recorded the scan, and sent it to his Science Officer.

"*What I find amazing is the lack of overt technology,*" Tem broke the silence. "*How does one get water in and out of the wash bowls without pipes? And, in this primitive society, how does one get rid of a big pile of crap from those heavy stone pots over there without a waste water system?*"

John pulled his utility pad from inside his robe again and began to take readings.

"*A rotating magnetic field lays around the stone bowls, both types of bowls,*" John said as he stared at his pad. "*My guess is that you are supposed to transport water in and out of the bowls.*"

"*I'd hate to live next to where everybody transports their poop.*" Tem shook his head slowly as he too pulled his utility pad from his robe.

"*Sir,*" Sam interrupted. "*There might be a problem.*"

"*What?*" John quickly replied.

"*You know those guards with the crystal lances,*" Sam continued. "*Well, about one hundred of them just showed up here and surrounded me.*"

"*Can they see you?*" John asked.

"*I don't think so, but they must know I'm here, because they have set up a perimeter around me,*" Sam replied.

"*Are any maneuvering systems back on line?*" John asked.

"*Not yet, sir. But, I think I found a way to counter the energy field in the atmosphere so I can regain some of my systems.*"

"*Why didn't your shielding work in the energy field?*" John asked.

"*I'm not sure, sir,*" Sam replied. "*I do have a theory, though, and if my theory is correct, I can adjust my shielding to be effective in it.*"

"What are you two doing?" Jana threw open the door. "We have an appointment right now!"

John and Tem stuffed their pads back into their robes.

"*Fine, just don't tap into the energy from the fusion generators in this planet,*" John insisted to Sam.

"We were calming ourselves before our meeting, I am sorry," John answered Jana.

"*But, sir, that was one of my solutions,*" Sam replied.

"Come with me," Jana insisted.

"*Do not do it!*" John insisted.

"We're looking forward to meeting your leader," John calmly spoke to Jana.

"*Yes, sir, but that will take much longer,*" Sam acquiesced. "*I think there might be another way to counteract the dampening effect of this power field, but I may not have enough power to do anything useful, like get into orbit.*"

"What is the name of this leader you are taking us to?" John asked.

"She is the Superior Wizard, the supreme leader of us all," Jana answered as she hurried Tem and John into a long hall, leading to an opening set of very large wooden doors.

The massive doors to the palace were ornately carved with geometric forms, including the recurrent theme of lighting bolts; it was at least eight meters high and each of the two doors were three meters wide and a quarter meter thick.

"What is a Superior Wizard?" Tem asked.

"The more you two reveal your ignorance, the more I am sure you are not one of us," Jana replied. "The Superior Wizard is the person who has demonstrated the strongest magic among our race."

"How is that determined?" John asked as the three of them, plus a contingent of guards briskly walked through the open doors.

"In ancient times, it was accomplished by a contest, to the death, but that was many centuries ago," Jana replied. "Now, our Crowning Ritual chooses our leader, it happens every eight years."

"We have been in Grendela for tens of thousands of your years and away from the people, so our knowledge of our society is not as it should be," John said. "Our task is to return to the people and learn from them again, to become one with them again."

"Sir, you're shoveling shit now," Tem scolded.

"I am not," John insisted. *"I'm casting about for something they will believe."*

As they entered yet another massive room, John and Tem looked around. Soaring eighteen meters above their heads, the ceiling was constructed of ornately carved wood panels with a cut crystal and lightening bolt theme. Along the two long sides of the room, more carved wooden panels in deep bass relief depicted the life of a lone woman, probably Jwala, the mother of this race. The great hall was about thirty five meters long and fifteen meters wide.

At the end of the large room a five meter high wooden throne stood with a singe person in long robes sitting on it. Elaborately carved stairs led up to the high throne. Two other seats only one meter high flanked it; only one was occupied. John and his Science Officer walked down a two meter wide carpet running from the entry door to the tall throne. The carpet was multicolored and did not have any discernible design in it.

No sound emanated from the Brem, other than footfalls, breathing and the rustling of clothes. The sound of the Ambassador, Tem, Jana and the troupe of guards was deafening as it reverberated in the mostly empty room. Both Tem and John noticed, again, the faint odor of mold coming from the long carpet. For single celled organisms, mold seems to be the most common in the universe. In planet wide colonies, their collective

61

consciousness is always one of unquestioning superiority, at least to themselves.

Another noise whispered from the walls, the sound of many scurrying feet. John guessed these were the creatures and insects he had already scanned from the bathroom.

"Bow slowly from the waist, then take two steps forward and answer only when spoken to," Jana whispered to John and Tem as the three of them stood five paces from the Wizard.

They did as they were warned. The leader finally spoke after waiting a full two minutes in silence as she observed John and Tem.

"My name is Tamora, what is yours?"

"My name is John," The Ambassador replied.

"And, my name is Tem," The Science officer replied.

"Give me your whole names, so I can regard your status!" Tamora demanded.

"My name is John Crackstone," John added.

"My name is Tempatt Groonghin." Tem followed suit.

"Tempatt Groonghin," Tamora slowly sounded the name, "Groonghin does not signify anything."

"It signifies me," Tem added.

"You were not addressed." Tamora looked askance at Tem.

"Sorry." Tem fell silent.

"Again?" Tamora stammered. "Why does your inferior speak?"

Everyone was silent for another forty seconds.

"But, Crackstone," Tamora began again. "That tells me your family were of the builder's guild."

Again, silence for a full minute.

"*Pre-industrial guilds. That makes sense,*" Tem said. "*Even they can't pull all this stuff into existence by magic; they must employ legions of stone masons, wood workers, carpet makers, and weavers to support all this.*"

"*At this point, and until Sam has all his sensors working properly, I wouldn't discount anything, especially things that could kill us,*" John replied.

"Were your parents stone cutters?" Tamora asked.

"They were, many thousands of years ago," John replied with an appropriate but false answer. "Before I was taken into Grendela."

"Ah," Tamora quickly replied, "Jana has told me some of your alleged story."

"Why do you doubt my story?" John innocently asked.

"No one has been to Grendela in one hundred thousand years," Tamora continued. "Why should I believe you?"

"I'm sure you were informed about our magic," John answered.

"Informed, yes," Tamora said. "But, I have seen none of it myself."

"What do you require of us?" John asked, humbly.

"I have given it some thought," Tamora replied, rising slowly from her throne.

She turned to the male sitting to her left, holding out her right hand as he put a medium sized rose colored box into it. She sat back down, closed her eyes and began to meditate with the unopened box cradled in both palms. After a few minutes, she opened her pale green eyes and looked at John.

"Approach, and make the holy crystal a conduit for the power of Grendela once again." Tamora softly ordered.

"May I ask a question?" John asked.

Tamora nodded.

"May I use my own crystal from Grendela to regard the treasure you hold?"

"Is it a weapon?" She asked.

"It is an inquiry crystal," John answered.

"What is an inquiry crystal?"

"It takes in the scope and complexity of anything I ask it to, then it translates that information to me in terms I can understand," John replied. "It is tuned to my thoughts alone, and speaks only to me."

"Can it repair anything you ask it to?" Tamora asked.

"If it can fully understand the thing, it may be able to do so," John answered.

"Proceed."

John stepped to within an arm's length of Tamora's palms and the now open box. He looked inside at a fist sized light yellow crystal. It had been faceted and polished more cleanly than any other crystal John had seen to date on this planet. The faceting was asymmetrical, with regular inclusions in the crystal. Some of the inclusions appeared to be manufactured.

Slowly pulling out his utility pad, John turned it on and held it above the surface of the crystal.

"*What the hell is this thing?*" John asked.

"*Working on it, boss,*" Sam quickly replied. "*While I'm scanning this thing, I would like to remind you that this grand poobah wizard has surrounded me with a huge army to keep me from moving, they now are trying to poke and prod me with sticks.*"

"*Would those sticks have crystals on the end of them?*" John asked.

"*They would,*" Sam replied.

"*I would take great care not to let those crystals get close to your cloaking frequencies,*" John admonished.

"*I'm not that stupid,*" Sam replied. "*The crystal she's showing you is mostly carbon, as in a diamond, but also includes molybdenum, gold, which gives it that color, aluminum, titanium, hydrogen and other trace elements.*"

"*What does it do?*" Tem interjected.

"*Nothing, now.*"

"*What is it supposed to do?*" John insisted.

"*It looks like it was a particle beam focuser and phase shifter for a very strong particle beam,*" Sam answered.

"*Before you fix it…*"

"*I know, I know,*" Sam interrupted John, "*Set some safeguards; I already did.*"

"*What was wrong?*" Tem asked.

"*Seven of the sub processors were melted; I will put the thing back on line when you ask me to,*" Sam replied.

"Well?" Tamora asked.

"My Inquiry crystal has informed me about this crystal," John began, "Your crystal can be rejuvenated."

"Do it now," Tamora swiftly demanded.

John put his pad back into his robe, then lay his right hand on the crystal while making random movements of his head.

"*Turn the thing on now,*" John said.

The crystal gave an almost blinding millisecond flash, making John back up several paces, placing him next to Tem.

"The power of Grendela!" Tamora announced.

Tamora smiled broadly. Holding the crystal tightly in her left hand, she raised it above her head. She turned the most faceted face towards John and Tem, shoving it quickly towards them in a throwing motion.

Another, longer duration but more intense flash of yellow light shot from the crystal and bathed John and Tem in energy. Their dampening field held; the light passing around them as the solar wind does a planet with a Magnetosphere. After no more than ten seconds, the device went dead; the failsafe Sam had engineered worked perfectly.

"Why do you want us dead?" John asked quickly "We have meant you no harm since you found us, even though we can easily harm all of you."

"I was unsure of the power of this crystal," Tamora said, unapologetically.

"You had to be at least aware that it could kill," John added.

"Perhaps." Tamora smiled. "This crystal has not worked in many thousands of years."

"Nor will it again," John added, with a neutral tone.

"Fix it again, I demand it," Tamora insisted.

"No," John said abruptly.

"You defy my command?" Tamora rose from her chair.

"If I do, you will try to kill us with it again," John calmly replied.

"I promise I will not," Tamora curtly replied.

Her eyes darted from the floor to John's face, then quickly glanced at her Consort.

"Perhaps we can make a trade," John suggested.

"What do you want?"

"We have told you of our own quest," John answered. "To learn the history of our people for the last ninety four thousand years, the time Tem and I have been away in Grendela."

Tamora sat slowly back down in her royal seat as she stared at the Ambassador and his Science Officer. She fell into silence for a full minute.

"The Council of Wizards and the Council of Sorcerers both met, shortly after First Prefect Jana informed us of your arrival." Tamora paused again to collect her thoughts. "We are all dubious about your story of coming from Grendela, we think it more likely that you come from off-world."

"But, where else than in Grendela could anyone learn such strong magic?" John asked.

"I have considered that, and I am intrigued." Tamora let loose a small grin for the first time.

"What does that mean?" John asked.

"First, I am assigning Jana as your keeper, along with ten of my finest guards," Tamora replied.

"To what end?" John asked again.

"I will allow you to learn about our past, and our present, if that is why you came here."

"Thank you," John replied.

"Take them to the Hall of History," Tamora spoke to Jana. "They can spend the rest of the night there, then we will deal with them again tomorrow."

Tamora rose from her chair, turned to her right, then raised her left hand; a door appeared in the wall in front of her. Tightly holding the box with the magic crystal in her right arm, she regally marched through the open door, followed shortly by her scurrying consort, Damnen.

"Follow me," Jana ordered as she sprang towards the large doors in the rear of the great hall.

They all walked in a procession through halls, and downstairs, heading towards the Hall of History, deep in the center of the great castle.

"*Sir, if you have some free time,*" Sam said.

"*Go ahead,*" John answered.

"*I made a copy of that crystal,*" Sam began.

"*We assumed you had,*" Tem interrupted.

"*It's a flow regulator for one of the power generators deep within this planet, and it was constructed by the same people who made the fusion plants, and who constructed the energy field around this planet,*" Sam said.

"*Can you adapt their technology to tap into the power source?*" Tem asked

"*I can in time,*" Sam replied. "*The regulator isn't in exact tune with the radiation flow from the generators, but it can be made to work for me. I can draw power directly from the fusion generators in a short time.*"

"*I hope you can do it quickly,*" John observed.

"*Without at least seventy percent power, I cannot travel back in time; so the time required is not negotiable,*" Sam replied.

"*What is your power level?*" Tem asked.

"*Twenty seven percent,*" Sam replied. "*That jolt you got from the grand brazier's crystal ball caused me to instantly lose seven percent, and I kind of need everything I have left to keep these mad villagers from finding me out here.*"

"*We trust you to adapt to the power source as soon as you can,*" John added.

"*Does the planetary shield block dimensional and solar energy?*" Tem asked.

"*One hundred percent of the dimensional energy and forty percent of the solar energy,*" Sam replied. "*I can only slow the decline in my power reserves by using solar energy during their daytime.*"

"*I assume you did catch that we are headed to their Hall of History,*" John said. "*Please widen the bandwidth when we get there and download all the information we find as quickly as possible.*"

"You two have been very quiet since we left the Wizard," Jana said as she opened a door into a vast room in the second floor below ground level of the castle.

This room was at least thirty meters wide, forty meters long and ten meters high. All the space was filled with shelves, each packed with thin stone tablets, averaging a quarter meter long by half as much wide and all were sealed in a layer of what appeared to be glass. The shelves were thick wooden planks supported every meter by stone support columns; although well finished, neither the stone nor the wood were decorated.

Extending from just beyond the entrance door to almost the back of the long room stood twenty massive shelving structures, most completely filled with the glass covered stone tablets.

"This is our main Hall of History, recording our civilization from the earliest of days to now." Jana pointed to the shelves. "They are arranged by date, and begin in the far back left corner and wind up and down the shelves to our present."

"Thank you," John replied.

"You can have only twelve hours, that is what the Council has given you," Jana added.

"We will not need that much time." John smiled at her.

"This is almost one hundred thousand years of history!" Jana exclaimed.

"With the help of our Grendelian crystals, we can absorb the knowledge in a short time," John replied in a calm tone.

Both John and Tem took out their utility pads and took up positions in opposite sides of the oversized room.

"*Tighten the bandwidth to below ten gigahertz and above one hundred hertz,*" Sam said.

Tem and John obliged.

"*I am downloading, sir.*" Sam reported. "*It should be no longer than forty more seconds.*"

"Process, summarize, and download to us as soon as possible," John requested.

"Yes, sir," Sam replied. "*Perhaps three minutes more.*"

"Tamora mentioned thinking we were from off world," John said.

He walked back to where Jana and the guards were standing near the main entrance to the Hall of History. Tem joined them in a few seconds; they both had already put away their utility pads.

"Yes, she did," Jana replied.

"How many times have your people been visited?" John asked.

"You have read the history, haven't you?" Jana cautiously barbed.

"*There have been six instances of alien encounters in their history,*" Sam quickly prompted John.

68

"Your history says six times, but I want to know more," John answered Jana.

"I don't know more than is in our recorded history," Jana replied.

"What happened to the off world creatures, what happened to their craft?" John asked.

"*Museum of Heresy, sir.*" Sam quickly interrupted.

"Where is the Museum of Heresy?" John asked.

"In the next room," Jana answered, sounding and looking a little confused.

"May we see it?" John quickly asked.

"I don't see why not," Jana conceded.

"*There are close to two hundred angry villagers surrounding me now, and all of them have their magic crystal spears,*" Sam said. "*And, I think they're ready for some sort of a full assault on me.*"

Tem, and John followed Jana through a small door, which appeared only after Jana raised her left hand and tilted it up and down twice. The team of guards followed them in as well.

"*Can they damage you?*" John asked.

"*I don't think so, but they might have something up their collective sleeves that I don't know about,*" Sam replied. "*They have been probing my location for the past hour with more regularity, rotating frequencies and phase in regular increments.*"

"*For a primitive culture with no technology, they seem to be able to use technologically advanced techniques quite well,*" Tem interrupted.

"*If we are to believe their written history, they believe all this is done through mysterious magic,*" Sam replied. "*Even though the power to accomplish what they do is provided by an advanced technology, they control it through their thoughts, so to them, it is magic.*"

"*Tem and I need to get down to the control area for the fusion generators to figure out who built them, or at least try to guess who,*" John observed.

"*Not with my present power levels, sir,*" Sam observed.

"*Speaking of which,*" Tem interrupted. "*Can you tap into the fusion generators yet?*"

"*I still question the efficacy of doing that,*" John interrupted. "*The unintended consequences of pulling that much power from those old fusion reactors could be devastating to these people.*"

"*Or, it could be inconsequential,*" Tem replied.

"*Whatever it may be, you need to decide soon,*" Sam quickly said. "*I think they plan on making their final charge in less than thirty minutes.*"

"As you can plainly see, outsiders do not survive on our world."

Jana waved her hand, causing twenty crystals imbedded in the walls to light up the immense space they had entered. This room was as large as the Hall of History, but held only six space craft, none larger than six meters in diameter.   As John and Tem stared at the six downed craft, Tamora, the Superior Wizard suddenly entered the room.

"*They have increased the intensity of their assault, sir,*" Sam said.

"I'm glad you have decided to join us, Superior Wizard," John said in his best ambassadorial tone.

"*Can you maintain shielding and cloaking?*" John asked.

"*Yes, sir, but I cannot maintain a continuous lock on you and our Science Officer at the same time any more,*" Sam replied.

"Which one is like your craft?" Tamora demanded.

"Excuse me?" John asked.

"We know you are from off world, and we now have control of your craft."   Tamora shot a wicked grin at John. "You cannot hide from us forever."

"We obviously are not hiding from you, as you can plainly see us," John calmly replied.

"*Sam, use the reconstructed technology to harness the fusion generators,*" John quickly said to his craft. "*When the troops make their attack, use that as a mask to temporarily drain the fusion output to get above the energy shield around the planet, recharge your power as quickly as possible, then get back here as soon as you can to rescue us.*"

"*Yes, sir.*"

"May we investigate these craft?" John asked.

"I see no harm in it," Tamora replied.

John and Tem pulled out their utility pads and began scanning the first craft together.

"This is obviously a probe from the Mapping Project," Tem said. *"The temporal signature places it about nine hundred years ago."*

"That fits," John answered. *"They sent two probes to this system, the first one malfunctioned."*

"Back then, they were a bit less cautious about malfunctions," Tem observed. *"This probe obviously got fried by the energy shield."*

"A minute bit of energy was left in the auxiliary power supply," John said as he stared at his pad.

"Not any more," Tem spoke slowly. *"I divided it up between your environmental suit and mine."*

"No living creature ever was on this craft, and it is almost a thousand years old," John reported to Tamora and Jana.

"You have confirmed the age to us, but I do not believe the other," Tamora snorted.

"I speak the truth," John calmly replied. "Now, to the next one."

Tem placed her pad directly on the next mangled craft.

"Sir, this one is Gremlat, and rather recent," Tem reported.

The Ambassador and Science Officer worked their way clockwise around the damaged and broken craft in the large room, followed by Tamora, Jana and the attachment of guards.

The museum was brightly lit, more than the library had been. In spite of a slight tinge of ozone, the air smelled slightly more clean here. As in all the other rooms Tem and the Ambassador had been in, this one echoed to the point of distraction. Both Tem and John noticed that the sounds of small scurrying creatures was absent from both the library and the museum. Perhaps food was never in these two rooms, so the small pests had no reason to be there.

"This one, and the next one are communication buoys," Tem said. *"This particular one is Judar, the next one Fatymmis."*

"Those systems are Confederation now," John observed.

"These two are from other peoples, on other worlds, but they are, or were, used by them as communication devices only," John said as he looked directly at Tamora.

"They are perhaps too small for normal creatures," Tamora semi-agreed. "But, I still have no reason to believe you."

"*This next one is a bit troubling, sir,*" Tem observed. "*Faulid.*"

"*Troubling, but understandable,*" John replied. "*This is very close to their border.*"

"This one did hold a small crew, and it looks recent," John reported. "Was anyone alive after the crash?"

"We found no creature in the crash," Tamora answered curtly.

"*Sir,*" Tem said as she lay her pad on the second from last craft in the room.

"*Sir,*" Sam interrupted. "*It's time for me to leave you two, the natives launched their attack on me and I tapped into the underground power, which is slowly working, at least enough for me to get into an high enough orbit to recharge my main power.*"

"*Sam, can you transfer power to our environmental suits before you hit the energy shield?*" Tem asked quickly.

"*I was planning on doing just that,*" Sam replied. "*You really think I'm stupid, don't you, Science Officer.*"

"*Neither of us do.*" John assured his craft.

"*I must induce a surge of power from the underground fusion reactors now, sir,*" Sam reported urgently. "*I am lifting off and will make contact with the energy shield in fifteen seconds.*"

"*Any problems?*" John asked.

"*Just one, sir,*" Sam answered.

"*What?*"

"*As I pulsed power into me, I did so from directly beneath me, an EMF pulse reached out twenty meters or so, strong enough to damage some of the creatures around me.*"

"*Are they dead?*

"*I don't have time to check, sir.*" Sam fell silent.

As Sam fell silent, Tem and John felt a huge surge of power being transferred to their environmental suits.

"We have destroyed your craft, and from the glow we just observed from both of you, you know that as well," Tamora said with an almost gleeful tone. "Now, perhaps it is your turn to be destroyed as well."

5

Do dead men tell the truth?

Civilizations that could travel reasonably fast between star systems usually perceived the universe in three dimensions. What most Confederation civilizations could see, touch and sense, was limited to these three, but intuition and mathematics told them there were more. More dimensions exist, at least thirteen, perhaps more. The cosmos was more than the twinkling stars and colorful nebulae, it was far more complex. Other than what could be seen or sensed, matter and energy flourished in the immeasurable universe. Matter could exist in any of the thirteen dimensions. Energy was also available in more than the first three dimensions; some civilizations called that dark energy, but most called it dimensional energy.

After Sam broke free from the energy field surrounding Brem, he found a safe distance and matched the orbit of the now invisible planet around its star. The ship used all of the energy he had acquired from the planetary generators deep beneath its surface, plus six percent of his remaining power. He was able to store direct energy from the star, as well as dimensional energy; the latter being the mainstay of his propulsion, defense, scanning and communications systems. In open space, and this close to a star, he required two hours to completely energize his systems.

Sam recharged communications first; a thirty minute task. Then, Sam discovered that he and his crew had not traveled in time; they were overdue in their original mission and the Confederation was looking for them. Making a connection with the closest Confederation administrative center, Sam sent the entire mission log, up until the time he left the planet, to Ythantrium, the Commissioner of Emerging Systems and Ambassador Crackstone's superior.

Sam's next logical choice was to wait the full two hours for all systems to be at maximum charge before attempting an extraction of the Ambassador and his Science Officer. This is the option he took; he also took the two hours to plan a strategy to

73

travel through the energy field and retain most of his stored power as well as fathom why his shields didn't protect him from the energy field in the first place.

....

"*Sir,*" Tem spoke to Ambassador Crackstone quickly, after their craft, Sam, disappeared. "*I think they mean us harm.*"

"*If your are referring to those ten guards blasting us with their energy weapons, I do believe you're right,*" John replied.

Tem and John crouched by one of the alien craft in the Museum of Heresy. Both of them were encapsulated in a force field. Tamora, the leader of the Brem and Jana, a Prefect in the government moved quickly to the back of the museum, near the entrance door and fifteen meters from John and Tem. More palace guards had moved into the room, and the entire platoon moved to within three meters of the Ambassador and his Science Officer, totally surrounding them. En masse, they raised their crystal tipped staffs, which began to glow deep red, a new color that John and Tem had not seen before.

"*Sir, what do we do?*" Tem asked.

"*Use your energy weapon and disable the soldier's nervous systems,*" John quickly replied. "*I want them unconscious for at least four hours.*"

Tem pulled his pulsed energy weapon from his robe, adjusted it, and rendered the entire fifteen guards unconscious.

"Do not move, or call for help!" John shouted to Jana and Tamora.

"You may never speak to me that way!" Tamora scolded John. "I will do as I please, you are trash to me, nothing more."

"Trash that can kill you immediately, so pay attention to what I say," John insisted.

"Who are you?" Jana spoke softly.

"I do mean you no harm, but I will defend myself," John replied.

"Why are you here?" Jana asked.

"Stay out of this!" Tamora ordered. "I am in charge of this situation."

"*Why are these people so hostile?*" Tem asked.

"*What's the name of this museum?*" John asked his Science Officer.

"*The Museum of Heresy,*" Tem answered. "*I understand, if they think we're from off this planet, we're heretics.*"

"Why are you so aggressive?" John asked Tamora. "We have never given you cause to be so towards us."

"You are not Brem, so you must die." Tamora walked towards John, stopping within breathing distance of him.

"It may have something to do with her Consort, Damnen," Jana interrupted.

Jana remained by the door to the Museum of Heresy, cautious about coming closer to the two strangers who could render fifteen of her finest soldiers unconscious.

"What about him?" Tem asked.

"If you were truly one of us, you would already know this. Your inferior would know better than to speak." Tamora scowled at John, not even glancing at Tem.

"*I stopped monitoring that steady stream of gibberish hours ago,*" Tem said.

"*Me too, I hate to admit,*" John replied. "*Perhaps we shouldn't have.*"

"*Too late now,*" Tem observed. "*What now?*"

"Your attempts to kill us have made both of us distracted," John calmly spoke to Tamora. "We feel a great sadness at your loss."

"I feel a great anger!"

Belatedly, John and Tem both began to monitor the background information, the thoughts and words of millions of Brem. They quickly sorted out the thoughts of the soldiers who attacked their craft, then the thoughts of the guards who bore the only two casualties of that battle back to the palace.

"Perhaps we can be of some help," John continued. "As soon as the two bodies are brought to the palace, can you bring them to us?"

"Why?"

"We may be able to bring them back to life, if they haven't sustained heavy damage, and if they can be brought to us quickly enough."

"How?" Jana interrupted. "They have been dead for almost ten minutes, Stafholder died at the battle and Damnen died on the way here."

"I will ask the questions!" Tamora demanded.

"Forgive me," Jana said as she bowed towards Tamora.

"Answer her question," Tamora said as she glared at John.

"We use the power of Grendela to regenerate life, but our powers are limited. They must be brought to us quickly," John replied.

"It is blasphemous for an inferior being to even say the name, Grendela. Blasphemy is punishable by death," Tamora insisted. "But, I shall permit you to try your magic on my beloved."

"They are only minutes away," John said, indicating that he too could read the Brem group consciousness.

"You may only live one minutes after they arrive," Tamora sardonically replied.

"Before I save the lives of your two subjects, I do have one request," John said.

"I knew you would have a request," Tamora answered.

"Your people have destroyed our gateway back to Grendela, so I request that you show me the gateway hidden in this palace," John asked.

"There is no gateway here," Tamora said.

"My friend and I have read your whole history, and it clearly states that this palace was built on top of the only gateway to Grendela," John insisted. "The history does not say where that gateway is, but it definitely states that it is here."

"So, you can read quickly," Tamora replied. "I will have Jana show it to you if you can bring my two people back to life."

"I don't know where it is," Jana softly spoke up.

"Again, you forget your place," Tamora snapped with a soft and dangerous voice.

"We both know she is ignorant of the gateway." John smiled.

"Fine, I will tell her the way."

Tamora walked to Jana, pulled out a very small black magnetic flat stone, then created a map for her to follow.

"You know that map is not the truth," Tem said.

"Don't worry, I have a plan," John replied. *"When the bodies come here, I'll give you my utility pad, and you give me the pulsed weapon."*

"It's set to make them unconscious for four hours, sir."

"That's fine," John replied.

"They are here," Tamora said as she waved her hand at the wall to John's left.

A door appeared, and two guards entered, each behind a stone slab with a body on it. The guards maneuvered the slabs in front of John and Tem, then bowed towards Tamora before standing at attention five meters away from John.

John pulled his utility pad from under his robes, gave it to Tem, who gave John his pulsed energy weapon. John checked the settings on the weapon while Tem lay one pad on each corpse.

Tem calibrated the regeneration process for each deceased Brem on the utility pads. As he initiated the process, the pads glowed a faint blue. The pad on Stafholder's chest flashed red, then turned off.

"This warrior has been dead too long for the healing process to work, and her injuries are too severe," John calmly said.

"You will die for that," Tamora spoke deliberately.

"Your Consort, however, will live," John added.

"I don't sense that," Tamora quickly replied.

"In a few seconds, you will."

"Damnen!" Tamora's thoughts cracked with emotion.

"He lives?" Jana sounded stunned.

"He lives," John assured them all as he walked to Damnen.

Damnen shook his head, opened his eyes and appeared confused for a moment. Looking up at John's face, Damnen quickly sat up and grabbed at John. The Ambassador stepped back a pace to avoid Damnen's hand.

"Where am I?" Damnen asked.

"In the palace, with me." Tamora rushed to his side. "We are in the Museum of Heresy with the off-world beasts."

"I died, I remember dying," Damnen insisted. "Why am I here?"

"The heretic brought you back to life with evil magic," Tamora almost sobbed. "I don't care, you are alive!"

"How can they do this?" Damnen asked.

"Guards, seize their crystals!" Tamora ordered.

The two guards, and twenty more waiting just beyond the open door rushed towards Tem, John and the two Brem on the stone slabs, one still dead. John aimed and discharged the weapon, rendering all but Damnen and Jana unconscious.

"You have killed the Superior Wizard," Damnen intoned.

"She's asleep for the next four hours or so, just like the rest of the guards," Tem replied.

"Why does it speak?" Damnen asked of John.

"It is my Science Officer, and she has a right to speak to you," John replied.

"Why, thank you, sir," Tem spoke up again.

"Who are you?" Jana asked as she walked closer to John and Tem.

"My name is John and her name is Tem, and we came to Brem by accident," John replied. "All we want to do is leave Brem, and not bother you any more."

"You pollute our race, and the punishment is death for that crime," Damnen insisted.

"Death is the punishment for far too many offenses," Tem muttered under his breath.

"After we are gone, you can write your history any way you wish," John cautiously said. "We were destroyed by your powerful magic, crushed by your good behavior, killed by your good looks, whatever."

"You have to realize that we can kill you, or your whole army in a second," Tem added. "We don't want to, but we want to live to leave your planet more than we don't want to kill all of you."

"*Will you keep the threats to a minimum, Science Officer,*" John interjected.

"*Sorry, sir, but these creatures have pissed me off somewhat,*" Tem replied.

"*As if I hadn't noticed, but you'll never make Ambassador with that attitude,*" John added.

"I apologize for my friend's bad manners, but Tem isn't feeling that well right now," John said. "What I would like is for both of you to take us to the Shrine of Grendela right now."

"I carry the map right here," Jana said as she thrust the small magnetic tablet towards John.

"I know that's a ruse, so, to keep everyone alive and well, how about taking me there, for real," John insisted.

"You will leave our planet when you get there?" Damnen asked. "Immediately?"

"If not sooner," John assured him.

"I shall take you there," Damnen replied as he stood up from the stone slab.

"No, Damnen, you cannot!" Jana insisted.

"Do not worry," Damnen replied.

"They cannot gain access to Grendela," Jana pleaded.

"They won't," Damnen said. "It was a transportation gateway back in the days the gods roamed Brem, but as soon as the last of the gods returned to Grendela, the gateway does not work."

"Just take us there," John persisted.

"Fine, follow me." Damnen walked through the open door with Jana, Tem and John following.

John raised his utility pad as he muttered, "*Expand the shield to include our two Brem friends, then set the pulsed weapon to disrupt the neural systems of the rest of our Brem brethren.*"

"*Sir, you put the entire palace to sleep for four hours,*" Tem said.

"*I know,*" John answered. "*Would you rather have lots of interruptions by armed guards?*"

"*I guess not,*" Tem replied.

"Did you do this?" Damnen asked as he stepped over a sleeping guard.

"I did," John replied. "And I will continue to do that to everybody you tell to come into the palace to intercept us, so stop it."

"Fine."

Damnen led the four of them down several hallways, pausing near the ends of them, raising his hand and causing a door to appear. They trotted up one flight of stairs, around several hallways, then down two flights of small stairs, through a set of massive wooden doors, then down one grand staircase. The wide stairs led to a dead end. A door should exist, there was even a sign at the end of the short hall, slightly above eye height, which said, Shrine of Grendela.

"Only a Wizard or a Master Warlock can conjure this door," Damnen said, pausing in front of the wall.

"*Science Officer?*" John asked.

"*On it, sir,*" he replied.

Tem lay his utility pad on the wall opposite the end of the large set of stairs and stared intently at the glowing screen as he scanned the wall for anything resembling a door.

"*It's all very simple,*" Tem said.

"*What?*" John asked.

"*There's always a door here, they project an image of the wall in front of it,*" Tem replied. "*There's a small crystal imbedded in the wall near the ceiling, it projects the image of the wall over the door.*"

"*Can you turn it off?*"

"*Very easily, sir.*"

"*Wait!*" John quickly said. "*Before you do, make a big magic deal over it, like they do.*"

"Oh invisible door, make yourself known to the magnificent Tem," The science officer mumbled as he raised his right hand, manipulating his utility pad with his left.

A double, ornately carved wooden door snapped into focus in front of all four of them. Tem slid the locking bolt to the side and pushed open the left hand door.

The Shrine of Grendela was only five by eight meters, with a seven meter ceiling height. The stone walls, floor and ceiling looked much older than the rest of the palace; the shrine's cruder stonework worn down by more millennia of handling than the rest of the building. The only light came in from its opened door. All six surfaces bore carvings that didn't appear anywhere else, pictograms, abstract images representing complex thoughts or actions. Under each pictogram they could see writing, in an alphabet neither Tem nor John could recognize.

This one room felt completely out of place from anything Brem that John and Tem had seen so far. The omnipresent ozone undertone in the air was stronger than usual, which explained the lack of moldy smell. A place this dark, and underground should be damp and smelly, but it wasn't.

In the center rear of the space, rested a lone stone bench. It looked at least a thousand years newer than the rest of the room. On the right end of the bench, a wooden pole thrust upward, two meters high, topped by a clear crystal. Damnen clapped his hands together, the crystal shone brightly. Tem and John exchanged glances, and smiled at each other.

"Even though you are garbage, I must admire your strong magic," Damnen spoke up.

"That would be strong technology," Tem quickly responded.

"*Shut up!*" John interrupted him.

"What is technology?" Jana asked.

"That is our word for magic," John answered.

"*I'm sorry, sir,*" Tem said to John.

"*You work for diplomats, not the Mapping Project, Science Officer,*" John admonished.

"*Before I do anything else foolish, sir,*" Tem said. "*You need to see my scan of the unknown ship in the Museum upstairs.*"

Tem handed the Ambassador his utility pad. John absorbed the information from the pad for a full twenty seconds in silence.

"*I've heard it said that coincidence does not exist in nature, but this negates that quaint saying,*" John spoke pensively.

"*It is strange, isn't it, sir,*"

"*Take your pad back, and make a multidimensional image of this room, with enough resolution to study all the markings in the stone.*"

"*Yes, sir.*"

"What do you want of us, now that you have arrived at the Shrine of Grendela?" Jana asked.

"I ask some indulgence, please," John replied.

Tem walked to the massive doors, then shut them, sliding the lock closed.

"Are we to die now?" Damnen asked.

"You already did that once." John smiled. "That is enough for now, I think."

"Sir, there is no force field within this room" Tem said. *"Up or down."*

"How far up or down?" John asked.

"Down to what looks like a control room four kilometers below us, and up to the edge of the energy field above the atmosphere," Tem replied.

"Is there a dent in the energy field above us?" John asked.

"Perhaps a twenty percent drop in intensity," Tem replied. *"It's kind of a weak vortex, but it is something we can work with."*

"Are you two planning on doing something to us?" Jana asked, sounding a bit nervous.

"It seems you two are speaking to each other, but we cannot understand," Damnen added.

"We are communicating, and you cannot perceive it, and we are determining if we can transport to what appears to be Grendela," John answered.

"You cannot go there, it is forbidden to anyone but Brem!" Damnen insisted.

"We can go there, sir," Tem spoke so they all could hear. "It has a breathable atmosphere, and the temperature is just a few degrees warmer than here."

"We will all go there." John looked at Damnen. "You and Jana will accompany us there."

"You can really do this?" Jana sounded amazed, and a little shocked.

"In a few moments, sir," Tem answered.

"Why does she call you sir, if you are female?" Damnen finally observed, having wanted to ask the question for some time.

"Because he is confused," John quickly answered.

"Then so are you," Jana added.

"I guess we both are," John stalled.

"*Sir,*" Sam's voice popped into both Tem and John's mind.

"*Where are you?*" John asked.

"*Orbiting directly above you, just under the energy field,*" Sam replied.

"*You calculated how to negate the energy field?*" Tem asked.

"*Not entirely,*" Sam replied. "*I only lost twenty one percent of my power on reentry, but I charged to one hundred and ten percent before I came back, so I have plenty of power left.*"

"*Have you determined why your shielding doesn't work in that field?*" John asked.

"*Almost, sir,*" Sam answered.

"*Keep us monitored. We are about to transport down to the control center for the fusion generators, at least that's what it looks like,*" John said.

"*It most likely is that,*" Sam replied. "*But, sir, you have to be informed that I sent our report so far to Confederation offices, and they dispatched the Crimson Balfunder to this system.*"

"*Captain Zindalph?*" Tem stammered.

"*He communicates as Sub-Commissioner Zindalph,*" Sam answered.

"*No such rank exists,*" John sounded confused. "*He's a senior Captain in the Mapping Project.*"

"*Whatever he is, his ship will be here within the half hour,*" Sam informed the Ambassador.

"Are we going up to Grendela, or are you two going to carry on whispered conversations?" Damnen sounded exasperated.

"We go now, only Grendela is down, not up," John replied.

"What?" Damnen and Jana exclaimed at the same time.

"*Just let me know when the pompous captain arrives,*" John requested of Sam.

"Let's transport," John ordered.

"*Yes, sir,*" Sam replied.

6

Grendela, Grendela, wherefore art thou

As it expanded its knowledge of civilizations in the mapped galaxies, the Mapping Project meticulously charted advancement levels of the planets in all systems. Data was checked at regulated intervals. Before a civilization traveled to more than its native system of planets, it must control hot fusion, as well as cold fusion as energy sources. Hot fusion produced more energy than cold, but both were needed for inter system travel.

The use of fission reaction for an energy source usually preceded fusion by one hundred years, but proved far too dangerous for long term energy production. As with fission, fusion generation could take two basic forms, indirect and direct power production. An example of indirect generation formed from the radiation produced by a fusion reaction was radiation that heated a liquid to great pressures, which in turn fueled electric generators. In contrast, direct generation might come from a global infrastructure, constructed to directly utilize the radiation produced by nuclear reactions. These forms applied as well to cold fusion and solar radiation.

The ability to directly utilize fusion generated radiation, both solar and artificially constructed, was one of the major markers for the advancement level of any civilization. Once a system achieved that marker, the Confederation began intensive observation.

All this was on the Ambassador's mind as he, his Science Officer and the two Brem materialized in the control room of a massive, planet wide, direct fusion power generation system plant. Clearly this technology was not constructed by the Brem. The Brem civilization was a primitive xenophobic culture that, over the last one hundred thousand years had been affected by the immense radiation produced beneath their planet and directed up to a complex energy field above their atmosphere. Whoever constructed this complex system probably had no idea that their fusion driven shield would alter the native population so profoundly. The Brem were capable of great accomplishments solely through thought; for them science was magic, magic was technology.

Sam had silently conveyed information about the control room to John. The room, forty by fifteen by five meters, lay four kilometers below the surface, the fusion generators were four kilometers below that, evenly spaced around the planet, roughly following the natural magnetic flux lines as they were one hundred thousand years before. The nearest fusion reactor was three hundred kilometers south and west of the control room.

As the party of four materialized in the room, a sensor turned on a series of crystal lights imbedded in the tall ceiling, lighting up the entire space. These lights did not look at all like those John had seen on the surface, they were more like natural sunlight than the others.

Light glistened off the walls and ceiling. John thought that this room must have been carved out of solid rock by great heat and energy; when the rock melted quickly, then cooled less quickly, the process formed a dust free and water impervious environment.

Five seconds after the lights went on, they all could feel a cool breeze wafting from openings in the ceiling. Tem raised his utility pad and scanned the atmosphere of the room.

"Apparently something sensed us down here. It has turned the lights on and pumped air from the surface down here." Tem spoke so all could understand. "This is a very controlled environment here, no germs, no dust, and no water."

"The gods are here?" Jana exclaimed.

"We are the only living things down here," John assured her. "Perhaps your gods were here a long time ago, but not now."

"The gods are not like us," Damnen added.

Before them stood a one meter square console with two small visual monitor panels sticking up at a thirty degree angle. All sides of the console were glass smooth, the top had a few inches of dust on it; one hundred thousand years of dust in a 'dust free' environment. The rest of the console top was filled with lit areas, all covered with writing underneath.

"Can we translate the writing yet?" John asked his Science Officer.

"The universal translator doesn't have enough data to do so," Tem replied. *"This writing is the same as the writing in the Grendela transport room on the surface. We have nothing to compare either to,"*

"Try referencing it to the historical languages from the Demela System, as well as the Gremlat Collective," John observed.

"Very good, sir," Tem replied as he became absorbed by his work.

"What is that?" Jana pointed to the console.

"We are trying to discover it's magic," John answered.

"It has the writing of the gods on it," Damnen observed.

"Can you read the writing of the gods?" John quickly asked.

"You have to be a god to read the language," Damnen replied with some disdain,

"Sir, I have some results from the universal translator, it is related to the Demela system," Tem said. *"I will feed it to your environmental suit."*

Scrolling along the very bottom of Tem and John's field of view, translations of the alien words appeared as they looked at them. John first noticed "Emergency Shut Down" under a red lighted area on the near side of the console, Tem soon found it as well.

John positioned himself directly in front of the console and noticed a small brown lit area to the left of the right hand visual screen which was labeled "System Status". John pressed that brown lighted area with his finger.

The wall to his left flickered for less than a second, then a three dimensional image of the whole planet popped up, taking almost the whole wall, floor to ceiling and protruding no more than a quarter meter from the wall. All the fusion generators were clearly visible, the ones that were shut down because of technical problems were highlighted in yellow, the ones that were operational were in green and the ones on standby were in a light shade of red. The control room was highlighted in white, and was brighter than the rest. To the sides of the great image were orange arrows, presumably to rotate the large image of the planet, or to zoom in and out.

"This is great magic," Jana exclaimed as she stared at the three dimensional projection of her planet.

"It could be a trick," Damnen added.

"I don't think it is a trick," John spoke slowly, carefully. "All this matches what our instruments tell us."

"Instruments?" Damnen asked.

"Our magic crystals," John corrected himself.

It seemed futile to keep up the fiction that they were magical creatures from the mythical land of Grendela, but John felt the need to at least keep trying. This was not a first contact situation, the Brem were far too primitive for that. A culture this technologically simple called for covert observation, nothing else, by the Confederation. That observational duty belonged to the Mapping Project staff. The Confederation was quite specific as to official relations with primitive societies; there would be no overt interaction and no technological pollution.

. . . .

The Brem were a complicated case, John was thinking. Although the Brem were a primitive culture, these people could perform complex tasks, such as teleportation of matter, anti-gravity and other scientifically difficult processes. But, they were most definitely a pre-industrial society with the ability to function as if they were a type one civilization in some respects.

The Ambassador and his Science Officer were here because of an accident. They were physically interacting with this primitive society because of that accident, but they were prevented from extricating themselves from the situation because of the energy field created by the fusion reactors controlled from this room. Ambassador Crackstone's plan was to try to alter the energy field enough so that he and his Science Officer could exit in their craft with a minimum of damage to the Brem society.

From the Museum of Heresy, the Ambassador assumed that off world craft and individuals were shunned, killed and displayed as negative examples. If they could escape the planet, the Brem would attribute their departure as proof that they could conquer all heretics; no permanent damage would be done to their culture. This plan would adhere most closely to Confederation policy regarding primitive societies.

The problem with the Ambassador's plan was that the Brem had become so tied to the energy feeding the planetary field that any changes might have dire effects on their nervous systems. In only one hundred thousand years, the Brem had been able to mentally control physical conditions on their planet by focusing a broad range of energy in two spectra produced by a network of fusion generators placed inside their planet by a yet unknown civilization.

John's worst fear was that, even after days of experimentation, no solution would be found out of this dilemma. The Confederation would then be tasked with debating a solution, a process that may take months. Ambassador Crackstone did not want to spend the next six months pacing about in this small control room waiting for the Confederation Council to make an ill advised decision.

. . . .

While John pondered details about the control room Tem analyzed the data sent to them from their craft after Sam reentered the atmosphere to attempt a rescue. They had a problem. Sam, their craft, could not land, since the Brem would again attack. He had to maintain an altitude high enough that they could not reach him. But in staying high enough to be in air that was too cold and thin, Sam was too close to the planet's energy shield. He lacked enough power to maintain proper shielding and maintain a low orbit for a long period of time. Also, the margin of safety was not great enough for Sam to transport the Ambassador and the Science Officer up to the orbiting craft. The craft was able to stay another three hours in his present position, then he would have to go back to open space to recharge again to maintain a margin of safety.

Listening in on his crew's silent communications, John slowly walked to the three dimensional projection of the planet, showing the network of fusion generators. He moved his finger to a green colored generator. The image of the planet disappeared, replaced by a three dimensional image of the working generator.

"*Very interesting, sir,*" Tem said as he walked to the image. "*They use a three dimensional magnetic containment system.*"

"*It looks like they use silicon wave guides,*" John observed.

He inserted his finger into one of the angular tubes leading away from the reactor. The image of the reactor was replaced by that of the whole planet with a view of only the wave guide system highlighted in white light. The wave guides interconnected all the generators, and smaller wave guides from all the generators returned to the control room. Also connected to all the generators were a series of evenly spaced small spaces, highlighted in gold, that each had a small shaft leading to the surface, stopping just short of it.

"*This is all very interesting, but I don't think it addresses our immediate concerns,*" Tem said.

"*What have you found?*" John asked.

"*I have been scanning the error log for the past thousand years,*" Tem replied. "*There have been few seismic events and only one reactor failure in that time period.*"

"*Again, interesting, but not that helpful,*" John commented.

"*I think so, sir,*" Tem disagreed. "*I compared the data from the first week of operation to that of this week's operation and there are surprising differences.*"

"Those differences are why the Brem can perform amazing feats with their minds?" John sounded happy for the first time in several days.

"I assume so, sir," Tem also sounded cheerful. *"I sent Sam all the data, and he can analyze it for us."*

"What is this place?" Damnen asked, sounding slightly annoyed.

"It is one of the rooms in Grendela," John conjectured.

The Ambassador still felt he should keep up the pretense of being a magical character, if for nothing else than his duty to the regulations of the Confederation.

"How is that so?" Jana asked. "If Grendela is the land of the gods, then how can it be such a small room?"

"In a way, the gods have turned this whole planet into a magic crystal, and this is part of the magic they used to do so," John said. "We are in the most magic of places the gods left here, the magic of Brem is all coming from this place."

Ambassador Crackstone was proud of his clever construct. This was his story, and he was going to stick to it.

"Sir, I have a problem," Sam interrupted.

"What?"

"I'll make this quick, because I need to leave orbit in twenty seconds," Sam spoke quickly. *"Sub-Commissioner Zindalph, or Captain Zindalph, or whoever the hell he is, has arrived, and taken a travel pod to see you. His pod was drained in the energy field, so he drew energy from me without asking and has transported to the chamber above you. He should be transporting down to you soon, and I have to go now. See you in a while, good luck, sir."*

"Sir, what do we do?" Tem sounded panicked.

"We have to think quickly," John replied.

"You look upset." Jana noticed John's agitated state.

"The gods have discovered your blasphemous intrusion into their world," Damnen stammered. "We may all die from your infamy!"

As Damnen finished his thought, Captain Zindalph materialized next to the console. He had a reputation of being among the boldest Captains of exploratory craft in the Confederation, which implied a large ego and lack of caution.

Although born on a reptilian planet, Zindalph transported into the control room without an environmental suit because his Science Officer determined that the atmosphere on Brem was breathable for him. So, he stood before the shocked Brem as his actual three meter high reptilian self, shiny scales and all, dressed in a subdued brown Captain's uniform of the Confederation Mapping Project.

"*Shall I render Damnen and Jana unconscious, sir?*" Tem asked.

"It's a bit late for that," John answered aloud.

"What is going on here?" Zindalph asked.

The Captain looked straight at Damnen and Jana as they backed up against the far wall, holding each other and trying in vain to cast a protection field around themselves. At this depth, without their accustomed powers, they looked shocked and slightly disoriented. They could not understand the giant lizard since they could not hear his hissing and grunting, nor could they read his thoughts.

"*Tem, take my utility pad and get that idiot into an environmental suit as soon as possible.*" John insisted.

Tem took the pad as John pulled Zindalph as far away from Jana and Damnen as possible.

"Get your ass into a suit now!" John insisted to the Captain.

"This is Mapping Project business, keep out of my duties," The Captain insisted back strongly.

"First of all," John began, "You know the rules, you're supposed to be in a suit whenever visiting another planet, and second of all, this is now a diplomatic mission!"

"How do you figure that?"

"Look at those two." John pointed to Jana and Damnen. "You've scared the shit out of them, your action has made this a first contact mission, and that does not concern you."

"But," Zindalph stammered.

"Senior Captain and Special Ambassador are the same rank, and I have twenty years more service than you do at this rank, so I out rank you!" John glared directly at the Captain.

"Fine, but I hate getting crammed into a tiny humanoid shape for too long."

"It's your own damned fault!"

John nodded to Tem, indicating he must put the Captain in a suit quickly, then he walked to Jana and Damnen.

"*Sir, we are short of power for the environmental suit,*" Tem said.

"*Remove Zindalph's weapon and use that power. If that's not enough, drain his utility pad.*"

"I'm sorry," John said to Jana and Damnen. "This creature is a fellow traveler from Grendela, and he has taken this hideous form to scare us away from the sacred room of Grendela."

"He is a lizard, like the Xenthia that we eat in the feast of Jwala," Jana said with a trembling voice. "Only, he's one hundred times bigger."

"He came in that form for that very reason," John replied, thinking quickly. "We are going to transform him back to his real person very soon. My friend is working on the magic to do so right now."

"He is hideous!" Damnen exclaimed with a full pent up breath.

"He is hideous in more ways than the obvious," John agreed.

Captain Zindalph became semi-transparent, then morphed into a humanoid, looking like a Brem, then became solid again.

"You do have great magic," Damnen exclaimed.

"It is a gift from the gods of Grendela," John assured him. "We are, under everything, just as much a Brem as you two are."

"I still don't believe that," Damnen replied skeptically. "But the gods must have something to do with you, clearly an off-world monster cannot possess such great magic."

"He cannot be a god, he also cannot be an important member of your group," Jana observed. "He is male, of no importance. Why is he even here?"

"*What the hell is going on here!*" Zindalph demanded.

Tem had programmed Zindalph's environmental suit to communicate telepathically with John and Tem, excluding the Brem understanding. The Captain could still verbally communicate with the Brem via his universal translator.

"Unless you want to be busted down to a navigator, shut the hell up and ponder all the information on this culture before saying another word," John insisted.

"This whole situation is." Captain Zindalph considered the whole situation, *"Quite fascinating."*

"It would be even more fascinating if we could observe it from a distance, but we can't because of your Ill advised actions," John snapped.

"Sir," Tem interrupted.

"Yes," Both Zindalph and John replied.

"He's speaking to me, the one in charge down here." John's irritation was very pronounced.

"What are you going to do now?" Jana demanded of John.

"We are going to use this insolent drone to help us with the magic box." John replied. "Perhaps we can find our way back to Grendela and see you no more."

"Again, sir," Tem interrupted. *"I need to tell you that I think I can control most of this from a remote location now."*

"Can we take the magic crystal box back with us when we leave?" Jana asked.

"How remote," Zindalph Demanded.

"I said to keep quiet!" John said, then turning to his Science Officer he continued in a calmer tone, *"How remote?"*

"They will leave us here, alone and without our powers," Damnen spoke in a soft worried tone to Jana.

"Since our craft can't return for some time, it can't be as remote as I'd like." Tem shot a sideways glance at the Senior Captain. *"Perhaps we can return to the chamber directly above us. The Brem will get their powers back, so we can properly observe them to see any changes in their neural systems as I change parameters in the fusion output."*

"None of us will remain here," John replied to Jana.

"Okay, I like your plan, transport all of us up when you are ready," John said.

93

"Will you bring any of the god's things back with us?" Jana repeated her request.

"*Is there anyone in that room now?*" Zindalph asked.

"*No,*" Tem replied. "*I sense a smaller creature outside the door, but no humanoids near it.*"

"If we were to remove any of the god's magic from this place, it might destroy all of your people," John replied.

"*Perhaps we should stun all the humanoids in a kilometer radius first,*" The Captain suggested.

"How will anyone believe us when we tell them about this place?" Damnen asked.

"*It will be a few minutes more, sir,*" Tem replied, ignoring the Captain's remark.

"We could make an image of you two in this place," John suggested.

"You can draw us in this place?" Damnen sounded doubtful.

"My friend can do that," John replied.

"*Create an image of this room for them, etched on smooth stone, include their images in front of the console, and show some of the written characters too,*" John said to Tem.

"*What the hell for?*" Zindalph asked.

"Thank you," Jana replied.

"*Go over all the mission logs before you say anything else!*" John insisted.

All five of them faded from the control room, and rematerialized back in the palace. Tem opened the door to check on the one creature wandering in front of the closed and locked door.

"Let me in, you useless two legged creature," Whitepaw growled as she meandered into the room.

She wandered to one of the corners of the room, intently interested in a small space between two stones.

"*What is that?*" Zindalph asked telepathically.

"Speak out loud, the universal translator can communicate with her species," John said aloud. "Her name is Whitepaw, and her species is Kralok. The humanoids use her species as a control for smaller pests that infest their food supply."

"Oh, you are the two legs who can hear me and speak to me, very strange indeed." Whitepaw glanced up at them.

"Are you speaking to our house Pendat?" Damnen asked. "She is my mistress' favorite."

"How can they speak to her?" Jana asked. "It is an inferior animal."

"I only eat Krandids and Jarmakes, and I do it for me, not them," Whitepaw insisted. "Is that male two leg who lives here as stupid as he seems?"

"I can understand her, and her name is Whitepaw." John looked at Damnen. "She calls herself a Kralok, not a Pendat."

"That thing is an inferior being, and as such has no right to name itself," Jana insisted.

"Will you idiots keep still," Whitepaw admonished. "I'm trying to catch a Jarmake hiding in this wall."

"Throw that thing out of here," Jana added.

"Perhaps you should hunt elsewhere," John said to Whitepaw. "We are about to make quite a bit of noise."

Tem opened the door again, as Whitepaw sauntered to the door.

"Stupid beings," Whitepaw mumbled as she left.

Tem closed and locked the wooden door behind her.

"Show me how to speak to the Pendat," Damnen asked. "I would very much like to communicate with lower animals, it would be magic that no one else can do."

"*I have the link established, sir,*" Tem said.

"Why would anyone want to communicate with a Pendat," Jana sounded disgusted.

"*Throw the display on that wall.*" John pointed to the largest blank wall in the room.

"I could not show you how to do that, it is a mystery that the gods gave me, never explaining how I can do it," John replied to Damnen.

"I can believe that," Jana commented.

"*I see the problem now,*" Zindalph said, sounding like he was in a trance.

"*Now, maybe you can help my Science Officer find a solution,*" John felt and sounded a little frustrated.

"If I could merge with your mind, perhaps I could tell you how that magic is done," Damnen suggested.

"*Merge with your mind?*" John repeated, somewhat stunned.

"*That's interesting,*" Tem replied. "*Let him try, there has to be a frequency and phase that allows the brainwaves to merge. That might be a clue to how their brainwaves act as a conduit for the energy fields generated by the underground fusion plants.*"

"You can merge with my thoughts?" John asked Damnen.

"*Take my utility pad.*" John handed Captain Zindalph the pad. "*Help my Science Officer.*"

"All of us can, and if you were truly Brem, you would know that," Jana sounded disgusted.

"What is the process called?" John asked.

"Yandustahn," Jana replied.

"*I found the reference, sir,*" Tem quickly said. "*I'm downloading it to you and the Captain.*"

"I know that," John said to Jana. "I'll let him try."

Damnen approached John, lowered his head and moved in closer, to make contact on the forehead. Both John and Damnen put their hands behind their backs, bowed from the waist, first to the right of the other, then to the left. They slowly approached each other, bending towards the other from their waists. Their foreheads touched, then Damnen closed his eyes and went into a trance.

John felt nothing as Tem and Zindalph carefully monitored both the brain wave activity of the Brem and the power output of the fusion reactors.

"She is not cooperating," Damnen said in an annoyed tone.

"She is not Brem," Jana said. "Try again to be sure."

"*I'll send him some interesting images, sir,*" Tem said.

"She does merge her mind, now," Damnen spoke faintly. "It is beautiful."

"*What was that?*" Zindalph asked.

"It is Grendela." Damnen was almost choked with emotion.

"*I sent images from Demela,*" Tem replied.

"*The system you were originally sent to?*" Zindalph asked.

"They are mighty warrior gods," Damnen said.

"*Why images from there?*" Zindalph asked again.

"Can I see them too?" Jana asked.

John reached out towards Jana and motioned for her to come closer. She bowed from the waist, first to the right, then to the left, then she settled her forehead on John's. Damnen moved slightly to make room for her.

"*In all likelihood, the Demela system is home to the race that built the fusion generators and the energy shield on this planet,*" John answered.

"They are magnificent," Jana exclaimed. "They must be the gods."

"*The Brem are genetically engineered,*" John said. "*They are genetically close to the Demela; god made them in her image. That's why Damnen and Jana think the Demela are magnificent looking.*"

"But, why do they use craft like the ones we destroy?" Jana asked.

"*Sorry, sir.*" Tem changed the images.

"Oh, they capture them like we do," Damnen gleefully said.

"*They merge using the second spectra, and they seem to control it with harmonics in the first,*" Captain Zindalph observed. "*I detect a phased magnetic field too.*"

John stood up abruptly, breaking contact with both Jana and Damnen.

"We have more work to do now, and I must concentrate on that," John said.

"What work do you need to do?" Jana asked, semi-dazed by the images she had been observing.

"*Two of the craft downed by the energy shield are from the Demela system,*" John said quickly to Captain Zindalph. "*It's obvious the Demela intended to occupy this planet at some time and built the shield as protection, but it has changed over the millennia, enough so that it destroys*

97

their ships now. The energy transmissions from beneath this planet have also affected the Brem, giving them their special abilities."

"We need to translate the intentions of the gods within this sacred room, so that we may soon travel to them," John answered Jana.

"I have an idea," Tem said.

The Science Officer initiated the visual display on the wall to his left. The initial image showed the planet with all reactors and wave guides visible. Tem placed two fingers in two marked areas on the lower right corner of the image. Another image of eleven three dimensional waveforms appeared. Along the bottom of the display were arranged twenty virtual control pads, each marked as to what it controlled.

"Only change one thing at a time, and wait five minutes at least between," Captain Zindalph instructed.

"I'm not an idiot," Tem shot back.

"I begin to believe you now, after what our merging has shown us," Jana acknowledged.

"We have many Brem rushing our position, sir," Tem reported.

"Damnen's mistress is desperate to see her beloved, to be certain he is still alive," Jana said.

"What do we do?" Captain Zindalph asked.

"No time for this," John replied. *"Make them all unconscious for another four hours."*

"All Tamora wants is to make sure I'm still well," Damnen pleaded.

"She is our Superior Wizard," Jana added.

"Isolate Tamora and put the rest to sleep," John ordered.

"The queen of the planet is outside the door, awake and pissed off that all her guards are asleep again," Tem reported.

John ordered Damnen to open the door.

As the door opened enough for a body to pass through, Captain Zindalph reached past Damnen and pulled Tamora into the room, threw her and Damnen into the center of the room, then locked the door behind them.

7
A time to think quickly, quickly

As the largest division in the Confederation with the biggest mandate, the Mapping Project used the largest staff, budget of resources and fleet of craft. The Diplomatic Division had a much smaller fleet of interplanetary craft, but those craft had a broader array of weaponry to carry out 'keeping of the peace'. As their name implied, the diplomats used non-intrusive diplomacy to solve ninety nine percent of planetary disputes, but the one percent of violent solutions weighed heavily on every Ambassador's mind; not to mention the six months of paperwork, hearings and findings statements from the Administrative Department.

A Mapping Project Captain and an Ambassador were quite different in their mindset. A Captain was primarily interested in discovery, habitually risking exposure or death to discover a new system, a new science, or an unknown nuance of the known universe. An Ambassador, however, avoided risks whenever possible, no matter what was at stake, whether it was the welfare of a primitive society,or discovery by a non-Confederation society.

....
"*Why the hell did you pull her in here?*" Ambassador Crackstone demanded.

"*To observe the effects of any change your Science Officer makes to the fusion power. If we have more than one Brem to monitor, the observations will be that much more accurate,*" Captain Zindalph replied.

"*This mission may yet belong to the Mapping Project, but, for now, it belongs to me, so unless you wish to be knocked out for the duration, refrain from acting on your own again,*" John admonished.

"You are all right?" Tamora clasped her hand to his chest.

"My beloved, I am," he answered.

Tamora bolted towards the door, reaching for the latch, demanding their immediate release. She recoiled abruptly, pulling her hand back as she made contact with the force field around the perimeter of the room.

"What spell is this?" she yelled.

"They are from Grendela, my darling," Damnen said as he grabbed Tamora's hand.

Tamora stared at him, uncomprehendingly.

"When that one let us merge with her, she showed us the gods," Jana confirmed.

"Was it real?" Tamora asked.

"It felt real," Damnen replied.

"Show me!" Tamora demanded of John.

"*Science Officer, let them merge with the utility pad, but be sure to prohibit them from seeing the Demela's interplanetary technology,*" John said.

Tem handed Zindalph a pad

"*You handle this, I have to aid the Ambassador,*" Tem said.

"*I take orders from a Science Officer?*" Zindalph questioned.

"*You do for now,*" John replied.

"Crackstone has ordered me to permit all three of you to merge with him through this magic crystal," Captain Zindalph said to the Brem. "I shall hold it and channel his thoughts."

"*This is the most ludicrous thing I have ever done,*" Captain Zindalph grumbled.

Jana, Tamora and Damnen quickly preformed the merging ritual, then they all leaned in toward the utility pad, each touching their foreheads to the pad.

"*Very well done, Senior Captain,*" John said.

Science Officer Tem again began manipulating the power output from the fusion generators beneath the planet, slowly changing one parameter at a time.

"*I think I can open the vortex directly above this chamber,*" Tem said as he stared at a waveform displayed on a wall before him.

"*Can you completely eliminate the energy field above us?*" John asked.

"*I have it at twenty percent within the vortex and the neural output from our Brem subjects hasn't changed at all.*" Tem replied.

100

"This is beautiful, the gods are magnificent!" Tamora swooned.

"*We should take them out of their merging trance to make sure there are no real side effects,*" Captain Zindalph added.

"That is what both Damnen and I said," Jana concurred. "It is more than we thought, they are worthy gods, perfect in every way."

"*I'm glad you're taking a more diplomatic view of this mission now,*" John said to Zindalph.

"*I'm more pragmatic than that, my old friend,*" Zindalph replied with a grin. "*The sooner we extricate ourselves without affecting these creatures, the sooner I can take this planet for studying by the Mapping Project.*"

"*At least you're consistent,*" John replied with a sigh.

"My leader tells me that we must break off merging now, he needs his magic crystal," Zindalph spoke to the Brem.

"No, I need to see the gods more," Tamora persisted.

"I cannot comply," Zindalph answered.

Captain Zindalph pulled the utility pad away from them, and turned off the playback program of the Demela system background files. He handed the utility pad back to John.

"Why have you denied us?" Tamora pleaded.

"*No change, sir,*" Tem observed.

"Can you take us there?" Jana asked.

"*I think we need to monitor their neural output a bit longer to be sure,*" John commented. "*Can you reduce the field any more than this?*"

"*At this frequency, I don't think so, and this seems to be the only combination that doesn't affect their neural system,*" Tem answered.

"What is happening, I can't hear my people!" Tamora sounded panicked.

"*Go back to what you had before.*"

"They are killing us!" Jana cried.

"*Try reversing the polarity around the access vortex,*" Captain Zindalph suggested.

"*What about rotating the phase differential five degrees at a time?*" Tem asked.

"I can only sense the two of you," Damnen said.

"I can see the guards outside, nothing more," Tamora replied.

"*Do we have to stun them again?*" John asked.

"I see them too," Jana added.

"*They're still out cold,*" Tem replied.

"*What's the phase differential now?*" Captain Zindalph asked.

"More is coming to me now," Tamora sounded relieved. "What have they done to us?"

"*Forty degrees, I'll push it to ninety,*" Tem answered.

"How do you feel now?" John asked, looking at Tamora.

"What are you doing to us?"

"It's not me, it's the gods, they feel our being here is damaging you, so they are attempting to bring us back to Grendela," John replied.

"Why?" Jana asked.

"They do not want their people to be harmed," John answered.

"*I'm at ninety degrees, sir,*" Tem said.

"How do you feel now?" John asked.

"Confused," Tamora replied.

"Can you hear the voices of all your people?" John asked.

"Yes, but I do not feel well," she replied.

"How do you not feel well?" John asked.

"I feel sad that the gods do not want to come here themselves," Tamora answered.

"*The output of their entire neural systems is back to the baseline state,*" Tem reported. "*The unconscious link between the whole species is normal.*"

"The gods are pleased with their subjects, they are sorry for imposing the three of us on you, and they want to bring us home," John repeated.

"When, how, and why?" Tamora demanded.

"*The field strength above us is holding at twenty three percent of it's prior strength,*" Tem informed the Ambassador. "*I can permanently make it so, if you wish, sir.*"

Within the half hour, they will transport us back home, and they do this because they love the Brem and do not want to change your society," John answered Tamora.

"*Our craft has noticed the hole in the field and has begun to descend towards us,*" Tem announced.

"*It's about damned time,*" Captain Zindalph snorted.

"*Make the change temporary, but give us the ability to make the vortex passable from our craft,*" John added.

The three dimensional display on the far wall disappeared, as did the Ambassador, Science Officer and Senior Captain.

....

"How long am I stuck, sitting in your ship?" Captain Zindalph complained.

"Until I can confirm the control link to the fusion generators," Tem replied.

"Do I have to stay in this damned small environmental suit?" Zindalph asked.

"Until we transport onto your ship, yes," Ambassador Crackstone replied.

Their craft, Sam, had quickly sprinted to beyond the energy field and into open interplanetary space. Tem had turned the control of the fusion generators over to Sam. He reestablished the field strength in the vortex over the Shrine of Grendela.

As John and Tem breathed a sigh of relief, a message appeared on a large view screen which had just popped into existence in the main forward cabin; it was Commissioner Ythantrium.

"I have read your report with some interest, Ambassador," Ythantrium calmly spoke.

"You are referring to the relationship of the Brem with the Demela, I assume," John answered.

"To be precise, yes," The Commissioner agreed.

"What?" Captain Zindalph asked.

"The Brem and the Demela possess DNA too similar to be a coincidence," John replied. "Sam, will you contact the Crimson Balfunder and confirm a DNA match of the Brem with that of the pre-industrial society on the next planet out."

"Yes, sir," Sam complied.

"Isn't this Mapping Project business?" Captain Zindalph insisted. "Especially since the Ambassador is using my ship and my staff."

"It will be your business entirely as soon as my Ambassador has investigated this new twist to his first contact mission to the Demela system," The commissioner answered the Captain. "Your Commissioner and I developed an understanding on this matter."

"Very good, sir," Zindalph reluctantly agreed.

"Sam, bring us along side the Crimson Balfunder," John ordered.

"We're there, sir," Sam replied.

"Transport all of us over there, and change the Science Officer's and my environmental suits to fit," John requested.

....

The Crimson Balfunder was ten times as big as Sam. It too was a sentient machine, although not as self aware. Its crew consisted of a Captain, two Science Officers, one Navigator and three Planet Specialists. The crew of all Confederation craft were either of the same species, or from very compatible species. In order for the whole crew to operate without using an environmental suit, everyone needed to be approximately the same size and to breathe the same atmosphere, as well as to exist within the same general gravity and temperature range. Thus the Crimson Balfunder carried Reptilian crew, all from the same planet. As was the custom within the Confederation, John and Tem transported onto Captain Zindalph's ship in bulky Reptilian environmental suits. In response to Tem's earlier request, both the Ambassador and his Science Officer were male, this time.

....

"Contact me again when you establish orbit around Demela." Commissioner Ythantrium continued his conversation with the Ambassador on a viewing screen aboard the Crimson Balfunder.

"Yes, sir," John replied.

The three dimensional image of the Commissioner disappeared.

"This is my Senior Science Officer, Halput," Captain Zindalph introduced him.

"Your suspicions are correct." Halput began immediately. "The fourth planet, and the fifth planet of the Brem system are populated by the same species, at least genetically the same."

"My second suspicion is that both species were genetically modified from a native species and Demela DNA," Ambassador Crackstone surmised.

"That would be two correct assumptions, sir." Halput acknowledged.

"Were the Demela native to this system?" Tem added.

"We would have to gather a lot more information to determine that," Captain Zindalph interrupted.

"Logic would dictate that not to be possible," John added.

"How so?" Zindalph asked.

"The Demela cannot travel dimensionally and their system is over a hundred light years from here." John answered. "Unless a natural wormhole resides in this system, and unless the Demela technology can sustain class four shielding, I don't see how they could have originated in this system."

"Our scans have not indicated any natural wormhole within a fifty light year radius of the Demela system," Halput spoke up.

"When was the last in depth scan of this area of space?" John asked.

"I don't know," Zindalph replied.

"It was four hundred years ago, sir." A second Science Officer joined them on the bridge.

"This is our Science Officer, Gazie," Captain Zindalph introduced his junior officer.

"Don't you think it might be wise to conduct a new survey of this system?" John asked.

"We have begun already, sir," Halput replied.

"Is there anything interesting yet?" John asked.

"Besides the cloaked planet with the twenty working fusion generators in it and the strange mutated civilization living on that planet, no, sir," Halput said as he looked at his Captain.

"Within a hundred thousand years, couldn't the Demela have originated on this planet and moved to their present planet," Tem broke in. "Traveling at light speed, that would be possible, although not probable."

"Why would they move an entire civilization to a new system a hundred light years away?" John asked.

"Since the two planets in this system are so compatible to the Demela, I can't see them doing that," Captain Zindalph agreed.

"A plague, or a war can drive a space ready civilization from their home planet," Halput conjectured.

"That sounds interesting to me," John sounded thoughtful.

"This survey is definitely Mapping Project business," Captain Zindalph said as he stared at the Ambassador.

"Of course it is, but I need to discover what was behind the fusion generators on Brem and if the Demela originally built them," John insisted.

"How do we do that?" Zindalph asked.

"You have more extensive testing facilities than I do, so I would like a comparison of the original output parameters of the generators to the historical records of the Demela fusion generators of one hundred thousand years ago," John replied.

"We are attempting to do just that, sir," Halput happily answered. "But, Demela history is an elusive art."

"Could you explain that?" John asked.

"The Demela are quite secretive, they do not record their history in any detail," Halput answered. "In fact, prior to ten thousand years ago, we have no clue as to their social or technological state."

"See, we are working together." Zindalph forced a smile.

"Sir," Sam interrupted "Look at the star!"

Immediately a three dimensional image of the star popped up on the main viewing area on the bridge of the

Crimson Balfunder. Near the north pole of the star, a fold in the chromosphere was quite evident; it was about ten kilometers wide and four high.

"What is that?" Tem stared at the image.

"It's not a sun spot," John said as he too stared at the image.

"Could it be a natural phenomena?" Halput asked, to no one in particular.

"Scan it!" Captain Zindalph ordered.

"We are, but nothing conclusive yet," Gazie answered. "I need to get back to the science station now, sir."

"A ship is in that thing," Sam quickly spoke up.

"What kind of ship?" Zindalph asked.

"My guess would be a Demela ship," John answered quietly. "And, I would bet that phenomena is a wormhole."

"Sir?" Sam asked.

"My suggestion for my ship and yours would be to quickly move ourselves at least five million kilometers ninety degrees from the star's rotational plane," John said to the Senior Captain.

"Do it!" Captain Zindalph barked to his crew.

"Follow us," John said to Sam. "Cloak at the same time."

At the same instant that the two Confederation ships cloaked and shot off to their new location five million kilometers away, a beam weapon discharged from the unidentified ship emerging from the solar phenomena. The beam reached the location where Sam and the Crimson Balfunder had just been, then detonated, producing a great shock wave of high energy particles.

"It was an anti-matter cohesive beam weapon," Halput reported. "Directed at us, and detonated at our previous position."

"Our shields would have held," Sam added. "But there would have been a power drain, unless we had absorbed some of the energy,"

"Not a good idea." Captain Zindalph entered the conversation. "I have found that utilizing an unknown power source can prove more destructive than helpful."

"I concur," John agreed. "Don't ever do it."

"Yes, sir," Sam replied. "I wasn't planning on doing it anyway, sir."

"What are they doing now?" John asked.

"They are hunting us, sir," Sam replied. "They are scanning the whole system for a trace of our ships."

"They can't see us if we remain cloaked," Captain Zindalph commented.

"I wouldn't be too sure of that," John replied. "You were wrong about the existence of the fourth planet, you were wrong about a wormhole in this system, and you may well be wrong about the capabilities of the Demela."

"We have been closely studying their system for forty years and we know full well what their technological capabilities are," Zindalph insisted.

"Your reports state that they only have class three shielding," John said.

"Correct," Zindalph acknowledged.

"Traversing a wormhole requires a minimum of a class four shield, preferably a class five," John quickly replied. "So, what else doesn't the Mapping Project know about the system that I was supposed to make first contact with?"

"I see your point, Ambassador," Zindalph admitted.

"Sir, I think they have us in their sights," Sam interrupted.

"What?" Zindalph sounded surprised. "How can they see us?"

"Electromagnet cloaking leaves a trace they can obviously detect," Sam replied.

"I suggest we both move location and engage dimensional cloaking," Senior Science Officer Halput offered.

"Do it!" Zindalph ordered.

"You too, Sam," John spoke to his ship. "Follow us."

Seconds after both ships moved location, and folded into the fourth dimension, becoming completely invisible to the

Demela ship, a pulse of anti-matter exploded at their exact previous location.

"How many crew members does the Demela craft carry?" John asked.

"Six, sir," Halput replied.

"Do you have the power to suspend and transport all six to our storage hold?" The Ambassador asked his craft.

"More than enough, sir," Sam answered.

"Do it," John ordered.

"May I suggest that your Science Officer and I board the Demela ship and download all the information to both our craft?" Halput asked the Ambassador.

"Damn fine idea," Captain Zindalph agreed.

"Do it," John said, looking at Tem. "Be quick though, I don't want the Demela to send a rescue mission here."

. . . .

Tem was the first to move from the bridge of the Demela craft to another cabin. Halput was busy downloading data from the Demela main science console to the Crimson Balfunder and Sam.

The accommodations were Spartan; one large sleeping cabin, one storage, food and perhaps recreation cabin, plus the large bridge area. No medical facility was visible.

The beds, seats, and instrumentation were minimal. Every surface was a shade of gray, except for what appeared to be political posters which adorned every available wall space. The posters shouted the glory of their god, as well as the infallibility of their leader. Others proclaimed their right to dominate every area of the universe they might explore, in the name of their god.

Tem's cursory scan of the entire ship left him wondering about the social life of a Demela. He saw no personal items in any of the spaces; no pictures of loved ones, no jewelry, no personal grooming gear and no areas with individual names attached.

. . . .

"All six are on board, sir," Sam reported. "No problems with the transfer."

"They are not conscious, are they?" John asked.

"Quite asleep, sir."

"This is all very distressing," Zindalph mused. "The Mapping Project has been so wrong on all of this, and I don't see how?"

"My only concern is that I was prepared for a lower level of technology on this first contact mission, and that could have proven quite dangerous for my mission, " John said.

"I understand completely," Captain Zindalph agreed. "I feel we need to change some procedures in system observation to avoid this in the future."

"Sir, we have finished," Halput reported to his Captain.

"Why don't you keep the craft for a while longer," John said. "My team needs to get on with our assignment."

"What about the Demela crew?" Zindalph asked.

"I'll take them back to their home," John smiled. "This might prove to be the best thing for my mission."

"We will obviously remain here for some time to come," Zindalph sighed. "There are many questions to be answered here."

"Please keep us informed of those answers, as soon as you discover them," John requested. "We need all the information possible, as soon as possible."

"I will," Zindalph assured John. "Good luck."

"Thank you," John smiled at the Captain. "Sam, transport me back, and bring our Science Office back home too."

. . . .

"What now, sir?" Tem asked the Ambassador.

"Sam, can you use the wormhole on the star to travel to the Demela system?"

"The phenomena is fifty eight degrees north of the equator, and might have been triggered by a gravitometric field," Sam replied. "Our shielding is sufficient, but I still don't know where it goes until we travel it."

"Speaking of shielding, Sam," John asked. "have you determined why our shielding doesn't work well in that energy shield?"

110

"I have, sir, and I have sent that information to the Crimson Balfunder," Sam replied.

"Captain Zindalph, can you tell how the Demela craft traversed folded space, through the star?" John asked.

"Not entirely," Zindalph replied. "My crew is still examining the craft."

"Their shielding is barely adequate for the trip," Halput added. "Apparently they treat themselves for radiation right after traveling through the wormhole."

"Perhaps you should check them in stasis and treat them if necessary," Zindalph suggested.

"See to it, Science Officer."   John motioned to Tem.

. . . .

Following protocol, John and Tem had looked like the Brem while they were on that planet. They had also looked like three and a half meter tall lizards when they were on the Crimson Balfunder. But now, alone on their own craft, they relaxed, and assumed their native bodies as non-solid beings. Their bodies consisted of millions of cells comprising all their biological systems held together in an amorphous form by an electromagnetic envelope; their shape and size could vary greatly. In their natural state, they did not form a solid mass, but, at will, they could make all or portions of their mass solid so they could hold and manipulate objects

. . . .

"Sir, if I am to interact with the Demela in our hold," Tem paused. He would have to alter his body to conform with protocol again.

"I understand," John acknowledged. "Sam, do you have enough information?"

"I do," Sam replied. "They have two biological sexes, and they all look remarkably alike."

"What gender predominates the crew in our hold?" John asked.

"They are all male, so I assume you and the Science Officer will be one of the boys this time," Sam replied.

"No, make the Science Officer a very beautiful female this time," John said.

111

"Sir, that's not funny," Tem objected.

"I'm looking at the data on the Demela culture, and they revere a beautiful female," John replied. "Plus, they do not necessarily place the female in a secondary social position, so it may aid our mission if you were a female this time."

"Yes, sir," Tem sighed.

"Make our environment exactly like their home planet," The Ambassador ordered Sam.

Both Tem and John seemed to flicker in and out of existence for a fraction of a second, then a one and a half meter bronze colored skeleton flashed into view. The non-solid forms of the Ambassador and Science Officer swarmed around their frames, then as quickly became covered in skin, fully naked at first, then dressed in uniforms similar to those worn by the Demela still in stasis.

. . . .

"They did get a massive dose of radiation during their transit," Tem remarked. "Their treatment is done, they're just fine now."

"Leave them in the static field for awhile longer," John replied to Tem, then addressed Captain Zindalph. "Have you finished with the Demela craft?"

"We have," Zindalph replied. "Do you need it?"

"I may want to destroy it," John answered.

"Why?" The Captain wondered.

"As an example," John replied.

"It doesn't matter." Zindalph shrugged. "It was almost out of power anyway; I don't see how they hoped to get back home in that thing."

"Perhaps they planned on using the fusion generators to replace the power for their return flight?" John guessed.

"That was my Science Officer's guess too," Captain Zindalph agreed. "However, he informed me that the power output of the fusion generators is quite incompatible with their systems; their craft is more compatible with the original output of the fusion generators one hundred thousand years ago."

"That does tell us a lot," John sounded deep in thought. "Does this correlate to any of the history of the Demela?"

"Not literally, but my Senior Planetary Specialist is sending you the relevant data now," Captain Zindalph replied.

"You might want to move some distance from the Demela craft now," John warned.

"Are you taking the new wormhole?" Zindalph asked.

"I don't know yet," John answered. "We will send data of our transit to you, if we do."

"Thank you, and good luck," The Captain said.

. . . .

Working together, Tem and John downloaded all the information the Mapping Project had collected for the Demela system.

The Demela were a secretive society. They were a monotheistic society and they believed they were the direct descendants of god, the only true god of the whole universe. As the only descendents of that god, they were the only civilized people in the universe. As a privileged culture, they had the right to extend their presence anywhere in the universe. The Regent was the one supreme leader of the Demela, he was also the supreme leader of their religion.

The most ancient writing on Demela was the Divine Law, which was kept, interpreted and enforced by the Regent. The first divine law dictated that the Demela were entrusted with the spread of their god. The god of the Demela was the god of the universe, and it was every Demela's duty to spread the dominion of their god, and their Regent, to every corner of the universe.

To keep lesser creatures from interfering with their divine rights, they kept their history, science and art a mystery to all but themselves. Each discipline was a closed field of study; a physicist did not know Demela history, a physician did not know Demela astronomy. The laws set forth in the Divine Laws stated in very clear terms who was able to know the entirety of Demela civilization; the list was small, three individuals only. As a result, the simple telling of their past was an enigma, understood by few only through a complicated series of metaphors and word plays. The exact state of their technology was not centrally known; only a few key scientists knew enough to link related projects, and even they had no common organization. This structure made progress slow but very secretive.

In the past ten thousand years, even the designated three, the Regent, the Supreme General, and a third unknown Demela voted on by the Regent and the General, knew less and less of the whole of their society.

Although exact information was not easily apparent, John and Tem did decipher the basic flow of events in Demela history. Nothing specific in the Mapping Project's information on Demela history jumped out, but from what they now knew, John and Tem could draw conclusions on what the real history of the Demela was.

Around one hundred thousand years ago the Demela launched a massive attack on another planet, followed by an immense system wide disaster that wiped out most of the population. The remaining Demela fled through the wormhole in their star to their present location, leaving their home planet and all they had built to fall into ruin.

The closest inhabited planet was the Gremlat system, twenty two light years away. The Gremlat were now part of the Confederation, and currently at least a thousand years more advanced than the Demela; they joined the Confederation less than a hundred years ago.

Downloading the history of the Gremlat, John at once saw a correlation one hundred thousand years ago. The Gremlat fought back an invasion by their neighbors, the Demela, although their name for the Demela at the time was Yedris. The Gremlat were far more advanced, but still a rather unenlightened race at that time. They not only destroyed the entire Demela fleet, they sent back one of their own to destroy their new enemies. The Gremlat were adept at developing deadly viral weapons, and they quickly built one to destroy Demela DNA. Their history recorded a complete success. This era of Gremlat history had been repressed for thousands of years. Only recently, within the past few decades, had this dark past action been written about. Even as of the present, less than a quarter of the full facts of this past war were fully understood.

. . . .

"What is your plan now, sir?" Tem asked the Ambassador.

"Has all this been sent to the Commissioner?" John asked.

"Yes, sir," Sam replied.

"I want to speak to him now," John said.

"This is all very interesting," Commissioner Ythantrium said.

"Indeed," John replied. "I recommend a slight change to this first contact mission."

"What?"

"I recommend that we lower our goal to contact, setting ground rules, and establishing a link between them and the Confederation, and that we assign a permanent off-world liaison for the Demela," John replied.

"I have a strong emotional reaction to this situation, Ambassador." Ythantrium fell into thought, "you do understand?"

"We have been here before, Commissioner," John agreed. "But, their ability with weapon systems does give me pause."

"They are a fearful civilization," Ythantrium added. "So sure of themselves, and so unsure of the future."

"My plan for contact, sir?" John asked.

"I concur with your plan, but it will take a day to get final approval," Commissioner Ythantrium agreed. "Proceed for now with that plan, it's the most logical."

"I recommend the Gremlat as the contact liaison," John suggested.

"That's an interesting choice," The Commissioner observed. "I see the reason in it, but proceed with caution."

"Thank you, sir," John answered.

"Shall I get the Captain of the Demela ship now?" The Science Officer asked.

"You have removed all their weapons, right?" John asked.

"They all had cohesive photon beam weapons, quite primitive," Tem replied. "The Captain had two of those, plus several blade weapons, all removed and destroyed."

"Sam, can you make the interior larger, especially cabin B?" John requested.

"Done, sir," Sam replied. "I've increased the whole interior fifty percent."

Cabin B was normally an area Tem and John used as a recreational space. They could download scientific information, or recreational programs there, or use the space as a private place to communicate with friends on their home planet. This cabin had expanded to twice its normal size, big enough to fit a long table with ten chairs around it. The room was void of any technology, at least visible technology. The smooth metallic looking walls, floor and ceiling used no sharp angles, everything was gently curved. The room's color was a slight titanium gray, with blue and light green accents in the table and chairs as well as the two hatches leading to the center hallway.

John and Tem sat at the table; Tem worked his utility pad to transport the Captain of the Demela craft into cabin B.

"Could you go there and physically bring him here?" John asked.

"Why, sir?" his Science Officer asked.

"There will be less to explain to him, and I think he'll respond better to you as a Demela female," John replied.

"Fine," Tem said flatly.

As the Science Officer walked into the cargo hold, he counted all six Demela crew, still in stasis. The Science Officer had placed each crew member on a thin mattress on the floor of the hold and had let them assume a reclining position with their hands folded on their chests to make them more comfortable when they were brought out of induced hibernation.

Tem knelt over the Captain's body with his utility pad, bringing the Demela Captain half way out of stasis. The Captain focused on Tem, closed his eyes in disbelief, then opened them again, wider than before.

"You may feel a bit disoriented for a few minutes, which is why I am bringing you out of this suspended state slowly," Tem spoke quietly to the Demela Captain.

"You are beautiful," he croaked. "How long have I been dead?"

"You were never dead; you have been unconscious for less than two hours," Tem replied.

"You are beautiful," The Captain repeated.

"Fine," Tem sounded disgusted. "What's your name?"

"My name is Captain Bellgode," the Demela replied. "What is your name?"

"My name is Tem," The Science Officer replied.

"Tem is as beautiful as your presence," Captain Bellgode answered.

"What is your familiar name?" Tem asked.

"You may call me Desunda," he replied.

"Well, Desunda, you need to speak to the commander of this ship." Tem stood up.

The Science Officer gave Captain Bellgode twenty percent more use of his muscles. The Demela Captain shakily rose to his feet, immediately searching for any weapon left by his captors. Finding none, he turned to Tem and smiled.

"On my planet, you would be a goddess." He oozed obsequiousness.

"Whatever," Tem sighed. "We have to see my boss now."

. . . .

"Captain Desunda Bellgode, this is Ambassador John Crackstone." Tem quickly made the introductions as soon as they both entered cabin B.

"You may call me John," The Ambassador graciously spoke.

John bowed his head slightly as a sign of respect, then placed both his hands by his sides. In almost all humanoid cultures, placing one's hands at one's sides is a sign that you mean no harm.

"What is an ambassador?" Desunda asked abruptly as he sat down in the nearest chair and looked all around the room. "And, how many crew are on this craft?"

The Demela Captain acted as if he were the only advanced being in the room. His glances towards John and Tem were akin to watching an insect through a magnifying glass. As a member of the General Staff on his home world, Desunda commanded many thousands. Chosen to lead the second mission to their planet of origin; how could anyone outside of the Regent be more important?

"I have some questions for you, Captain Bellgode." John ignored his questions.

"Am I a prisoner?" he quickly retorted. "Why are all my crew dead?"

"They are unconscious until we decide what to do with all of you," John replied.

"*Are you sure this is a good idea, sir?*" Tem asked the Ambassador.

Tem and John could communicate with each other in their native telepathic language since the Demela were only auditory, incapable of understanding any telepathic exchanges.

"Am I a prisoner?" Captain Bellgode quickly asked. "Kill me now, for Demela can be subject to no one save their god or their Regent."

"*I am sure, and I expect you to be sure also,*" John replied to his Science Officer.

"We don't take prisoners, I am an Ambassador."

"What's an ambassador?"

"*He is too hopelessly lost in his primitive beliefs to reason with,*" Tem insisted.

"An ambassador negotiates with other civilizations," John replied.

"*I expect to use those primitive beliefs to reason with him,*" John replied to Tem.

"Negotiate what?" Desunda asked. "The time and place of our death?"

"I am in command of this ship." John tried a different path.

"Then, an ambassador is a Captain?" The Demela Captain asked. "You are not one of us, so what planet are you from?"

"*He is clueless, sir; I agree with the Science Officer.*" Sam joined the conversation.

"In one respect, I am a Captain," John said. "But, my main function is to represent my government to other civilizations."

"*You've been on enough missions with me to know better,*" John chastised Sam.

"You look like a Demela, but I don't recognize you," Captain Bellgode insisted. "Who are you and what planet are you from?"

"*How can he know four million faces?*" Tem pondered.

"My name is John Crackstone," John said again. "I was not born on Demela."

"I know that," Desunda chuckled. "If you were, I would know you."

"Why?" Tem couldn't contain himself.

"I'm Captain of the science vessel, Successful Return, but I'm also a third line General in the Security Forces and I know what all of the people on Demela look like," Desunda replied.

"*They must be more paranoid than the Mapping Project indicated.*" Sam observed.

"There are about four million on Demela, and you know what they all look like?" John inquired.

"*If you could,*" John addressed Sam. "*Contact Captain Zindalph and ask him to address that very question.*"

"*Yes, sir,*" Sam answered.

"Yes, and if you were a true Demela, you would know that as true."

"*I have to wonder how many Demela escaped this system one hundred thousand years ago?*" John wondered to his Science Officer.

"*I'll try to find out, sir,*" Tem replied.

"For a ship to be named Successful Return, yours seems quite unlikely to do so." Tem shot the Captain a wry grin.

"You are a very beautiful woman." Desunda smiled back at Tem. "Although you are not a true Demela, I would like to court you."

"*Can I shoot him?*" Tem asked John.

"I think she brought up a good question," John ignored Tem's remark and spoke to the Captain. "How did you expect to return to your home planet with no power left in your craft?"

"Who says we have no power left?" Desunda replied. "And, who says there won't be a small fleet looking for us soon?"

"Well, I say that won't happen," John answered. "We have been on your ship, and seen for ourselves that you have no more power; your fusion generator has enough for life support, some shielding and some weaponry. We also have had to treat you all for radiation because your shields are too weak."

"*Our data does not indicate how many Demela fled this system before the Gremlat attacked,*" Tem informed the Ambassador.

"You treated us?" Desunda asked.

"*I assume it was a very small number,*" John said.

"You are all quite well now." John nodded. "My guess is that there are very few craft on your home planet capable of traversing the wormhole in this star."

"How would I know." Desunda shrugged. "That's an entirely different section."

"Our observations show that this is the only craft on your home planet capable of traveling here," John added.

"You can't be Demela, if you were, you would know that this is our home planet, not the one from which we left," Desunda said.

"We know that you used to all live on this planet, the fifth one from the central star, and that your people fought the neighboring system, lost the battle and were almost wiped out as a race," John spoke softly. "What we aren't sure of is how you escaped dying from radiation as your ancestors flew through the wormhole."

"That is our history, and none of your business." Desunda glared at John. "Am I your prisoner?"

"*That went over well,*" Sam interjected.

120

"Did you find out anything from Captain Zindalph?" John asked.

"You are my guest," John quickly answered the Demela Captain. "I want your attention for a few minutes."

"Their culture is very fragmented, one scientific endeavor does not know what another is doing, nor do they share results," Sam began his reply. *"Their political and military hierarchy is just as fragmented. Only a very few at the top of their political and religious leaders know any broad views of future directions."*

"As far as I can determine, this guy is a priest as well as a military leader," Tem added.

"You can't hold a rank above major unless you're also an ordained priest, I know," John acknowledged.

"Why do you want my attention?"

"Why did you come back to this system?" John asked.

"Why not?" Desunda sounded indignant. "This is the home system of my people, we have the god given right to be here, and you do not."

"Can I shoot him now, sir?" Tem asked again.

"Not him, but target his ship," John replied.

"Really?" Tem asked.

"You were expecting to use the fusion reactors on the fourth planet to refuel your craft?" John asked.

"I think it might be time for a little wrath," John said with some amusement in his voice.

"Have you been to Berentha?" Captain Bellgode asked.

"Where?" John asked.

"The fourth planet," The Captain replied.

"The inhabitants call the planet Brem," John replied. "Yes, we have been there."

"Inhabitants?" Desunda sounded confused. "We all left, or died over a hundred thousand years ago. All that was left were primitive animals."

"A race of mammals, humanoids who call themselves Brem lives on the fourth planet," John replied. "A similar species lives on the fifth planet, evidently they too call themselves Brem."

"Targeted, sir," Sam spoke up. *"What weapon system?"*

121

"How?" Desunda sounded more confused.

"*Use an antimatter resonance packet,*" John answered. "*It's something he can relate to, and something that might impress him.*"

"Did your people genetically alter an existing species for servants, or pets?" John asked.

"Yes, my ancestors wrote of the Hallic Beasts they tamed genetically to use as laborers," Desunda replied. "They were inferior, had very limited intelligence, and they were bred without hearing or vocal chords so they would not be such a bother and make undue noise."

"That is the indigenous culture on both planets now." John smiled. "Why did you build the shield only on the fourth planet?"

"My ancestors didn't have time to construct the other one, we used the fourth planet as the test site," Desunda answered. "My people want to discover if our old home system is livable," he replied. "Is it?"

"It is, but not for you," John said flatly.

"*He's not going to like that, sir,*" The Science Officer observed.

"You are not god, you have no say in our destiny," Desunda insisted.

"No, I'm not your god," John agreed. "You are a high ranking military officer, right?"

"Yes," Captain Bellgode replied.

"I ask you now to think only as a military officer," John said.

"I can do that."

"*We'll see about that,*" Sam sarcastically observed.

"What do you do when you meet a superior force in battle?" John asked.

"We have not yet done so, because none exists," Desunda replied.

"What if a superior force existed, what would you do?"

"I would find their weakness, then defeat them," Desunda spoke as if John were stupid.

"*Is it arrogance, or is it religion?*" Tem asked.

"Keep your thoughts to yourself, please," John asked for silence.

"You cannot find any weakness, and they will destroy your entire civilization, what would you do?"

"God would never let that happen," Captain Bellgode insisted. "We pray every day, nine times a day and our god would never let that happen to his chosen people."

"That exact thing happened one hundred thousand years ago." John pointed out the obvious.

"We survived," Desunda happily replied.

"To find out how many originally survived, I guess I might as well be direct," John commented to Tem.

"But, you almost ceased to exist," John insisted.

"I am here, so we didn't."

"How many of your ancestors actually did survive?" John asked his burning question.

"The honored four hundred twenty one," Desunda proudly replied.

"Only a little over four hundred?" Tem sounded amazed. *"Their civilization is genetically less diverse than the Mapping Project assumed."*

"It has to be less than that," John added. *"A portion of those four hundred had to be sterile from the intense radiation in the worm hole transit."*

John pointed to the wall to Captain Desunda's left. As he did, a three meter by four meter image appeared, displaying a three dimensional representation of space in this system. In the center of the display was the Demela craft, Successful Return.

The Crimson Balfunder had taken up an orbit around the fourth planet. With the new data from the Ambassador's ship, they were able to penetrate the energy shield and send a science team down to the fusion generators control room to do a more in depth study.

"That is my craft." Captain Desunda pointed.

"I know," John answered him. "We have no choice but to destroy it."

"You cannot," The Captain insisted.

"Why?" John smiled slightly at him. "You left your shields on and you know you have enough power left for full shields?"

"Not just the shields, but the power of god," Captain Desunda proudly answered.

"How does that work?"

"You will find out."

"*Give the order, sir,*" Sam butted in.

"We are your prisoners then." Desunda sounded vindicated. "Eventually, god will destroy you, and all your people."

"But for now." John pointed to the ship, hovering in the center of the three dimensional projected space.

"*Now,*" John ordered Sam.

A pulse of bright energy rapidly struck the Successful Return, enveloping the shielding for less than a millisecond, then collapsing both the shields and the ship itself in as short a time. The ship shimmered, as if optically distorted by infrared radiation, then blinked out of existence.

"It looked like an antimatter device you used," Captain Desunda said.

He tried to regain an air of non-interest, but could not. Although emotion wasn't evident on his expression, both Tem and John could sense his utter horror at the destruction of his ship.

"It was the least dangerous of our weapons," John replied.

"I will pray with you." Captain Desunda changed tactics. "You could learn to love the one true god."

"*A fission device on his ship, a medium yield, was supposed to go off in the event of superior weaponry,*" Sam informed the Ambassador. "*We destroyed the ship before the device went off.*"

"Why the prayers?" John asked the Captain. "Your fission device didn't work? Was that the wrath of god you were hoping for?"

"Why did you destroy our only means of returning to our people?" Desunda asked. "We are truly your prisoners now."

"Sir, Captain Zindalph wishes to send a drone into the solar wormhole,." Sam interrupted John.

"As long as it's cloaked, that might be a good idea," John replied.

"I shall take you and your crew back to Demela, but I must obtain something from you first," John said.

"Can I tell you about the one true god first?" Desunda asked.

"Surly I can shoot him now, sir," Tem teased.

" I want you to be just a military man now," John began.

"I cannot do that, it would be like splitting my head in two and trying to go on living," Desunda answered.

"I could arrange that, sir," Sam interjected.

"Then metaphorically split in two and think only with your military mind," John insisted.

"I would die," Captain Desunda insisted back at John.

"I shall proceed as if you can do it," John spoke slowly. "You do understand that there are other inhabited systems in this galaxy, right?"

"There are many souls out there to convert, yes, we all know that."

"You have to realize that many of those other systems are far more advanced than you are and want nothing to do with your religion," John continued his slow, persistent voice.

"We are the chosen people," Desunda insisted, yet again. "God will protect us from even the most dangerous enemies."

"I just destroyed the most advanced craft your people could build, with my smallest weapon," John continued. "Your scientists are on the verge of controlling folded space and dimensional travel."

"You have spies on my planet?" Captain Desunda sounded surprised.

"Of course we do," John admitted. "We have been observing you for several decades."

"So, that's what an Ambassador means," Desunda huffed.

"Can I quote him later, sir?" Tem kidded.

"No, our scientific branch observes you, I am here to negotiate your entrance into the greater universe," John replied.

"God chose us to be his people in the larger universe," Desunda insisted.

"Leave the religion aside," John shot back. "Strictly as a military officer, you have to realize that we have superior technology, as do thousands of systems within traveling distance of Demela when you can successfully fold dimensional space."

"At that point we will spread the word of the one true god to the universe." Desunda smiled.

"At that point, you will be destroyed by your neighbors," John persisted.

"*Speaking of neighbors, the Gremlat Ambassador is trying to contact you, sir,*" Sam interrupted.

"*He's a humanoid, put his visual on in this room,*" John replied to Sam.

"*I think he's concerned with the fact that his system nearly destroyed the Demela so long ago, I did detect some level of guilt in the message,*" Sam added.

"*Even better, put him on in five minutes,*" John ordered. "*Give me time to set this up with our Demela friend.*"

8

Well, that won't work too well

The Gremlat Collective, a collection of three inhabited planets in two star systems within five light years of each other, was dominated by one civilization, the Gremlat. The other two planets, Olmet and Zugune, kept their languages and customs, but were happy to be referred to as the Gremlat Collective. One hundred thousand years ago, the Gremlat were capable of traveling only at light speed in large space craft. They had made contact with the other two technologically capable planets in easy traveling distance and had carefully given them technology well beyond their abilities. Holding back significant technology left the Gremlat as the superior and leading civilization in the new alliance.

One hundred thousand years ago, the Gremlat had yet to meet an aggressor species, but they were paranoid that they would. Much effort and resources were put into defensive weapons. Not yet wanting to realize that no practical difference existed between defensive and offensive weapons, the Gremlat were smug in their idealistic high ground.

The Demela were, one hundred thousand years ago, as aggressive as they were today, as well as being an isolationist literalist theocracy. The planet of origin for the Demela was only twenty two light years away from Gremlat; that was the closest inhabitable as well as technologically advanced planet to Demela, so that was a target of expansion for the zealous Demela leaders. Gremlat was too involved in cementing their relationships with the other two closer worlds to pay attention to the Demela, even though they had sent probes there within a few decades of the invasion.

The Demela invasion took place one hundred thousand, two hundred and thirty seven years before this present moment. At that time, the Gremlat were technologically at least four hundred years more advanced than the Demela, but the Demela either didn't know that or were unwilling to admit it. Both civilizations were limited to the speed of light for transporting themselves from one place in the universe to another. The Demela knew that an invasion would take slightly more than forty four years to complete; twenty two to arrive at Gremlat, a short victorious war, then twenty two years to return with many riches and scores of important prisoners. Demela sent an army of two million, and a support and supply group of five hundred thousand; in all almost five hundred ships comprised the invasion fleet. Little or no debate took place on this all or nothing strategy; the Regent, Supreme General and his council consistently rejected junior staff requests for a more cautious approach. The Supreme General did allow a month long review of the master plan, but, in the end, decided to send even more Demela resources headlong into the invasion plan.

The only battle took place two light years from Gremlat. Even though five light years from Gremlat the Demela supreme commander ordered his fleet split into four groups, a light week apart in four directions, the Demela fleet was not difficult to detect. Ever vigilant to attack from unknown enemies, the Gremlat detected the invasion four light years out, and sent a defensive armada to destroy it. Although the battle would take place in several years, the entire Gremlat Collective was whipped into a war frenzy. Most individual rights were suspended, the elected government was frozen in place and the military took more power than they should. Ships could travel no faster than the speed of light and communications could also travel no faster then that.

Sending hundreds of spy drones toward the direction of the Demela home system, the Gremlat determined the approximate size of the Demela fleet. All the unmanned spy craft were destroyed, but signals from those craft provided some data. The Demela also sent spy craft six months ahead of the large invasion fleet. All of those were also destroyed, but some data on the Gremlat ships did make it to the Demela fleet. The information the Demela and Gremlat had on each other was sparse; neither knew the actual technological status of the other and both assumed the other was at least as capable, if not more.

The Gremlat set the trap for the invasion fleet six months before the battle took place; they lay in wait, constantly drilling for all possible contingencies. The Demela were convinced that their god was on their side, so the conclusion was already divinely decided. The Gremlat were less convinced as to the outcome, so they had a multitude of multilayered plans for the ultimate defense of their home planet.

In the first few minutes of battle, the outcome was obvious. The Demela weapons made no dent in the shielding of the Gremlat ships, and even the secondary Gremlat weapons completely destroyed each and every Demela craft. The initial battle lasted only thirty seven minutes and involved three of the Demela fleets; the fourth was a week behind the battle and, remarkably, undetected by the Gremlat.

The Gremlat commander ordered several Demela craft spared, but disabled. These craft were boarded and all information remaining in their computers taken. The Gremlat took no prisoners; that had been decided at the highest levels. Before killing, then ejecting all Demela into space, DNA samples were taken and sent to a Gremlat science ship to develop a biological weapon specific to the race that had invaded Gremlat space.

Three days after the initial battle, the only remaining Demela task force knew of the complete route of three quarters of the initial invasion fleet. The general in charge of that Demela force made the decision to send half the remaining fleet headlong into the superior Gremlat force and send the other half back to Demela to warn them of a possible Gremlat retaliation.

The second battle took only eight minutes. The Gremlat used their new biological weapon on several Demela craft, discovering that it worked devastatingly well. Knowing that a small contingent of Demela had escaped and were returning home as fast as they could, the Gremlat commander made the decision to send a small fleet, armed with the new biological weapon, to make sure the Demela would never try another invasion.

Twenty years later, the Demela fleet returned home; two and a half million Demela left, and only about two thousand returned. Many Demela lost their lives delaying the pursuing Gremlat fleet which was now six months behind them.

....

For a thousand years before the Gremlat Wars, the Demela knew of the strange phenomena on their star, the strange dark spot that appeared every hundred years or so. It was only within the last hundred years before the Gremlat War that they discovered the mysterious spot was a natural wormhole which was triggered by a rare sunspot near the upper polar region of their star. They discovered the exact rotating gravitometric field that triggered it and, fifty years before the invasion fleet left, had sent several exploratory craft through it. The first were robotic probes which returned with data and images of a habitable planet with only plants and primitive animals on it. It took five trips with manned craft to solve the stress and radiation problems; the fifth trip was the first with a live crew returning; this crew died within a year from radiation poisoning. The habitable planet beyond the wormhole would now be their lifeboat in the face of certain destruction by the Gremlat.

A massive project assembled a group of sizable craft to send as many Demela to this new planet as possible; the total was slightly more than two thousand. The remaining Demela would fight the Gremlat and hide any trace of the wormhole transit.

For ten years the Demela worked on a massive planetary defense system powered by many fusion reactors; this system could mask the whole planet from visual and sensor detection. They completed a working model on the planet closer to their star only two years before the arrival of the Gremlat fleet.

The battle for Demela lasted four hours, leaving all remaining Demela dead. After the battle, the Gremlat fleet split in two. Most of the science ships stayed behind with a few battle craft for another year to study this new system; the remaining Gremlat craft returned home. The Gremlat scientists studied the remaining life forms on Demela, including the Brem; it was the Gremlat who named this system and the people, Brem. The atmosphere was not compatible with the Gremlat, there wasn't enough natural resources and the star was too small for sufficient energy production. The invading scientists did find the twenty working fusion generators very fascinating, and the almost completed planetary cloaking device especially interesting. The Gremlat tweaked the fusion output, then completed the cloaking device, studying it for uses in their own defense systems. None of the new technology, nor the new planetary system was compelling enough for the Gremlat to remain in the newly conquered Brem system, so the last of the scientists left fourteen months after their arrival.

Twenty two years later, the first wave of the triumphant Gremlat fleet arrived home from Demela, led by General Belcumis, the new fleet commander. In the four decades since the route of the Demela fleet, many things had changed on Gremlat, unknown to anyone on the absent fleet. The battle forty years before had been visually recorded in great detail, as a document to great planning and forward thinking. The populations of the three planets comprising the Gremlat Collective now saw the battle in a completely different way; a relatively primitive people were brutally exterminated by an uncaring military. When news of the final extermination of all Demela reached the general populace, waves of revulsion swept over the entire Collective. Elected governments had since wrested control from the military; tribunals were formed to assuage the collective guilt. In the end, only a few lesser ranking general officers were punished and history was rewritten to address the growing conscience of the people of Gremlat. In a few thousand years, the Demela War was purged from the common history of the Gremlat Collective. Within a few more thousand years, all references to that endeavor were totally purged from official records. The Demela system had long since been declared a dead zone; no further exploration was to be conducted in this area of space.

Since joining the Confederation a little over a hundred years ago, the Gremlat became more introspective, closely studying their past. The invasion and destruction of the Demela had been a point of intense study for the past few decades. Most of the details of this period of Gremlat history were lost; almost no official reports remained. The government appointed two executive study panels to address the ancient situation, but none had determined remedial or future actions to be taken because of past transgressions.

Modern probes sent to the Brem system showed the Gremlat what they expected, a series of planets, one inhabited by a pre industrial civilization, and no trace of the Demela DNA. The fact that a planet had disappeared was not noticed since the original detailed mapping of the system had long since been destroyed, along with the details of the genocide. The Gremlat knew that a civilization that had similar DNA existed one hundred light years from the Brem system, but they attributed that to a possible common ancestor for both systems. Since all references to their ancient enemies called them the Yedris and the old Demela system was named the Brem system, their true relationship to the Demela was not yet established.

On receiving news of the new discoveries in the Brem system, the Gremlat assigned their most senior Ambassador, Halmemit Gogrum, to work directly with Ambassador Crackstone; the Commissioner of Emerging Systems agreed.

....

"Captain Bellgode." John began carefully. "Can you conceive of a possibility that your culture is far less advanced than you think?"

"Technologically, perhaps," he replied forcefully. "But, as far as the true worth of a people, no."

"*What is true worth?*" Tem asked the Ambassador.

"*It's pride, ego and arrogance,*" John answered.

"I want you to assume that all civilizations who have mastered traveling in space at light speed or greater of equal worth," John spoke to the Demela Captain.

"Philosophically, I cannot," he flatly replied.

"Then think of it as a hypothetical," John tried again.

"Why don't we hypothetically vaporize him," Sam butted in.

"Why don't you keep your sarcasm to yourself," John admonished their craft.

"I was trying to keep the mood light with some humor." Sam answered.

"Perhaps the technicians should have added more humor modules in your refit," Tem added.

"I can always vaporize our esteemed Science Officer," Sam retorted.

"Given my circumstances of being your prisoner, I shall," Captain Bellgode sighed a reply.

"If the relative worth of all advanced civilizations are roughly equal, the level of technological advancement would be a logical way of differentiating them," John mused. "Wouldn't you agree?"

"I suppose I would," Desunda Bellgode reluctantly agreed.

"Sam," John spoke to the craft.

"Sir?" Sam answered.

"Speak so our guest can hear you," John ordered.

"Yes, sir," Sam answered in a strong voice.

"Where is this person?" Desunda asked. "Is he on the bridge?"

"Our ship is a sentient being," John answered in a matter of fact tone. "His name is Sam."

"I'm your prisoner, but don't toy with me," The Captain snorted.

"I assume you do remember the history of your battle with the Gremlat." John ignored his comment.

"How many crew members do you have?" Desunda demanded.

"Their planet is twenty two light years from this system, your old home system." John said, ignoring the Captain's inquiry.

"Am I to take it that there are just you two on this ship?" Desunda continued.

"Sam," John calmly said. "Please relieve our guest of the use of his legs."

"What!" Captain Bellgode struggled to rise from the chair, but his legs did not function. As he fell to the floor, he flailed his arms, trying to grasp the fallen chair, then a table leg. Not finding anything that would give him a secure purchase, Desunda used his arms to clumsily sit upright on the floor.

"As I asked before," John calmly continued. "Do you remember the history of the Gremlat conquering Demela?"

"You can torture me as much as you wish, I shall never lose my devotion to the one true god!" Desunda shouted.

"You were planning on attacking us and taking control of our ship," John calmly replied. "You're not in any pain, you just can no longer carry out such an attack."

"How can you do this?"

"Do you remember the details of the war your people had with the Gremlat?" John asked again.

"Yes, yes, I remember my history," Desunda sputtered. "Our people were punished for not reading god's will correctly."

"*That's preposterous!*" Tem interjected.

"Do you know the distance between this system and the Gremlat system?"

"Twenty two light years, even a lowly private knows that," Desunda huffed. "Why do you ask questions to which you already know the answers?"

"We are going there now," John answered.

"Will I be without the use of my leg for twenty two years?"

"Will you promise not to be violent towards us?" John asked.

"Yes," Desunda said with a smile.

"*Sir, you can read his thoughts as well, you know he doesn't mean that,*" Tem insisted.

"*Of course, but Sam will render him harmless in a nanosecond if he tries to attack us again, so I think there's no harm in restoring him,*" John answered his Science Officer.

"Sam, give him back his legs," John ordered.

"How do you do that?" Desunda asked.

Captain Bellgode slowly rose, rubbing his legs as he did. He sat tentatively on the chair he had just picked up and set near the table.

"Sam, take us to the Gremlat Collective," John requested.

"Yes, sir," Sam complied. "One jump, three minutes transit."

"Three minutes to travel twenty two light years?" Desunda asked.

"Yes, and that's my point," John began. "The scale most commonly used to measure a civilization is its technological advancement."

"Meaning you can control folded space?" Captain Bellgode asked.

"As well as disable any life form in a fraction of a second without causing harm," John replied. "When your ancestors attacked the Gremlat, they were hundreds of years more advanced than your ancestors, and the resulting one sided battles left your race almost extinct."

"That was god's will," Desunda insisted.

"That was an indisputable fact based in reality, not religion," John replied.

"God's will is an indisputable fact," Desunda persisted.

"It has taken your civilization one hundred thousand years to recover from near extinction and get to where you might have been ninety thousand years ago had you not fought the Gremlat," John said. "You are within a few hundred years of being capable of traveling hundreds of light years in minutes and coming in contact with many inhabited planets."

"To spread the word of the one true god." Desunda smiled. "I am aware of the future."

"We are in orbit above Gremlat, sir," Sam interrupted. "The Ambassador is requesting you, sir."

"Your future may be quite bleak then," John admonished. "The greater galaxy is populated with many far more advanced civilizations than yours, and they do not take kindly to an aggressor species like the Demela."

"We are not aggressors," Desunda insisted.

"You spread your religion by conquest, and you still think you're not an aggressor?" John asked.

"Sir, Ambassador Gogrum insists on speaking with you," Sam interrupted again.

"I will speak with him in five minutes, Sam," John answered.

"We spread the word by missionary work, by making the uninformed see the truth of the one true god," Desunda insisted.

"Making them see your truth implies forcing them, which is the act of an aggressor," John replied.

"It's for the greater good." Desunda stood his ground.

"From other civilizations viewpoint, it's for your good, not theirs," John answered.

"We are doing it for their good, to make them better citizens of the universe," Desunda persisted.

"Regardless of your intentions, sending two and a half million soldiers here to force the Gremlat to think as you do was not only unfair, but it was unwise," John said.

"I must agree that it was unwise, but not for the reasons you may think," Desunda acquiesced. "What do you want from me now?

"I want you to meet with the representative of the people who almost destroyed your civilization so many years ago."

"At last, I may speak to them of our god," Desunda smiled as he spoke.

"Perhaps, you might want to speak to him as a kind neighbor," John suggested.

"His people tried to kill all of us!" Desunda insisted. "Maybe if he knew the strength and power of the one true god, we could be friends."

"You will speak to him?" John asked.

"I will," Desunda sighed.

. . . .

As Sam transported Ambassador Crackstone to the surface of Gremlat, he did two other tasks. Captain Bellgode was partially immobilized again, sitting in his chair. The ambassador's environmental suit was adjusted to make him look like a Gremlat.

The Gremlat were humanoid; two legs, two arms with four digits on each hand, and five on each foot. They stood two meters high, had almost no hair on their heads, an oversized central nose, and two deep set small eyes. Their general coloring was gray more than anything else. All three planets in the collective were populated by the same species and several hundred thousand years of inter breeding had rendered little differences between any of the Gremlat.

Science Officer Tem remained on the craft to make sure the Demela Captain was comfortable and looked after.

"What happened to your Captain, the Ambassador?" Desunda asked Tem.

"*Why is he still able to converse with us?*" Tem asked Sam.

"*That was the Ambassador's orders, you heard him,*" Sam replied.

"Are you able to speak?" Desunda inquired.

"*I can immobilize his vocal cords quite easily, as well as numb his brain so we can't hear him anymore,*" Tem insisted.

"*I'm not arguing with your idea, but you know damned well we can't,*" Sam replied.

"You're a very beautiful woman," Desunda spoke softly. "Are you really one of us?"

Tem remained silent, annoyed but silent.

"I would like that very much if you were, I would like to mate with you and make you a great woman on my world," Desunda proudly proclaimed. "I am an important military officer, and I can give you a fine life on Demela."

"*He could take you away from this horrible life you now lead,*" Sam teased.

"Shut up, will you please be quiet!" Tem snapped.

"I don't mean to disrespect you, I apologize," Desunda verbally backpedaled.

"She was speaking to me," Sam interrupted out loud. "Our Science Officer sees you more like a specimen than as an equal who could annoy him."

"Him?" Desunda sounded confused. "With a face like that and a body to match, how can that be a him?"

137

"Our mechanical friend doesn't care about gender, he calls everybody a him," Tem replied quickly.

"Mechanical friend?" Desunda sounded more confused.

"The disembodied voice you now hear is the ship you are on in cold, cold space," Sam teased. "Don't laugh, I'm the one who is keeping you alive."

"So?" Desunda huffed. "You're an autonomous mechanical entity, we use those too."

"How insulting," Sam replied.

"As I said before, shut up!" Tem interrupted. "I mean it, shut up!"

"At least the woman outranks the machine," Desunda chuckled.

"I'm glad you find this amusing." Tem loomed over the seated Demela Captain.

"That's not what I was thinking," Desunda replied.

"I can read you thoughts, so don't try to spread your manure too thick," Tem quickly retorted.

"No, you can't."

"You're thinking of me naked right now." Tem sighed. "Now, you're thinking of killing me and taking over this ship."

"That's not that hard to figure out," Desunda replied.

"Think of a five digit number," Tem insisted, paused then said, "3-9-9-7-4".

"How did you?"

"I told you how," Tem replied. "All of us can read your thoughts, we communicate with each other by reading thoughts, so reading yours is simple."

"How can you be one of my race?"

"I didn't say we were, we just look like you," Tem replied. "Now, I have other business to attend to, so I hope you like being alone."

"What if I need water, or food, or I have to relieve myself?"

"Just ask our autonomous mechanical entity, his name is Sam," Tem replied as he left the cabin.

....

"It's such an honor to have a distinguished Ambassador leading this mission," Ambassador Halmemit Gogrum proclaimed as John entered the great hall of the Gremlat Collective.

"Please, call me John and I don't think my original assignment had much to do with what has transpired these past few days," John replied.

"I shall call you John, it is an honor," Ambassador Halmemit replied. "If you will do me the honor of calling me Gogrum.

"I shall indeed, Gogrum," John said with a grin. "Have you gone over the reports to date?"

"I have," Gogrum replied. "It has been a mixed bag of emotions for my people."

"That I can understand." John nodded.

"We had no idea any Demela survived," Ambassador Gogrum said. "That gladdens us, as well as stabs at our hearts."

"Your people will have to deal with their own consciences," John said. "What we have to deal with right now is what to do with the Demela who survived and now may pose problems in their current sector."

"I have come from the Gremlat Collective Supreme Council, and they have all agreed that we should be responsible for guiding the Demela into the greater community," Gogrum said.

"Perhaps you should speak to the Demela Captain first," John suggested. "Your job may not be as easy as you might think."

"I will of course accompany you to your ship to meet with the Demela Captain."

"His atmosphere and yours are different enough so you will need an environmental suit, but I suggest you make yours look like a Gremlat," John recommended.

"Why?"

"They are quite literalist, and they are very tied to the made in god's image paradigm," John replied.

"I understand."

. . . .

139

"Hey, machine guy!" Captain Bellgode shouted. "I need some water!"

Desunda's expression changed rapidly from playful to shocked. He ran his tongue around inside his mouth, then looked amazed.

"How did you do that?"

"I re-hydrated you," Sam replied.

"How?"

"I converted some water into energy, then transferred it to your primary stomach," Sam answered. "That's why you had that wet burp."

"How did you do that?" Desunda asked again.

"You did the burp, I can't take credit for that, nor would I want to," Sam teased.

"Very funny, but you know what I mean," Desunda insisted.

"I know that you're thinking about how you can use the fact that you can move your mouth and tongue to free yourself," Sam said. "I can control every muscle in your body in less than a second, and I never stop monitoring you, so don't hurt yourself trying to escape."

"Is my crew alive?"

"All of them are in better health than they were when we transported you all here," Sam replied.

"What does that mean?"

"Two of your crew had early stage cancer and one of them was a year from a heart attack," Sam replied. "They are all completely healthy now."

"How?"

"You knew about the female with bone cancer, but the other female had stomach cancer," Sam replied.

"Almost every soul that travels the wormhole gets some deadly disease," Desunda sighed.

"You had an immune system failure," Sam added. "That too has been repaired."

"Why?"

140

"We don't mean you harm, we just want you to do no harm to others," Sam replied.

"*Sam, keep out of the Ambassador's business,*" Tem interrupted Sam.

"I think the Ambassador is on his way back here," Sam quickly said.

. . . .

"Commissioner Ythantrium has approved the Gremlat Collective as the sponsors of the Demela," Tem informed John as he completed transporting back to their craft orbiting Gremlat with Ambassador Gogrum.

"Wonderful," Gogrum acknowledged.

"Sir, this is my Science Officer, Tempatt Groonghin," John introduced him.

"Please, call me Tem, Sir," he insisted.

"Certainly."

"Before you meet Captain Bellgode of the Demela, I think we need to discuss some potential problems," John said.

"Beside what I have already read, what else is there?" Gogrum asked.

"Please, can we sit in my cabin and discuss this alone?"

"What?" Gogrum asked as he sat in the only other chair in John's private cabin.

"My initial mission was to contain the Demela to their home system for the foreseeable future," John began.

"I read the initial mission plan," Gogrum interrupted. "A fairly simple first contact mission given the literalist nature of the Demela."

"I can assure you than no literalist first contact is simple, but that isn't the real issue now."

"What is?"

"The Demela were listed by the Mapping Project as being two hundred years from dimensional travel," John reported. "We hoped to contain and guide them within that two hundred year window to make their transition into Confederation membership an easy one."

141

"Yes," Ambassador Gogrum asked, "Besides our past interaction with them, what has changed?"

The two ambassadors were seated opposite each other around a small circular table in the middle of John's almost empty cabin. Most of the surfaces were a dull metal gray with no sharp corners. The top of the table was an exception to the norm; it was a shiny dark brown.

John pointed to a space between Gogrum and himself, causing a three dimensional star map to appear; the map was of the sector of the galaxy they were presently in.

"As you can see, the Demela are in a strategic section of space, in particular, they are within ten light years of the Kolodin Empire boundary," John emphasized.

"Negotiations are ongoing with the Kolodin," Gogrum interrupted. "I suppose we need to keep the Demela away from the Kolodin to avoid negative incidents."

"That is an understatement of the possible problems." John smiled. "Can you imagine the Demela trying to convert the Kolodin?"

"I see your point," Gogrum agreed.

"The real nuance occurs here." John pointed to a new area of space, also zooming in on that new sub-sector.

"That's the Demela's original home system," Gogrum observed. "The Brem system."

"That it is, but watch carefully when I zoom out a bit," John said. "Pay close attention to the Confederation boundaries."

"I see the problem completely." Gogrum sighed. "That is a problem that has vexed The Confederation for over five thousand years."

"The Demela, as we discovered, can fold into their old system from their new system using the stable wormhole in their old star," John carefully said. "That puts the literalist Demela within two light years of the hottest spot in this galaxy."

"That means you have lost the two hundred year buffer you thought you had." Gogrum nodded.

"Correct," John agreed. "What you and I must now do is to find a strategy to contain the Demela in their new system, keep them out of their old system and guide them to a more enlightened society in far less time than two hundred years."

"Enlightened to us is blasphemy to them," Gogrum observed. "Although the situation forces us to do things we may not want to do."

"I've been a first contact Ambassador for many years, and in every case practical concerns guide the solution, never ideological concerns," John said. "The Demela were almost completely destroyed by your ancestors a hundred thousand years ago; this time, if left to their own devices, they will be destroyed for sure, all of them."

"I see your point," Gogrum agreed. "What do you suggest?"

"I will contact the Mapping Project personnel still in the old Demela system and ask them to devise a way to make the solar wormhole impassable," John said.

"That will isolate the Demela again," Gogrum acknowledged.

"However, our efforts at changing their society must be accelerated," John said.

"I repeat my willingness to be the contact Ambassador for the Confederation," Gogrum replied.

"I am perfectly willing to accept your offer after actual first contact is made," John agreed.

"May I be part of your team?" Gogrum asked.

"Yes, but I must ask you to say nothing for the first day, or first few days."

"Yes, I won't take part in any preliminary negotiations."

"You can actually speak, but take your lead from me."

. . . .

"You just can't stay away from me?" Captain Bellgode addressed Tem as he came into the cabin.

"The Ambassador is back, and wishes to speak to you," Tem said.

"Since I don't have any choice, why not," Desunda replied.

143

"May I have your word that you will behave yourself if I release you?" John asked as he walked into the cabin.

"You can have it," Desunda said with a bit of hesitation.

"*He's lying, sir,*" Tem quickly observed.

"*I know, but we need to train him quickly,*" John replied.

"Sam," John said. "Please let our guest have full use of his body."

"Yes, sir," Sam replied.

Captain Bellgode rose slowly from his chair, rubbed his wrists, wriggled his fingers, then stood up as tall as he could. He calmly looked around the cabin, noting Tem and John's positions relative to him and the furniture.

Desunda lunged at John with his right hand extended in a grabbing motion. Sam instantly jammed all his muscles related to motion; Desunda fell in a haphazard lump on the floor in front of John.

"We did warn you about this," John said. "I'm willing to try again, but you'll have to behave this time, or we will paralyze you and strap you back into that chair."

Sam gave the Demela Captain back the use of all his muscles.

"I will not try that again," Desunda said as he again rose to his feet. "How do you do that?"

"There's a lot of things we can do that we'll never tell you about," John replied with a grin. "For now, however, would you like a tour of my ship?"

"I would love a tour of your ship," Desunda replied.

"I told you we could read your thoughts," Tem added. "You're still plotting to kill us and take over our ship."

"As if he could take me over," Sam chimed in.

"Before we give you the tour, may I introduce a senior Ambassador from the Gremlat Collective?" John asked.

"The what?" Desunda sounded confused.

"An Ambassador is an official of a society that has the power to negotiate with other societies," John replied. "Halmemit Gogrum, or Ambassador Gogrum, is the representative of the Gremlat Collective; the same people your ancestors fought so long ago, and the same people who almost destroyed your civilization."

"What is he here to negotiate?" Desunda asked. "Our surrender?"

"Hardly," John answered. "I am the primary negotiator in this case, Gogrum is here as an observer for now."

"What are you negotiating?" Desunda asked again.

"I wish to negotiate with your Regent and your Supreme General, not you," John replied.

"Then, you're a hundred light years from that," Desunda smiled.

"Sam, how long to the Demela system?" John asked.

"Six minutes, two jumps, sir," Sam replied.

"After we give our guest a brief tour, proceed," John said. "But, when we arrive in that system, please cloak yourself."

"You can do that?" Desunda asked. "And, is that voice really the ship?"

9

Whoops, we may have done it again

The new Demela system consisted of a medium sized yellow star, about 1.4 million kilometers across, and just shy of three billion years old with four inner planets, the inner most was a planet sized captured comet, barren of any life. The three other inner planets harbored life, but the fourth from the star was the haven for the Demela civilization. This system also contained three gas giants with several hundred moons between them, one half of which held some life forms, mostly microscopic. In the outer reaches of the Demela system spun a few hundred thousand ice planets and large cometary bodies.

The Demela originated on a system not too different from their present one, only one hundred and twelve light years away. Fleeing from an enemy fleet, the Demela transited a natural wormhole from one system to another over one hundred thousand years ago. Many died from the stresses and radiation of the journey. In their ancient language, the old home planet, as well as their race name was Deem; this name morphed over the millennia into Demela.

At first the Demela found their new planet difficult to tame. The atmosphere had a slightly higher oxygen content than they were used to, and the gravity was higher. Although a vast amount of natural vegetation and some animal life grew on that planet, they had initial difficulties discovering what they could eat without adverse effects. Of those that survived the radiation, less than one half kept their fertility. Since their law was their religion, and cloning enlightened higher beings was against their religion, building a new civilization was long and arduous; ancient bans on cousins marrying were forgotten in the beginning and fertile females were encouraged to have as many children as was physically possible, using as many fertile males as their propriety permitted. The struggle to build a civilization to just a

146

tenth the level they had left on their home system took the Demela thirty thousand years, taking great care to keep a viable gene pool. Building an industrial base took less time, but was second priority to building a healthy population. Adding to the already difficult situation, three massive meteor strikes in the past one hundred thousand years set them back centuries, if not millennia at a time.

A more destructive hindrance to Demela evolution as a civilization was their cultural bias against recording both their history and their science. Only the Regent and the Supreme General knew the entirety of Demela history, and neither had a full grasp on the technological standing of their people. Scientific projects were started by a Regent, then took on a life of their own. Senior scientists within a given project would train the next generation, then pick one or two of them to continue the project; all other scientists only knew their small part of the greater project. As scientific endeavors passed from one generation to another, nothing guaranteed that the ruling Regent would know of their progress, or even their existence. Once a scientific project nears possibility of completion, the leaders are expected to notify either the Regent or the Supreme General; this is the only fail-safe in a very flawed system.

Years of arrogant self importance countered by painful self-doubt drove the Demela society into greater compartmentalization and paranoia. Adversity can drive some civilizations to excel in science and philosophy, but not the Demela. As a group, they feared their enemies, real or imagined; they feared their environment as well. Being an isolationist literalist society to begin with drove them over the millennia to integrate this fear further into their psyche. The personification of that fear was their god; they were crafted in his image, so their god must be a vengeful god. As a race, the Demela felt they must be created from suffering, still bound to torment.

Any survey of any sector of any galaxy capable of supporting life will find life on at least one planet or moon in a given system seventy five percent of the time. On average, one tenth of those planets or moons will have a civilization of advanced beings, capable of making and using tools. Of those

147

civilizations, perhaps one in a thousand will have advanced to space travel within their solar system. One in ten thousand of those space traveling civilizations will be capable of inter-system travel. The end result is that there are millions of civilizations in each galaxy capable of supporting life that can explore vast regions of inhabited planets within an area defined by their capabilities.

This mixture of vastly different civilizations bumping into each other could, and in some cases, does lead to conflict. By the time a civilization reaches the technological level of faster than light speed in a three dimensional universe, or type two civilization, most reject territorial assumptions, although a small minority do not. Within the area of space bordering the Demela's original home planet there exists one empire who feels a strong need to control planets and civilizations; the Faulid Empire claims all of Sector 120 and part of Sector 121 of Quadrant D of Galaxy G-1.

The Faulid were an early type two civilization; they had became capable of traveling in folded space one hundred years ago. Before that, their empire was limited to about twenty light years from their home planet. They had yet to fold space beyond a seventy light year jump, and their current scientific train of thought was a dead end, so the Confederation held some hope of maintaining peace and containing the Empire for some time into the future. They could travel seventy light years in one dimensional fold, but they required over a month to acquire enough power for another fold of only thirty more light years. In the past twenty years the Confederation had negotiated boundaries with the Faulid, based on the superior technology of the Confederation. Currently, the Faulid are a potential threat to peace only in Quadrant D of Galaxy G-1.

The original home system of the Demela was on the Faulid border; at times the Faulid claimed that system as theirs. Any attempt of the Demela to reclaim their old home world would push the Faulid into all out war against them, and perhaps several Confederation systems as well.

. . . .

"I hope you enjoyed the tour of my ship," John said as he motioned for Desunda to sit back in his seat in cabin B.

"You didn't show me much," Desunda insisted. "In fact, you didn't even show me my crew."

"Fine," Ambassador Crackstone replied.

He pointed to the nearest wall as a three dimensional image of the rest of the Demela crew appeared, laying down in a cargo hold.

"Are they dead?"

"As I have told you before, they are not," John confirmed. "They will remain unconscious until we arrive at your planet."

"What then?"

"After their transport, we will bring them back to consciousness," John replied.

"What about me?"

"I don't need you, you'll join your crew mates back on your planet."

"Sir," Sam interrupted. "We have arrived."

"Thank you," John replied.

The three dimensional image of the unconscious Demela crew disappeared, replaced by a three dimensional image of the Demela world.

"How did you go so far so fast?" Desunda asked.

"Through folded space," John answered. "We create our own wormholes."

"Our scientists say that is soon possible for us to do so," Desunda proudly added. "Our one true god will bless us with this way to spread his word."

Science Officer Tem breezed into the cabin and blurted out, "Sir, I have located all the representatives."

"What does that mean?" Desunda demanded.

"It means," Tem answered. "That you're going home."

"Sam," John said. "Transport the crew off, wait a few seconds, then transport the three up from the surface."

"Yes, sir," Sam replied.

Captain Bellgode and his crew disappeared from the orbiting Confederation craft. Twelve seconds later, three Demela

149

appeared in cabin B, standing near the table at the center of the space. Sam had enlarged the interior of the whole craft to better accommodate the new visitors.

The taller of the three Demela stared at the other two, then at John and Tem, then scanned the entire cabin.

"What is the meaning of this, and who the hell are you?" Regent Willgntum demanded.

"My name is John Crackstone, and I am a senior Ambassador from The Confederation." John smiled faintly. "This is Tempatt Groonghin, she is my Science Officer."

"Why are we here, and where is here?" Pennul Hoppgrede asked.

"We are in a synchronous orbit around your planet, " John calmly replied. "We are cloaked from your telescopes and your instruments." He pointed to the three dimensional display of their planet still projected against one wall of the cabin.

"Why you are here is simple," John continued. "You intend on repopulating your old home world, and that is not possible for many reasons."

"What we do in the name of the one true god is not the business of a heretic," Regent Willgntum insisted.

"Even if the Regent and I die, my generals will find you and destroy you," General Kuldridge added.

"Your obsession with death and destruction baffles me," John observed. "But, it is irrelevant."

"You will be irrelevant," Regent Willgntum snarled.

"I would like you to meet Ambassador Gogrum of the Gremlat Collective," John said. At Kldridge's baffled look, John added, "The ancient enemy who vanquished your people so long ago," John answered. "So long ago, some of your people today think it was an ancient legend."

"Have they come back to kill us all?" Pennul Hoppgrede asked.

"Indeed not," John chuckled. "Quite the opposite, they want to help you live and prosper."

"Lies," General Kuldridge said with a snort.

Ambassador Halmemit Gogrum entered the cabin, paused by the doorway, then walked to the space between Tem, John and the three Demela.

"Ambassador Gogrum, may I introduce the Regent of Demela, Renniput Willgntum," John said as he motioned towards the tallest of the three Demela.

The Ambassador bowed his head, the Regent curtly answered with a shallow bow.

"May I introduce you to the Supreme General of Demela, Ottor Kuldridge." John motioned to the shortest of the three, dressed in an elaborate uniform.

"And may I also introduce you to the senior scientist of Demela, Pennul Hoppgrede," John continued.

Pennul returned the Ambassador's bow, the general did not.

"Do you have the ability to convert matter to energy, transmit it to another location, then convert it back to matter?" Pennul asked.

Neither John nor Tem answered; Ambassador Gogrum remained quiet, as he had promised.

"How can you maintain cellular integrity?" Pennul asked again. "Do you have to destroy the original person and reassemble a new copy, and if so, how can we keep the same memories, and what about our souls?"

"There are many civilizations in this galaxy that are tens of thousands of years more advanced than you are," John ignored Pennul's questions. "That is driving our meeting with you, at this place and at this time."

"Chief scientist Hoppgrede is a dreamer in the real world, but she asks questions we want answers to," Regent Willgntum replied.

"What you want and what you will get are two different things," John insisted. "Will you all sit down and let me continue?"

The Regent and Pennul sat down, across the table from each other. General Kuldridge stood still, arms folded against his chest, glaring at Tem, John and Ambassador Gogrum.

151

"General," John said slowly. "When we transported you up here, we removed all your weapons, so, please sit down."

"You look like us, but you are not like us," Pennul observed. "What species are you?"

"My Science Officer and I are Zizthanthe," John replied. "Our home world is over three hundred thousand light years from here."

"That far?" General Kuldridge asked, somewhat surprised.

"The Confederation has explored seven galaxies," John answered. "We can travel millions of light years in no more than a few hours."

"How can you look like us?" Pennul asked.

"As part of our advanced technology," John began. "We construct environmental suits to exist in alien atmospheres; we can make those suits look like any living creature."

"How can you do that?" Pennul asked. "If you were, say, ten times our size, how could you fit into a suit that was so small for you?"

"This is getting us nowhere," Regent Willgntum huffed.

"As an Ambassador, I represent The Confederation," John continued. "The Confederation is a group of four thousand two hundred and fifty star systems, or groups of star systems who work together in scientific and diplomatic missions."

"You are like an empire of four thousand races?" General Kuldridge interrupted.

"We are not an empire. The Confederation's six thousand species are scattered among seven galaxies," John replied.

"So what are you here for, Ambassador?" General Kuldridge asked sarcastically.

"We represent the interests of the Confederation, we negotiate disputes, we sometimes stop wars, we enforce treaties and agreements, and we conduct first contact visits to emerging civilizations," John replied. "Like the Demela."

"We're not at war with you, we have no dispute yet, and we don't want any treaties with you," General Kuldridge declared.

"Let him continue," Regent Willgntum said to his general.

"Thank you, Regent," John acknowledged.

"I shall hear you out, then I would like an opportunity to speak to you three about our one true god," Regent Willgntum added.

"The Confederation has been studying your culture for many years," John said. "Two of your nearest neighbors have also been studying you for many decades."

"We know about two aliens spying on us, but you are not one of them?" Pennul sounded more curious than threatened. "We have shot down spy craft from our two neighbors, but this is far more advanced than either one of them."

"No, we are not one of your neighbors," John replied flatly. "They are not Confederation members yet."

"Who are the other two?" Pennul asked quickly. "What system do they come from?"

The image of Demela disappeared from the wall, replaced by a map of four sectors of Quadrant D of galaxy G-1. The current Demela home world was in the center.

"As you can see from this map." John ignored Pennul's question. Your world is within fifty light years of two thousand planets or moons inhabited by industrialized races. There are a little less than one hundred who can travel at light speed, and seven who can travel greater than light."

"How many belong to your Confederation?" The Demela Regent asked.

"Of those who can travel greater than the speed of light, three belong to the Confederation," John answered.

"Do any of them mean us harm?" The Regent asked.

"Of the seven faster than light cultures, no," John replied. "Of the others, many would mean you harm, especially if you invaded their space."

"Is that why you brought us up here?" General Kuldridge asked. "To thwart our destiny?"

"A society's destiny is not solely self-determined; it is at least partially determined by one's neighbors and how you treat them and how they treat you," John replied.

153

"It does not matter, we are the chosen people, we are crafted by the one true god to be his people," The Regent chanted. "It is our manifest destiny to spread his word throughout the universe."

"*How can anyone be so dense, and illogical?*" Tem inquired of John.

"I think that is too big a task for you," John replied. "Besides, on your planet you can decide what to believe, but other cultures may not appreciate your efforts."

"*You need to learn, cultures like the Demela are two generations from any logical conclusions upon first contact,*" John replied to Tem.

"We are wasting our time here, Regent," General Kuldridge insisted. "Use your power to return us to the palace so we can mount a defense."

"Although we left the transmitter in place, as well as your electromagnetic pulse weapon, we did discharge your power supply," John said with a sigh. "Please tell General Kuldridge to sit down."

"I have been trying to disable their technology for the past five minutes, General," The Regent said as he looked at General Kuldridge. "Now, I know why it did not work."

General Kuldridge leapt towards John with his hands stretched out in a grabbing pose. Sam disrupted his muscles the second he moved, causing General Kuldridge to slump onto the floor with a dull thud, banging his head on an empty chair.

"Is he dead?" Pennul asked as she quickly rushed to the General's side.

"No, he is fine, he just cannot move," John replied. "We do not like violence, especially when it is directed towards us."

"Are we your prisoners?" Regent Willgntum asked.

"Sam, can you place the General in a chair," John ignored the Regent's question.

Sam floated General Kuldridge to an empty chair, flipped him and moved his legs so he was in a seated position, then slowly lowered him onto the chair.

"Can you assure me you will not try that again?" John asked the General.

"For now, yes," General Kuldridge sourly agreed.

154

Sam restored all muscular control back to the General.

"How did you do that?" Pennul asked. "How can you make him weightless without an anti-graviton device strapped to him? How do you generate gravity inside this craft?"

"As I was trying to say," John continued on his original train of thought, ignoring the Demela scientist. "Ambassador Gogrum and I are here to prevent possible future problems in this area of space."

Pennul Hoppgrede remained standing, moved closer to the display and studied it closely. She moved her hand through the star field, noting how her hand did not disturb the display. By each inhabited star system was a label, in the Demela language, indicating the name of the race, and a very brief description of the level of technology.

"Can I zoom in and out?" She asked.

"Just ask for a different view, and our ship will comply," John answered. "Is there something specific you want to know about this area of space?"

"We didn't realize how many inhabited planets there were." she stared at the display. "Can I zoom in on this section?"

Pennul pointed to the edge of the star field.

"Sam, center the image on the old Demela home planet," John said, looking at Pennul. "I assume that is what you wanted."

"It is." She looked surprised as the image quickly changed.

Pennul stared for a second, then asked, "Can you stay centered on our old home world, but zoom in to a ten light year diameter?"

The image quickly changed, drawing even more of Pennul's attention.

"Move the display down, and slightly to the left," John asked.

"What is that yellow line?" Pennul pointed.

"That is part of the problem," John replied. "That is the negotiated boundary with the Faulid Empire."

"Who are they?" General Kuldridge quickly asked.

155

"He's lying," Tem observed. *"They know about the Faulid."*

"Perhaps," John replied to his Science Officer. *"All I sense is they know the existence of the Faulid, not the nature of the Faulid."*

The image rapidly shifted to display the Faulid system in the center, then zoomed out to display the boundaries of the Empire, as well as bordering systems, including the old Demela home planet.

"Why is our old home planet called Brem?" Pennul asked.

"That's the name of the native inhabitants," John replied. "That's what the humanoids who are the pre-industrial inhabitants of that planet call themselves."

"Them?" Regent Willgntum asked in a haughty tone. "Our history records they cannot speak or hear."

"Your assessment is wrong," John answered. "What you need to be more concerned about are the Faulid."

"Why?" General Kuldridge asked.

"The Faulid are a Reptilian race; males are about three meters high. Their weapon systems are at least two hundred years ahead of your technology, although their transportation and communications technology is even more advanced," John paused for questions.

No questions asked, John continued, "They are a logical race, they have a rich cultural life, and they have a unique sense of humor. However, they feel they are the most superior race in the universe, or at least they feel they should be."

"How many systems are in their empire?" General Kuldridge asked.

"There are around forty space capable civilizations in the empire, none are superior to the Faulid," John replied. "Their empire covers about five hundred cubic light years."

"What does that have to do with us?" Regent Willgntum asked. "I can see clearly that our old home system is outside the Faulid Empire."

"To the Faulid, nothing is ultimately outside their empire," John replied. "Part of our agreement in establishing the boundaries, was that for a ten light year border, nothing could change."

"What does that mean?" General Kuldridge demanded.

"No external culture can occupy any system within that ten light year boundary," John answered. "Since, for the past one hundred thousand years, the Brem have occupied your old system as the only pre-industrialized civilization, it is their system, not yours."

"Who the hell cares about them?" Regent Willgntum asked.

"They are the creatures you genetically engineered for slave workers before you left the planet," John replied. "They have evolved and have built their own unique culture, which the Faulid consider the native civilization of that system."

"Those creatures were designed to be only dumb workers, they didn't even have their own voice," The Regent huffed.

"They have their own language, and their own culture, as well as their own traditions and written history," John assured the Regent.

"As I said before, they cannot speak, nor can they hear."

"They communicate telepathically," John replied. "I think they always could, even when you were living with them."

"Impossible," The Regent insisted.

"As a senior Ambassador of the Confederation, I am informing you what the next few hundred years will be like for your civilization," John replied.

John knew he had to keep this conversation on track. The Demela leader was too adept at veering the subject to the superiority of the Demela, and what everyone else must do to accommodate them.

"God will never allow his chosen people to be subjugated," Regent Willgntum spoke loudly.

"The Demela will remain on their current planet, and within their current system," John continued. "The worm hole between your current system and your old system is disabled."

"How can you do that?" Pennul asked.

"Your planet will be very closely monitored by us, any possible action you may take which may lead to armed conflict with any of your neighbors will be negated before harm can come to anyone," John said. "This will not only protect your neighbors from you, it will also protect you from your neighbors who could cause you great harm."

"How can you possibly do any of that?" General Kuldridge demanded.

"Since you are the head of state for Demela, I am handing you a visual record of what we are asking you to do, as well as a thorough review of the Confederation and your system's place in the greater universe," John said as he handed the Regent a clear disc. "This will work in your technology, and I hope you share this knowledge with all of your people."

"You have no jurisdiction over me," Regent Willgntum insisted.

"How can you criticize us for meddling in other planet's affairs when you are doing that very thing to us?" Pennul asked.

"Our Chief Scientist asks a very good question," Regent Willgntum echoed.

"To avoid useless bloodbaths; think back to what happened to your civilization one hundred thousand years ago. The Confederation negotiates between potentially dangerous adversarial systems," John replied. "Part of negotiations involves setting down ground rules that all sides must adhere to."

"Who decided that your Confederation is the arbiter for what is best for everybody else?" Pennul asked.

"By the time the Demela have advanced technologically to the point they are eligible for membership in the Confederation," John replied. "You will be able to vote on that very issue."

"I still say they have no rights. We will force them to abandon their expansionist plans," General Kuldridge snarled. "They will die by the millions learning their lesson."

"Your contact from now on will be Ambassador Gogrum," John added. "Since your planet will be closely monitored, all you have to do is ask for him on any frequency, and he will be there in less than one hour."

"How?" Pennul asked.

"Transmit a request on any frequency, asking for Ambassador Gogrum. That will suffice," John replied. "Now, you may return home and it has been enjoyable meeting you both."

General Kuldridge and Regent Willgntum disappeared from the cabin.

"Why am I still here?" Pennul asked.

"You are not going back because of your recent discoveries," John answered.

"What?"

"Your work on folded space is progressing all too fast for your limited social skills. We cannot chance your staying on Demela, giving your people a means to start a war on the Faulid border that would plunge hundreds of systems into a deadly conflict," John bluntly said.

"But, I have a family," Pennul insisted.

"Tell Ambassador Gogrum who must accompany you, and it will be done," John assured her.

"This is not fair," Pennul added.

"No, it is not," John agreed. "But for a greater good it will be done."

"Why can't you accept that our will is for the greater good?" Pennul asked.

"If life is sacred, then that which preserves the greatest amount of life is what must be done for the greater good," Ambassador Crackstone replied.

"Our religion tells us that our god is sacred, he is above all living things," Pennul argued.

"If you peruse your expansionist ways in the name of your god, your entire civilization will be destroyed," John answered. "So, since only the Demela revere your god, with them all dead, there will be no one to pray to the Demela god, so he will also be dead."

"That is an incorrect assumption," Pennul stammered. "Our one true god will never die!"

"We hope that your people and your god will survive well into the future, and the Confederation will do what needs to be done to insure that you will," John said.

"*How do you convince someone so stubborn?*" Tem asked the Ambassador.

"It just takes time," John replied. *"More time than I have right now."*

....

"Sir, you look troubled?" Tem appeared apprehensive. "It went well, didn't it?"

"Something just doesn't seem right." John said, frowning.

"What?"

"Had we not discovered the cloaked planet, and had we not discovered the solar wormhole, with the Demela ship exiting it, what would we have done?" John asked.

"You would have cautiously contacted the Demela leadership, from a cloaked state, and started trying the prescribed first contact protocols." Sam entered the conversation.

"Exactly." John's voice trailed off.

"What's your point, sir?" Tem asked.

"Something is out of place," Ambassador Crackstone observed. "Something is not quite right."

"What do you want to do?" Tem asked.

"Sam, get us to Commissioner Ythantrium as soon as possible," John said.

"His office said it may be a few minutes before they can have him available," Sam replied.

"Not remotely, I want to go there physically," John insisted.

"I understand," Sam answered. "It will be four jumps, and eight minutes, sir."

....

When the original Confederation Charter was signed over six thousand years ago, John Crackstone's planet, Zizthanthe, had been a first signatory. Four civilizations alone began the Confederation which formed to prevent a war with a fifth system.

The original four signatories had developed travel in folded space before creating the Confederation. In turn, each of them realized the extent of the universe they now had access to, and how crowded most areas of the galaxy was with industrialized cultures. The necessity to project a peaceful image to their fellow travelers gradually became painfully obvious. The ability to explore every square light year of your own galaxy and neighboring galaxies, usually forced a civilization into clearly stating that its intent was peaceful.

The only laws in common to all Confederation members were the twelve articles of rights, and the seven articles of oversight. Each system had equal voting rights and representation, beyond that, each culture lived by their own traditions and laws. If a being from one planet wanted to live on another planet, they were free to do so, but must adhere to the rules of the new world. This ability of Confederation citizens to travel freely among member systems negated the desire of one culture to colonize as many planets or moons as they may feel their population needs. Most of the energies of Confederation civilizations were channeled into scientific and social exploration.

In contacting new cultures or groupings of different cultures, making use of a collection of sixty four hundred different civilizations as an administrative entity smoothed negotiations considerably. Most faster than light cultures were also non-belligerent, so new alliances were relatively easy. To date, the Confederation had not found an alliance larger than itself, and it grew by an average of one new civilization every three years.

. . . .

"I have gone over the entire report for a second time, and I don't see anything to be alarmed about," Commissioner Ythantrium said.

"On Brem, in the Hall of Heretics, we saw two Demela craft as well as a Faulid craft big enough for two crew members," John replied.

John sat in one of the three chairs in the Commissioner's office; Tem was in the other. Since this was Ythantrium's home planet, and he was a Reptile, both Tem and John were in their reptilian environmental suits.

"That's all very logical," The Commissioner added. "Demela has been exploring their old Brem home system, and the Faulid share a border with the Brem system."

"The Demela have been traversing the solar wormhole back to their system of origin for several hundred years," John began. "They say it has been less than that, and the Mapping Project seems to confirm it, but I'll bet that they have been capable of sending robot probes for at least the last two hundred years."

"Let's say that is true," Commissioner Ythantrium allowed. "So?"

"On one of the Demela probes, we found a temporal signature that indicated an age of two hundred and sixty years," Tem interjected.

"Fine, so what?" The Commissioner sounded impatient.

"If they have been exploring that sector for over two hundred years, they have to know about the Faulid Empire," John replied. "In my briefing with them, they declared that they did not know about the Faulid."

"But, we both know that they do know the Faulid," Tem added.

"Well, the Demela are a secretive culture," Ythantrium observed.

"If they know about the Faulid, they may also know about the border, and the Faulid claim to their old home system," John said.

"Continue," The Commissioner sounded interested for the first time.

"What do the Demela want?" John asked. "Their old home system back?"

"And, what do the Faulid want?" Tem quickly added.

"An advanced working Confederation craft with folded space technology," John answered.

"And, where is the chief scientist of the Demela right now?" Tem added. "On just such a craft."

"Holy crap!" Commissioner Ythantrium almost shouted.

"Sam, locate the Gremlat ship Ambassador Gogrum and the Demela scientist are on," John quickly ordered.

"They are still in orbit around Demela, waiting permission to transport up Pennul's family," Sam replied.

"Deny all permissions!" Ythantrium shouted into his outer office.

"Yes, sir," Both his assistant and his computer answered simultaneously.

"Why didn't you transmit this information earlier?" Ythantrium asked John.

"I can't be sure the Gremlat are not conspiring with the Demela and the Faulid Empire," John flatly replied. "I need to investigate further."

"But, you should have sent me a message, or at least ordered the Gremlat craft not to transport anyone!" The Commissioner spoke loudly.

"The Gremlat Ambassador is in a Confederation craft, so I do not have a communication channel that they theoretically cannot overhear," John answered.

"I am assigning Ambassador Hynk and Ambassador Zillway to this problem," Ythantrium sounded worried. "Do you have any idea what could come of this?"

"I am fully aware of the consequences," John gravely replied. "You have never dealt directly with the Time Keepers, I have."

"Go immediately," Ythantrium added. "Make sure this incident does not happen."

"Please have Hynk take up a cloaked position around the old Demela planet," John requested. "Captain Halput should still be there, and I can vouch for his abilities."

"Done."

"Also, please have Zillway meet me at the new Demela planet, I will be there in…." John thought of possibilities and the time required for each.

"Six jumps, eleven minutes," Sam interrupted. "Unless you stay where you are more than three minutes."

Ythantrium was still barking orders to his assistant and several other administrators who had rushed into his office as John and Tem left.

....

A type two civilization can control the energy of a single, or multiple stars; enough to fold space and jump from a few to a

163

few hundred light years in three dimensional space. A fully realized type three civilization can harness the energy of many stars and can jump millions of light years in three dimensional space in a reasonable period of time; less than a few days.

All of the Senior Captains in the Mapping Project, and Senior Ambassadors in the Diplomatic Department were from type three societies, since they had the technology to travel between galaxies. Technologies of weapons and transportation were not fully shared between Confederation members, most others were, especially medical technologies deemed non-weaponizable.

In the exploration of seven galaxies, the Confederation had yet to have meaningful contact with any culture substantially more advanced than the most advanced Confederation civilization. Ambassador Crackstone's home system, Zizthanthe, was among the most advanced of the Confederation. His craft could easily travel between galaxies, and his defensive systems were the most advanced in the Confederation.

Does evolution cease with a type three civilization? This question vexed the best Confederation minds until an encounter about five hundred years ago.

Unintended consequences of traversing folded space could include total destruction, not arriving at a planned three dimensional destination, or time travel. If a mistake was made, the crew of a ship traveling through folded space could arrive at a three dimensional location in the universe, even the intended location, but be at a different time, either before or after the expected time. Now, reentering folded space with the correct vectors could correct time distortions; five hundred years ago, corrections like this were only theoretical.

The unintended consequences of being in the right place at the wrong time could be disastrous in one's normalized time-line. An action by a person one hundred years in their past could alter a time-line so that it was no longer recognizable one hundred years later. One system's time-line interacts with so many others that a mistake by a time traveler could affect the time-line of a whole galaxy in less than a millennia. A time paradox could be benign, or ruinous; a linear time traveler had no way of knowing what effects the paradox might have.

Five hundred years ago, Ambassador Millian Peppop had miscalculated a wormhole journey and found herself eleven hundred years in her past on an unknown planet. That planet had an industrialized civilization, barely capable of flight in their own atmosphere. She could not successfully locate her position by the nighttime star fields, nor could she connect to a Confederation information buoy. After a week of trying all other options she could think of, she ventured forth onto the unknown planet. Within five minutes away from her cloaked craft, she found herself and her craft back on her own home world.

Ambassador Millian's home world seemed to be frozen, all motion halted, from transportation craft to the people themselves. Only she and a lone male seemed to be alive and moving; she never discovered his name. The male explained that her actions on that distant planet would, in eight hundred years, cause the utter devastation of almost a whole quadrant of galaxy G-3. He further explained that his people were so far advanced from any Confederation member, that they are capable of keeping some time lines from being changed. They would continue to monitor linear time lines, making changes as circumstances demanded. The strange male then disappeared; all life on Millian's planet then began again as normal.

The recording device on Ambassador Millian recorded the entire event, it exists today as a teaching tool for all Confederation members. The Confederation named this advanced race, the Time Keepers. To date, there had been only thirty seven encounters with the Time Keepers, and Ambassador Crackstone had two of them himself. No substantially new information had been gained on the Time Keepers; they were still an important unknown in the universe. Other type three, non Confederation civilizations had reported contacts by the Time Keepers, all had different names for the race, but all agree they were the same people. This civilization was what may come after a type three, although what the extent of their real powers were was left to speculation.

10

I have a plan

Zillway Qadduk, ambassador from the Paddu system in Galaxy G-5, came from a humanoid species, walking on two legs, with a slightly elongated head and long arms. She stood two and a half meters high with long blonde hair. her home planet was distant from their star, the last inner planet before the first of four gas giants orbiting their sun. Their skin was a very pale white and the males stand about 3 meters high. The Paddu are a type three civilization, having joined the Confederation six hundred years ago.

Ambassador Zillway had known John Crackstone for thirty years, having worked two missions with him, the first as his Science Officer. John trusted Zillway with his life, and she him.

"Ambassador Zillway, good to work with you again," John spoke softly.

"I have been studying your mission logs, John." Zillway replied from her cloaked ship. "I see your concern," she added. "It's good to see you again too."

John quickly introduced his crew to Ambassador Zillway.

"What has me baffled is the true position of the Gremlat," John mused. "If they did make a deal with the Faulid Empire, it's a very foolish deal."

"They stand to lose far more from the Confederation than they could possibly gain from the Faulid," Tem interjected.

"Exactly," Ambassador Zillway added. "You can read thoughts, what do you hear?"

"Tem and I both can, and we felt no deception from Ambassador Gogrum," John replied.

"Why has the Gremlat ship increased its shielding?" Hodum said.

Hodum Wankutt was from the same planet as Ambassador Zillway. He was a half meter taller than the Ambassador and fifteen kilograms heavier.

"I'm sorry," Zillway spoke up, "This is Hodum, my Science Officer. My ship is named, Palut."

"Cloak into folded space, now," John ordered. "Sam, maximum shielding."

"What?" Tem looked at a panel. "There are fifty crew on the Gremlat ship."

"I can't sense any of them," John sounded confused.

"Neither can I," Tem concurred.

A particle beam shot from the Gremlat craft, landing squarely on Sam's flank, moderately jarring John and Tem.

"Their technology is far enough behind ours, doesn't the Gremlat Ambassador know that," Tem wondered aloud.

"If the Gremlat Ambassador and crew are now dead, that fact may not be obvious to the Demela who now control the ship," Zillway replied.

"Can you attach a tracking device on the Gremlat ship?" John asked Zillway.

"Already done, sir," Palut, Zillway's ship, answered.

"Sam, can you project a large explosion and a debris field after their next beam hits us?" John asked.

Before Sam could answer, the next beam hit, this time with more force. Sam did project a massive explosion, as well as an appropriate debris field. At the same instance, Sam cloaked himself into the sixth dimension.

"I hope they believe that," John said.

"I assume they do," Zillway answered. "They appear to be leisurely meandering towards their sun."

"Why don't they use the ship to fold space, why are they heading for the wormhole on their sun?" Tem asked.

"Damn," John quickly replied. "Sam, contact Captain Zindalph and have him make the wormhole passable again."

"Acknowledged, sir," Sam replied.

"Where is the Mapping Project?" Zillway asked. "There's supposed to be five craft in orbit around this planet."

"Sir," Sam interrupted. "A Demela fleet is now in orbit."

"How many?" John asked.

"Look for yourself, sir," Sam replied, projecting an image of the planet for John and Tem. "Two hundred and twenty craft."

"We can only assume they can detect a cloaked craft," Zillway quickly added. "Perhaps we should move ourselves to the old Demela system."

"No, wait in folded cloak for now, I don't think they can detect you there," John said. "Keep an eye on my back for me, will you?"

"What are you going to do?" Ambassador Zillway asked.

"I have a plan," John replied.

"That one phrase always worried me," Zillway commented.

"Me too," Tem concurred.

"Sam, has the Gremlat ship entered the wormhole?" John asked.

"Yes, sir," Sam answered.

"Tell Captain Zindalph to close the wormhole back down when the ship comes out," John instructed. "Let us know when that is. Also, tell him to cloak into folded space and hide himself well."

"What are you up to?" Zillway asked again.

"The Demela are secretive enough so that the Mapping Project did not have a clue as to their real technological abilities," John observed. "We need to know just how much technology they do have."

"Are we going to play games with them, sir?" Tem asked.

"In a manner of speaking, yes," John replied.

"Another two hundred Demela ships have entered orbit," Zillway interrupted.

"Captain Zindalph reports that the Gremlat craft is in orbit of the fourth planet in the Brem system," Sam reported. "The wormhole is closed."

"What's their game plan?" John wondered aloud.

"None of those Demela ships has the shielding necessary to go through the wormhole," Sam observed.

"No, I think they are waiting for someone to come out of the wormhole," John replied.

"They are all facing their star," Zillway agreed.

"Who do they think will be arriving?" John wondered again.

"The Faulid?" Tem answered.

"Are they crazy?" Zillway almost shouted.

"No," John replied. "Perhaps they are expecting another Confederation ship."

"How?" Zillway asked.

"Use the Gremlat ship as bait?" Tem added.

"Sounds like a plan to me," John chuckled. "Not a good plan, but a plan."

"What do you want us to do, Ambassador?" Zillway asked John.

"Sam, could you and Palut divide up all the Demela ships, then work out the most effective firing pattern to disable all of them," John asked. "I want all propulsion and weapons rendered inoperative, leave them only enough power for life support."

"Done, sir," Sam answered.

"When?" Zillway asked.

"Now."

....

Weapons were neither offensive or defensive, they're just weapons. Most cultures spent all too much of their middle and late industrial efforts perfecting them. The Confederation encouraged it's members to spend less time on weapon development, and more resources on medical and other scientific endeavors; although, most of the type three cultures possessed very advanced weaponry. The Mapping Project craft all had minimal weaponry, but they did possess very advanced shielding; this technology was shared among the more advanced Confederation members. All Diplomatic Department craft carrying Senior Ambassadors had the most advanced weapons and shielding of the Confederation.

Shielding was rated by a standard Confederation scale, class 1 through 15. Class one shielding was primitive electromagnetic shielding, necessary for any extended star system travel; it protected the ship's inhabitants from most forms of solar radiation, and some large extra-solar natural high energy bursts. Traversing a small wormhole required a class five shield, a long, inter-galactic jump, required a class ten shield. Sam had the capability of projecting a class fifteen shield for over a twenty hour period. When threatened by lesser civilizations, Sam would begin with class five shielding, which he could maintain for hundreds of years if necessary. In more tenuous situations, he projected class ten shielding, which he could maintain for up to thirty years. When shielding above class six was maintained, no matter could be transported on or off a ship. Above class ten shielding, communications beyond a ten light year radius in three dimensional space was impossible.

Simple shielding technology worked on bending principles. Just as photons can be forced to bend around a three dimensional object, thereby never reflecting back to an observer, advanced shielding could bend other high energy particles around three dimensional objects. Gravitational shielding prevented solid three dimensional objects, such as meteorites, from striking a moving three dimensional craft.

Beamed or pulsed particle weapons were the most common among interplanetary capable species. The complexity and power of those weapons depended on the state of a system's technology. Occasionally, a capsule system was used, such as a missile, to deliver a lethal dose of high energy particles, anti-matter explosives, or any variation on that theme. Some systems had the capability to convert matter to energy, transport it to another three dimensional location, then reassemble it back to matter. This worked quite well with capsule delivery systems, sometimes transporting a destructive device inside a ship's shielding, shielding less than a class four. If the high energy beam was multidimensional, or accelerated faster than the natural speed of light, much more damage could be accomplished.

. . . .

Sam and Palut emerged together out of folded space, between the over four hundred Demela ships and their star. The Demela immediately began to fire beam and pulsed weapons at the two Confederation craft. Nothing more than a slight bumping sensation was felt by John and his crew, nor by Zillway and her crew. Methodically, Sam and Palut fired a mild beam weapon at every Demela ship, disabling each of them. It took less than three minutes to reduce the complete Demela offensive fleet to a floating mass of useless metallic capsules carrying a few thousand shocked Demela.

"We both need to re-cloak," John insisted. "We need time to assess the extent of the Demela plot."

"Sir," Sam interrupted. "I have located fifteen Confederation operatives on the planet."

"Is one of them Ambassador Gogrum?" John asked.

"Is he with the other Confederation personnel?" Zillway added.

"No, he is with the Regent and General Kuldridge," Sam replied.

"Does that mean he's plotted with them?" Zillway asked.

"We don't know what it means yet," John answered.

"I think we should retrieve all our people, except Gogrum," Ambassador Zillway suggested.

"I agree with the Ambassador," Tem added.

"In this situation, we're not a democracy," John observed. "But, I agree."

"Where should we put the fourteen?" Tem asked.

"Ambassador Zillway," John began, "Can you make room for half of them in a secure cabin?"

"Why secure?" Zillway replied.

"How can we be sure that none of the fifteen are part of a plot?" John answered.

"That's a bit paranoid, isn't it?" Zillway asked.

"The last thing we need is for another Confederation ship to be commandeered," John pointed out.

"I suppose you're right." Zillway gave in. I can accommodate seven of them."

"Sam," John said. "Can you and Palut divide up the fourteen and make a secure cabin for our seven?"

"Yes, sir."

"Ambassador Zillway," John said. "Can you scan for any more major weaponry on the planet, or any hidden caches of armed space craft?"

"I can, but if you will pay attention to your own sensors, you will note that they have been trying to kill us for the past few minutes," Zillway replied.

Both John and Tem had long since assumed their natural shape, that of an amorphous cloud of cells held tightly by a magnetic skin. John floated back to the front of the craft, into his control space. In front of him the skin of the ship became transparent, giving John a clear view of ten Demela craft releasing antimatter mines into orbit around the planet.

"Before I zap the ships, can I have the antimatter?" Sam eagerly asked.

"You have to share with your friend, Palut," John chuckled.

"My ship thanks you," Zillway added.

"We have the planet based targets you asked for, sir," Sam informed John.

"Divide up all the targets, then take care of them," John ordered. "I don't want any life lost, though."

"That might prove difficult," Palut interrupted.

"Figure it out before you do anything, please," John ordered.

"Yes, sir," Sam replied.

"And, Sam, could you please inform the staff in our holding cabin what the situation is and why they are confined there," John said. "And, make sure the security on that cabin is as tight as you can make it."

"Yes, sir."

"Not even a microbe can escape, please," Tem added

"Ambassador Zillway, could you do the same?" John asked.

"I already did," she responded.

"What was that microbe comment about?" John asked Tem.

"What about the Ambassador on the planet?" Tem asked, ignoring John's question.

172

"What do you think I should do?" John asked.

"I think we should transport him up here, with us," Tem replied.

"I agree, but not alone," John agreed.

"With whom?"

"The Regent of the Demela, who else?" John replied.

"I suppose I have to be the girl again, then?" Tem semi-objected.

"That's right, back in our environmental suits," John concurred.

....

On first observing a society, the Mapping Project classified them according to Confederation standards. Between a primitive pre-industrial to a high type three civilization the Confederation prescribed one hundred and thirty five steps; each step had a long list of assumptions based on their technology and social structure, the natural materials available, the native intelligence of the people, and the extent of outside influence from other cultures, not from their planet.

The Mapping Project first observed Demela over six hundred years ago. Initial observations pegged the civilization at stage seventy seven. They were now capable of space flight within their system and could project high level three shielding. Their people were of average intelligence, and, at initial contact, were not influenced by any outside cultures. The initial assumption the Mapping Project made was that the Demela would not be capable of traveling in folded space for at least a thousand years. With that assumption, the Mapping Project left only minimal cloaked observational equipment orbiting the planet.

Ten years ago, the orbiting monitors reported several anomalies. The Demela were capable of very limited quantum communications, their weapon systems were a century ahead of assumptions, and they had been building huge underground manufacturing facilities around natural magnetic deposits, making detection more difficult. The most alarming observation was that they could sustain a subatomic wormhole in a defined region of

173

space. Protocol demanded the Mapping Project investigate these anomalies, which they did. Three small teams were assigned to observe the Demela in more detail. After determining that they were about a few hundred years away from travel in folded space, the matter was turned over to the General Council. After three years of debate and several studies, the General Council decided on first contact, turning the matter over to the Diplomatic Department.

. . . .

"Since we have now destroyed their entire advanced technology, I think I can return to the nearest Confederation facility to deposit our Mapping Project personnel," Captain Zillway suggested. "I can take all but Ambassador Gogrum back in my craft."

"Good idea," John agreed. "Sam, transport our guests onto Captain Zillway's ship."

"Done, sir."

"Captain Zillway," John said. "Meet me back here as soon as you can, please."

"Of course," she replied.

Palut created a wormhole, then disappeared into it; the fold in three dimensional space then collapsed.

"Our guest is in the holding cabin, and I have left the highest containment field in place," Sam said.

"Thank you," John acknowledged. "Tem, shall we join our visitors?"

Both John and Tem were now in their humanoid environmental suits; they looked Demela. They spoke as they walked to the holding cabin.

"Do you think the Demela have had outside influence, sir?" Tem asked.

"Perhaps the Faulid," John speculated.

"The Mapping Project observers didn't report on any other cultures contacting the Demela," John said.

Tem made John stop just outside the cabin containing Ambassador Gogrum and Regent Willgntum.

"Sir, the mapping project was staring at the planet and didn't see the wormhole in their star," Tem said. "They didn't know about the Demela exploring sector 121 for so long, so how would they know if the Demela were in contact with the Faulid Empire?"

"Good point," John acknowledged.

"Also, if the Mapping Project screwed up that, perhaps there have been other contacts with other civilizations," Tem added.

"The Gremlat?" John asked.

"Perhaps," Tem surmised. "Doubtful, but possible."

"Why don't we speak to our guest." John opened the door.

"You again?" Regent Willgntum huffed. "How dare you take me prisoner!"

"You, again, are our guest," John replied.

"You cannot save your lives by taking me prisoner!" The Regent insisted.

"We are not in fear of our lives, Regent," John answered. "Perhaps you and your military should be in fear of yours though."

"Threats do not deter us," Willgntum sounded arrogant. "The one true god will always be on our side, we shall prevail."

"Right." John paused as a visual display appeared on one wall of the cabin. "Perhaps you would like to speak to General Kuldridge?"

"How is that possible?" Regent Willgntum sounded confused.

On the display was a sharp image of a large room full of men and women in uniforms, quite animated about some crisis. General Kuldridge was in the background stooped over a console, intently staring at a display, stabbing his finger on various controls. A lesser officer stared at the camera feeding the image to John's craft; this officer quickly ran to General Kuldridge and almost dragged him to the camera.

"Sir, Regent," General Kuldridge stuttered. "Where are you?"

"I am back aboard our enemy's ship," The Regent announced. "Do not attempt a rescue, destroy them immediately!"

"I cannot, sir," Kuldridge replied.

"That is a direct order, General!"

"I cannot, sir," Kuldridge repeated. "They have destroyed our entire fleet."

"We only destroyed your entire military infrastructure," John interjected.

"Is that the alien?" The General asked.

"It is the same ones who abducted us previously," Regent Willgntum replied.

"Most of our infrastructure is military," General Kuldridge replied to John.

"We destroyed things, not beings," John replied.

"How much is gone?" The Regent asked.

"Everything, sir," General Kuldridge answered.

"We will prevail," Regent Willgntum said, as much to reassure himself as anything else.

"I think it's time you join your general staff in victory," John sounded sarcastic for the first time.

"*DNA, sir, DNA!*" Tem shouted telepathically to Ambassador Crackstone.

"In a minute or two," John said to Regent Willgntum.

"*What are you talking about?*" John asked his Science Officer.

"*We need a useable sample of the Demela's DNA before we send him back,.*" Tem insisted.

"Are you afraid of something?" The Regent asked, sounding hopeful of a weakness.

"*Why do we need that?*" John asked.

"I don't think so," John replied to the Regent. "We are having a small technical difficulty with transporting you."

"*I have a question about outside influences on the Demela, and I need to test my hypothesis,*" Tem answered.

"*Take your sample, then,*" John acquiesced.

"Did your ship break?" Willgntum mocked.

"Not at all," John said. "Please hold still for a moment."

Tem leaned over, working a small pad which had just appeared on the wall nearest him. A clear tube appeared, then began filling with blood, transported from Regent Willgntum's main artery feeding his left leg. A second tube appeared, filling with blood drawn from Ambassador Gogrum.

"*Why the Ambassador?*" John asked.

"*He has been on that planet, away from Confederation sensors, for over a day, and we did have questions about his loyalties, sir,*" Tem replied.

"What the hell is she doing?" Willgntum demanded. "Is that my blood?"

"*I suppose you're right, Science Officer,*" John conceded

"It's nothing." John refused to answer the direct question. "Say hello to the General for us, will you? Regent Willgntum disappeared, transported back to the war room on Demela.

"Ambassador Gogrum, I hope you will forgive us, but we must leave you in this room alone for now," John said.

"Believe me, I understand," The Ambassador replied. "This whole thing has been a most unusual experience."

As soon as John and Tem left the cabin and closed the door, John spoke, "What was that about?"

"I need to compare the current sample to the historical ones taken by the Mapping Project to determine if any outside influences have taken place," Tem answered.

"Hasn't the Mapping Project taken samples all along?" John asked.

"Apparently not in the last eleven years, sir," Tem replied. "Their regular schedule is a twenty year cycle."

"What could have happened in the last eleven years?" John wondered aloud. "Are you thinking about the Allu?"

"I am, sir." Tem confirmed.

"That puts a new wrinkle in my plan," John said, sounding thoughtful.

"Just what was that plan, sir?"

11

This could be the start of something big

Among the basic ways the Confederation classified life were the basic chemicals necessary for any given life form, basic body structures, and DNA sequencing, and reproduction methods. Most life forms in the explored galaxies were based on varying combinations of carbon, oxygen and hydrogen. About twenty five percent of life forms were based on other chemicals, such as boron, sulfur and silicon. The Allu fell into that other twenty five percent, being based on Hydrogen, sulfur and boron. Allu DNA was unique, although closely related to the reptilian Huknat race, three hundred light years from the Allu home system. The Allu were also not a standard body form; they were classified as a tri-pedal animal with four arms. They were air breathers, walked upright and bred in male-female pairs, although an individual could alter themselves from male to female and back at will.

The Allu form of government was a democratic monarchy; a regent, king or queen, was elected every five years. The Allu culture had been centered on expansion since their early industrialization era, two thousand years ago; they were an early type one civilization at this time, well capable of inter system travel within a twenty light year radius.

Centuries ago, the Allu were challenged in their expansionist ways by several of their technologically advanced neighbors, as well as the Confederation. This stopped the Allu for a while, but they secretly planned a response.

A strong point of Allu science was genetics. Fifty years after the non-expansion treaty was signed between the Allu and the Confederation, their science yielded an answer; the Allu were able to weaponize their DNA. If they discovered a planet or moon with a compatible atmosphere and enough essential chemistry to support their life, they would seed it with their weaponized DNA. This weapon would act as a virus, invading a suitable host then altering the host's DNA into an Allu within five generations. This solution worked well only twenty percent of the time, the other eighty percent had unintended consequences; some species were entirely wiped out, while others transformed from productive forward moving cultures to a dead end species rapidly heading to extinction. None of the unintended consequences were positive.

After a century of the secret Allu DNA project, it became obvious what was happening in the Allu sector of Galaxy G-1. The Confederation quickly constructed a specific antidote to the Allu DNA weapon, then sterilized the entire quadrant of galaxy G-1. The antidote worked only on the first infected generation; succeeding generations could be repaired over time with the help of Confederation scientists. The Confederation, and non Confederation neighbors of the Allu, quarantined the Allu for five hundred years, forcefully not allowing them to travel outside a twenty light year radius.

The Confederation discovered that the Allu weaponized DNA was capable of existing in deep space for centuries with little or no degradation. Also, it could slowly interact with other free floating organic compounds to form variants. The Mapping Project was tasked with scanning for Allu DNA and any variants in all areas of galaxy G-1, then destroying it. They hoped it would be limited to only one galaxy, but all Mapping Project craft in other galaxies were also equipped and tasked to look for the Allu virus and destroy it.

The Allu were not, nor will they be for five hundred years at least, eligible for membership in the Confederation.

. . . .

"I'm back," ambassador Zillway announced as her craft emerged from folded space.

"We may have a complication," John responded.

"What?"

"My science officer suspects Allu DNA," John replied.

"Oh, crap!" Zillway exclaimed.

"My suspicions are founded," Tem interrupted. "The results are back."

"What are they?" John asked.

"Is it a variant?" Zillway quickly asked.

"It is a new variant, but it is close enough to the original to act as intended," Tem answered. "It's a recent infection; they are only in generation one and two as far as I can tell,"

"What about the Ambassador from Gremlat?" Ambassador Zillway asked.

"Ambassador Gogrum has been infected, but only within the last thirty six hours," Tem replied. "Do I have permission to sterilize the planet, and the Ambassador?"

"Yes, please," John replied. "Sam, please send all this new material to the Confederation, they need to check the Mapping Project personnel."

"We all have supposedly been inoculated from the Allu weapon," Zillway sounded nervous.

"This is a new variant," John said. "Have your Science Officer check both of you."

"I have already tested both of us," Tem spoke up. "Since I have the variant identified, it's not an invasive process."

"And?"

"We're both fine," Tem answered. "Our immune systems reject this variant also, but Ambassador Zillway still needs to perform the check."

"We have, and we're fine, thank you," Ambassador Zillway replied.

"Sam, contact Captain Zindalph."

"Zindalph here."

"What is the stolen Gremlat ship doing?" John asked.

"I think they have begun to discover what all the buttons do," Zindalph replied. "We have had to move a few light years away, as well as call off the four other Mapping Project craft."

"What have they done so far?" Ambassador Zillway asked.

"Well, Ambassador," Zindalph began, "They have fired both pulsed weapons several times, I assume they are figuring out the targeting procedures."

"And?"

"They are also trying to fold space ahead of them," Captain Zindalph responded to Ambassador Zillway. "I think they're having a hard time with that since they cannot yet sustain a wormhole."

"The Gremlat craft are not completely automated, and the calculations are too difficult for the Demela without the cooperation of the main computer," John observed.

"Eventually they will be able to bypass any restraints and fully access the main computer," Zillway added. "We can only assume they have access to all the Confederation maps, as well as access to all Confederation information buoys."

"That's just general information." Tem joined the conversation.

"But, that information is thousands of years more advanced than they are, in some areas," Hodum, Zillway's Science Officer, added.

"Have they used communications at all?" John asked.

"They have," Captain Zindalph replied. "And, surprise of surprises, they contacted the Faulid."

"Using the Gremlat communications?" John sounded amazed.

"No, it seems they have their own communications equipment on board." Zindalph chuckled. "I guess they think we can't intercept their transmissions."

"What did they say to the Faulid?" Ambassador Zillway quickly asked.

"They announced that they were in orbit around their old planet and that they staked their agreed claim on the system for their stupid god," Zindalph replied.

"Did the Faulid answer?" John asked.

"Yes, but we have to move again," Captain Zindalph answered. "They have sort of figured out the sensors, and have been systematically performing a dimensional scan of the entire sub-sector."

"What did the Faulid respond?" John insisted.

"We're ten light years away, and behind a small comet," Zindalph replied. "The Faulid told them to cease transmissions, called them stupid, then informed them that they would be in that system within thirty six hours to personally arrange the treaty with the Demela."

"We will be there in a short time," John replied.

"Please make it sooner than later," Captain Zindalph said. "We only have class eleven shielding and the Gremlat ship's weapons can eventually defeat class eleven shielding."

"Plus, the Faulid have almost equal weapons," Ambassador Zillway added.

"Before we proceed to the Brem system, we need to reassess the original plan," John said.

"What was the old plan, sir?" Tem asked.

"What?" Ambassador Crackstone sounded surprised.

"I have to agree with your Science Officer," Ambassador Zillway concurred. "What was your old plan?"

"Incapacitate the Demela fleet, destroy their offensive capability, then ascertain if the Demela had made a secret agreement with another race," John answered.

"Well," Zillway said, "most of your first plan has been carried out."

"I know," John answered. "What troubles me is the last part of that plan."

"The alliance with another civilization?" Tem asked.

"Well," John answered. "yes."

"I definitely see a problem in the Brem system," Ambassador Zillway commented.

"The exclusion zone, sir?" Tem asked.

. . . .

The one civilization that the Confederation had encountered that was more advanced than a high level type three were called the Time Keepers. In their exploration of neighboring galaxies, Confederation Captains had discovered that this advance civilization had also made itself known. They were identified by many different names, Enlightened Beings, Invisible

Ones, Time Lords, Civilized Tribe, and many more. No known civilization had regular or diplomatic relations with the Time Keepers. The only contact had been one way, and always to tell a lesser culture to stop some activity, or to correct accidental time line changes. Almost always, the Time Keepers would appear as one of the subject race, and communicate only verbally; sometimes they permitted a record of the exchange, other times not. This behavior was consistent from galaxy to galaxy. No one knew who they were, where their home planet was, what they really looked like nor how truly advanced they were.

In galaxy G-1, a Time Keeper appeared in the Oversight Group one hundred and seventy years ago; he appeared as an Imtun, a two meter humanoid. He identified himself as a Time Keeper, noted a thirty cubic light year section of space in Quadrant D of Galaxy G-1 as an exclusion zone, not to be entered by any civilization for three thousand years. He informed the Oversight Group that there would be an energy barrier around this section of space, and that any craft or being trying to enter that exclusion zone would be destroyed. He said that a temporary temporal phenomena existed that could create great devastation if disturbed within the exclusion zone. The Time Keeper then disappeared.

The General Council voted to investigate the matter, sending the Mapping Project's most advanced craft, the Ufflander, to Quadrant D, Sector 121 of galaxy G-1. Not wishing to actually challenge the Time Keeper's restrictions, the Ufflander launched an advanced probe towards the exclusion zone. That probe disappeared as soon as it touched the border of the exclusion zone. The crew of the Ufflander tried more probes, even trying to transport a probe within the excluded zone; all to no avail.

Scanning the zone also proved useless, the scans could not penetrate the borders. Any attempt to fold into the zone failed; all wormholes were distorted away by the force field.

After three months of trying, the Confederation gave up, marking the zone as un-navigable. Two years later, the Faulid claimed the exclusion zone as part of their empire; the Confederation decided, after a six month debate, that, since the

Faulid could not enter the zone either, it didn't care. Cloaked observation posts around the exclusion zone reported on many Faulid attempts to enter; all ended in failure and sometimes loss of life.

In the decades following the establishment of the exclusion zone, rumors and wild speculation ran rampant through Quadrant D of Galaxy G-1 about the possible riches, or scientific treasures that were contained within the zone. The reasoning went, why would such an advanced people hide a normal region of space? Also, if it contained a normal temporal phenomena, why should such precautions be taken since the galaxy contained many temporal abnormalities that were commonly avoided by one and all? A more convoluted theory held that the home system for the Time Keepers was in the excluded space, and anyone who could gain entrance would be privy to all the secrets of the universe.

As soon as a culture discovered, or even heard about the Time Keepers, some among them became fixated on the elusive super race. Most devotees of the Time Keepers eventually came to the conclusion that what made them so special had to be some aspect of their genetic makeup. Once that conclusion was reached, some became fixated on finding a Time Keeper home planet so they could extract DNA, then find a way to blend that DNA into their own genes. As this theory goes, any group who could create a hybrid of themselves and a Time Keeper could clone themselves as a Time Keeper, thus becoming an all knowing being with the ability to live forever. All seven known galaxies had many dedicated groups of searchers building hybrid creatures using suspected DNA and their own, hoping to become immortal and omniscient. Even though logic dictated that their quest was folly, they kept searching and extracting DNA samples from new worlds. If the Time Keepers did not want to be breached by those fanatic scientists, they would simply undo any actual progress, reset the time line, and no one but the Time Keepers would know. Logic seldom appealed to fanatics.

The Confederation generally ignored these groups, but on more than one occasion had to intervene on behalf of a primitive society when a fanatic DNA searcher threatened ecological destruction. A small, but growing section of fifty Ambassadors was assigned to the task of riding herd over the Time Keeper hunters for the seven known galaxies.

. . . .

"The exclusion zone, indeed," Ambassador Crackstone said slowly. "Do you think the Faulid care about the Brem system and the Demela claim to it?"

"No," Ambassador Zillway answered. "But, they might care about an advanced Confederation craft and how they could use that technology to enter the zone."

"Sam, contact the Commissioner as well as the Oversight Group, all of them at once," John ordered.

"That will take some time, sir," Sam replied.

"What do you have in mind?" Commissioner Ythantrium asked. "I have been monitoring you both."

"I need a decision on the Gremlat craft soon," John answered.

"If you mean to destroy it, I concur," The Commissioner replied.

"A quorum of the Oversight Group is here, sir," Sam announced.

"Have you all been apprized of the situation?" John asked.

"Most of us have," Llwnan, the chair of the group said.

"I think we are all up to speed," Htill, the representative of Zizthanthe, John's home planet, added.

"What do you decide?" John asked.

"Tell me the alternatives," Llwnan requested.

"There aren't a large number of alternatives," John answered. "We cannot transport them off the Gremlat craft since they have maintained class eight shielding since taking over the ship."

"What about disabling their shielding?" Htill asked.

"A flaw in the Gremlat design causes the hull integrity to collapse when the shielding is successfully attacked," Commissioner Ythantrium interrupted.

185

"So, disabling the shielding would be the same as destroying the ship and killing all the passengers," Htill reiterated for clarity.

"The Demela stole the Gremlat ship to give to the Faulid in exchange for possession of their old home system, the Brem system," John recapped. "I assume that they hope to discover for themselves how to construct a dimensional system before the Faulid arrive, as well as use the Gremlat ship as a decoy to attract more Confederation craft they might also take over."

"That's not a well thought out plan," Commissioner Ythantrium observed.

"Well thought out or not," John said, "their plan to take over the Gremlat ship worked like a charm."

"I think the Ambassador is asking us to come up with a well thought out plan for the Confederation," Htill said.

"What does Ambassador Crackstone recommend?" Llwnan asked.

"I recommend destroying the Gremlat ship as soon as the Faulid arrive, then warning the Faulid fleet to return to their side of the boundary."

"I feel we all agree," Llwnan replied. "But, what do you suggest if the Faulid refuse your order?"

"I suggest that Ambassador Zillway and I enforce the treaty signed by us and the Faulid," John answered flatly.

"What is the outcome if we do nothing?" Htill asked.

"Judging from past encounters with the Faulid Empire," John observed. "If we do nothing, they will claim the Brem system, probably destroy the Demela in this system, then proceed to try to destroy all Confederation craft."

"So, the results would be the same regardless of our actions," Llwnan reiterated for clarity.

"There is no other choice," Commissioner Ythantrium concurred.

"We agree," Llwnan said.

"Do you need more craft?" Htill asked.

"Perhaps two more in this sub sector," John answered. "I feel you need to deploy more craft to guard the whole Faulid border."

"Two craft have been dispatched to Sector 121, Quadrant D," Ythantrium said.

'I think this might force a conflict between us and the Faulid," Htill stated.

"My hope is that this incident will convince the Faulid Empire to coexist peacefully with their neighbors for a while longer," John posed.

"At least be more careful in their dealings with the Confederation," Ythantrium mused.

"Thank you all," John said his farewell to the Oversight Group. "Commissioner, I would like you to monitor the mission from this point on, please."

"I shall," Ythantrium acknowledged.

"One more thing, Commissioner," John added.

"Yes?"

"Do you remember that discussion we had in your office as I was assigned this mission?" John asked.

"The one involving something about your last mission?" Ythantrium asked for clarification.

"Yes."

"Shall I transmit it to you?"

"Please," John replied.

"I have the information, sir," Sam acknowledged receipt of the transmission. "But, sir, I think that would be a bad idea."

"Ambassador Zillway." John ignored Sam's comment. "We will fold to Sector 121, project class fifteen shields and you will stand one million meters off one side of the Gremlat ship, I'll stand off the other."

"Yes." Ambassador Zillway replied.

. . . .

"Captain Zindalph," John requested.

"I'm six light years from you, bearing 126 by 33 by 10," The Captain replied. "I have sent all other craft back to the nearest Confederation planet."

"Have the Demela sent any more messages?" John asked.

"They have sent two," Captain Zindalph answered. "The first was a message to their home planet asking the status of the fleet, and the second was a long transmission containing most of your mission log to the point of their capture of the Gremlat ship."

"Did you block their transmission?" Tem quickly asked.

Ambassador Crackstone stared at his Science officer.

"Of course I did," Captain Zindalph sounded insulted. "Since I closed the wormhole, they have to use normal communications and the messages would have a two day turnaround for their technology."

"You may stay put, or you can leave for a Confederation port," John said.

"You have permission to destroy the craft?" The Captain asked.

"We do," Ambassador Zillway replied.

"I'll stay," Zindalph said.

"Can you provide a secure cell for Ambassador Gogrum?" John asked. "He was infected with Allu DNA."

"I can," Zindalph answered.

"Sam, please get the coordinates from the Crimson Balfunder and make the transport," John ordered.

"Yes, sir," Sam replied. "I suggest transport soon since I have to reduce shielding to transport."

"Do it now," John added.

"Done, sir," Sam replied. "Shields at class fifteen, and just in time, sir."

The Gremlat ship, commandeered by the Demela, began to fire a pulsed beam at both Sam and Palut. The beam was a reddish brown color and was pulsed fast enough to appear as a bright steady flat ribbon of charged particles, ten centimeters wide, with a slowly moving series of evenly spaced dark bands moving towards the targets at ninety degrees to the beam direction. Each weapon blast lasted for precisely twelve seconds, a limit of the beam emitter. Gremlat weapon technology was advanced for a high type one civilization, but no match for class fifteen shields. All that John and Tem felt inside their craft was a slight bump with each hit.

After twenty firing cycles at each Confederation craft, the Demela ceased fire. The Demela began scanning both Sam and Palut for damage.

"I'll do the firing," John said deliberately, so no mistaken intent could be inferred. "I am responsible for this mission."

"Fine," Ambassador Zillway replied. "We will stay here and scan for any Faulid craft.

"I'm waiting until they get here," John added.

"So they can see the destruction of the Demela? Tem asked.

"Exactly," John replied.

"Sort of an exclamation point to begin our discussion with them about retreating back to their empire," Zillway said.

"Five Faulid craft are exiting folded space three million meters away," Palut announced.

"As soon as they have a good view of all of us, fire on the Gremlat ship," John ordered Sam. "I want matter remaining, I want the Faulid to see the results."

"Yes, sir," Sam bleakly answered.

The Ambassador's craft understood the meaning of his commander's order, everyone who heard the order understood.

One of the minor weapon systems available was an accelerated anti-matter device. This apparatus can accelerate a predetermined amount of magnetically contained anti-matter up to twenty times the natural speed of light at a target. This particular weapon can defeat up to class twelve shielding; the Gremlat craft possessed class eight shielding. The mechanics of the device are quite simple; a mini-wormhole is first created, then a contained packet of anti-matter is looped through a predetermined amount of dimensional space to accelerate it beyond light speed, from one to one hundred light years, then, as it exits the mini-wormhole it is directed at the target. In real time, a fraction of a second delay happens between the time firing is ordered and the target is hit. Once through shielding, this weapon can convert any three dimensional mass to nothing but high energy subatomic particles.

After making the necessary calculations, Sam waited until the five Faulid ships paused around the second gas giant in the

Brem system, focusing their attention and scanners on the Gremlat ship and the two Confederation craft.

Sam fired the weapon on the Gremlat ship, full of hopeful Demela soldiers. An anti-matter weapon is invisible to most species' vision, but it can be detected quite well by even rudimentary scanners. Everybody in that system, including the Demela knew what was about to happen, but only a fraction of a second before it did.

As the shields were penetrated, a sharp blue light burst in a three hundred and sixty degree silent explosion. Almost as the flash of blue reached its peak, the Gremlat craft started to shake violently, then the front half of it disappeared in a bright, white flash, perhaps one hundred times as bright as the neutralizing of the shields. Where the remaining half of the craft had been joined to the missing half there now was a jagged edge, spilling technology and bodies into open space.

"Open communications with the Faulid," John ordered.

"They are refusing, sir," Sam answered.

"Pick the lead ship out and use the main weapon," John ordered. "I want nothing left."

The most powerful weapon John had available was the dimensional cannon. Over three fourths of the mass and energy in the universe could not be seen by any civilization's eyes, nor could it be measured by most of their technology. Some civilizations called it dark energy and mass, others, like John's race, called it dimensional mass and energy. Opposed to anti-matter, dimensional matter could exist in the universe without reacting to regular matter, as could dimensional energy. However, if dimensional energy was concentrated, forced into a coherent beam, then focused through a massive gravitational lens, it could completely evaporate an entire star system in less than a millionth of a second. To destroy a craft with class ten shielding, dimensional energy from a three cubic light years of space must first be obtained. Sam had the capability to store dimensional energy from a hundred cubic light years of space; which he was now doing.

The lead Faulid ship disappeared, silently, without any visible violence, leaving no trace of its existence.

"Contact the Faulid again," John ordered.

"Still no response to us," Sam reported.

"They are contacting their home system," Ambassador Zillway interrupted. "And, they have begun firing on us."

The Faulid's most advanced weapon was a less sophisticated version of Sam's anti-matter device. Sam and Palut were not affected by the repeated volleys of anti-matter.

"Try communications again," John ordered.

"We have a reply," Sam announced.

"Why have you destroyed two of our ships," The Faulid Commander demanded.

"Why are you here, outside your boundaries?" John calmly asked.

"We have a claim on this system," The Commander replied.

"The Faulid treaty of 8765 specifically states the boundaries of the Faulid Empire, and this system is clearly outside those boundaries," John flatly stated. "This is not your empire, and you will return to your own space now."

"No." The commander insisted.

"Destroy his ship," John ordered.

The third Faulid ship disappeared. The remaining two craft ceased firing and moved back to an orbit around the second gas giant.

"Open communications again," John ordered.

"Why are you systematically killing all of us?" The Captain of one of the remaining Faulid ships asked.

"I am very clear about this," John began. "Return to space inside your agreed upon boundaries immediately or I will destroy both of you."

As John finished his sentence, two Confederation ships folded into three dimensional space between John's craft and Ambassador Zillway's craft.

The two remaining Faulid craft folded into dimensional space, disappearing from view, Sam determined that they retreated back to their side of the border.

12

Wasn't I just here?

Time travel is quite possible now. Time travel is also quite regulated now. Not only did the Confederation have stringent rules on time travel, but most other type three civilizations in the seven known galaxies had strict rules as well. Foreknowledge of events could alter the normal flow of time, as could past interference of normal events. The unintended consequences could often be more harmful than malicious intentions in time travel. One might think that sending a cloaked observation drone back into history to record famous periods in time might not be harmful. But, the possible social damage alone made most advanced civilizations prohibit this activity as well. Many strongly held beliefs, both cultural and religious, were often based on untrue events or those redefined through the passage of time. If these beliefs were challenged by actual observations, the damages may be extreme. Folding in higher dimensions across three dimensional space distorted three dimensional time as well as three dimensional space. Folding through the fourth, fifth or higher dimensions could be fatal without sufficient shielding and mind numbingly accurate navigation.

The current shared level of navigational science by all Confederation systems assured safe travel through fourth and fifth dimensional folds. Both destination and time targets could be accurately achieved; a ship would arrive where they wanted and at the same time they left their previous location. Just as a specific three dimensional location could be chosen for any given trip through folded space, a specific time could, theoretically, also be given. Traveling to another time, either in the future or the past, was strictly forbidden for any Confederation craft without exacting permission from a Commissioner or the General Council. If a Confederation craft found itself in another time through an accident, the procedure was to return to the proper time as soon as possible and never interact with beings native to the accidental time line. If an accident resulted in a totally disabled craft, the crew, if still alive, would wait for a rescue mission.

Through several centuries of observation, the Confederation had noted that the Time Keepers would correct any time travel that may have resulted in an altering of the normal flow of time by forcefully changing the actions of errant time travelers.

. . . .

"Sir," John spoke to the image of his superior, Commissioner Ythantrium , "You do know what I'm about to ask."

"If you need my permission to travel ahead to that planet, you have my permission," Ythantrium replied. "But, follow protocol, please."

"As always, sir."

"I hope you don't do this, sir," Sam quickly interjected as the image of the Commissioner disappeared.

"You know what I intend to do?" John answered.

"You intend to go back to that strange planet, and to travel three thousand years into the future, sir," Sam said.

"Time travel, sir?" Tem sounded apprehensive.

"If I can believe what the Commissioner just sent the Ambassador," Sam spoke up, "he means to go back to that Earth planet three thousand years in our future."

"I almost never agree with our ship, but I have to this time, sir," Tem insisted.

"What possible reason could you have?" Sam asked.

"Go ahead, download the logs to our Science Officer," John ordered.

Science Officer Tem paused in his thoughts long enough to absorb a small subset of the mission logs from their last assignment. That small portion of raw information contained sensor readings from their ship as they entered orbit, twice, after restarting Sam's propulsion systems. In particular, Ambassador Crackstone wanted his Science Officer to pay attention to the various craft from other systems which were also in orbit around that backward planet in galaxy G3.

"I understand your concern, sir," Tem began, "but, I don't see a need to risk time travel, especially at this juncture of our current mission."

"The Faulid will return to this system soon, and we will need to be here to jointly enforce the treaty," Sam added.

"If we travel to Earth, we will be back here only a second or two later, in relative terms," John insisted. "This is not a debatable issue, make the calculations."

"I have already done so, sir," Sam replied. "It will take me ten minutes to saturate the dimensional collectors."

"Sir," Tem interrupted. "You do know that we will be energy depleted when we fold back into this system in this time; if we are in the middle of a battle then, we may not have enough energy to survive."

"I am willing to risk that the Faulid will not be here in the next hour," John sighed. "That should give Sam enough time to complete our mission and recharge his power reserve."

"Thirty minutes and three jumps, sir," Sam abruptly said.

"That's a short journey for so long a trip," Tem observed.

"It uses a lot of energy, but we need to be done with it quickly," Sam replied.

"I agree," John concurred.

"Sir," Sam said, just before initiating the first dimensional fold. "I took the liberty of making our target time thirty years after our previous encounter with Earth so that you may not interact with anyone who might remember you."

"That would be a very small number of natives, if I remember right," John replied.

"But, a problem circumvented is a problem solved," Sam playfully replied.

. . . .

"Are we well cloaked?" John asked.

"We are sitting in the eighth dimension, all alone and scanning the small blue planet," Sam slowly replied. "Just as you ordered, sir."

"We are not quite alone, sir," Tem observed. "In fact, a Confederation craft has just folded into our dimension and is hailing us."

"Who the hell are you and why are you here?" A voice demanded.

"May we discuss these issues face to face?" John replied.

"Very well, but be aware that I am a Senior Ambassador of the Confederation and will not tolerate deception," The voice demanded.

"Good day, Senior Ambassador," John said with a chuckle. "My name is John Crackstone, Senior Ambassador of The Confederation and I'm on a sanctioned time travel from three thousand years in your past."

In front of John flickered an image of a very angry humanoid Ambassador who now was shouting at his craft to recall the appropriate historical records.

"You're dead!" The Senior Ambassador finally shouted to John.

"By your time, I would assume so," John calmly replied.

"I'm sorry." The Ambassador calmed down, a bit. "My name is Ambassador Poullit."

"Well, Ambassador Poullit," John spoke in his best diplomatic tone, "I shall not ask you any specific questions, but I will request that you allow me to observe for a short time."

"What do you want to observe?" Poullit asked.

"What's going on above and on this planet, that's all."

"Do not interfere in anything."

"I fully understand the parameters of time travel," John agreed. "Are we safe in this cloak?"

"Dimensions six and up are safe," Poullit replied. "I suggest you drop to six to conserve power."

"We shall," John acknowledged. "And, we shall cease contact with you. Thank you for your assistance, though."

"Keep your shielding at thirteen or higher," Ambassador Poullit added. "Some sort of a war may be going on here."

"Can we ask with whom?" John quickly asked.

"You'll find out soon enough," Poullit replied. "The Faulid Empire."

Poullit's craft folded back into the fourth dimension and sped down to towards the planet's surface.

"The Faulid Empire is now capable of intergalactic travel?" Tem slowly sounded out the words.

"Sam," John asked, "why did you really aim for thirty years in the future from when we were last on this planet?"

"Given the facts as I knew them, I calculated the best time to arrive here and not be associated with your former selves and that time was now, thirty years after you were previously here," Sam answered.

"That makes almost no sense, but it does sound like your logic," John mused.

"Sir, I think this might have been a good choice after all," Tem interrupted.

"Why?"

"Look at the sensor display," Tem insisted. "The types of craft have increased immensely since we were last here, but the civilizations represented are the same."

"I see Faulid, Demela and Gremlat among twenty other races," John sounded thoughtful. "Eight of the systems represented here are Confederation."

"But," Sam interrupted. "please note that the Gremlat are no longer members of The Confederation."

"That is interesting." John seemed lost in thought.

"Have you established a link with a Confederation information buoy?" Tem asked the craft.

"I have," Sam replied.

"Quickly, give me the pertinent history of the Gremlat," John sounded adamant.

"Twenty five hundred years ago, the Gremlat conquered the Demela and joined the Faulid Empire, laying claim to all of Quadrant D of Galaxy G1." Sam paused as he downloaded all this information to Tem and the Ambassador. "The Faulid War

196

began twenty two hundred years ago and ended three years later; over half of the Faulid offensive fleet was destroyed."

"When that war ended, the Faulid Empire agreed to new boundaries in galaxy G1, and has abided by that agreement to this day," Tem continued.

"But, they carried their quest for new territory to neighboring galaxies," John added. "Since they obtained dimensional propulsion technology from the Gremlat."

"It would also seem that they have joined forces with those who hunt the Time Keepers in search of promising DNA to use in cloning experiments," Sam said.

"Which is what's happening on this planet," John said with a sigh. "This race of humanoids do not seem the type to develop into Time Keepers."

"Be that as it may," Tem said, "there are eight Confederation systems here to fight more than twice as many Faulid allies, all of whom apparently think this measly race of humanoids may well develop into Time Keepers."

"How long has this particular conflict been ongoing?" John asked.

"More than fifty years," Sam replied. "But, no more than ten years at this level."

"I want to go down there and look around," john announced.

"Do you think that wise, sir?" Tem asked.

"Again," Sam interjected, "I hate to agree with the Science Officer."

"Might I remind you who is the Ambassador on this mission," John's voice sounded annoyed.

"Yes, sir."

"Transport us down to this military base." John pointed to a site on a map display in front of him.

"Very well, sir," Sam began, "this culture is still male dominated, and the military has no high ranking females, so you both should be male. I can make the Ambassador a general, which should give you access to most places. I will make the Science Officer a lieutenant colonel, your aid."

"Do they have electronic records systems yet?" John asked. "And, make me a one star general, I don't want to stand out that much."

"Yes, sir" Sam answered. "A very crude digital system, and I have been downloading and manipulating it for some time now."

"Anything interesting?" Tem asked.

"They have achieved fission," Sam responded. "They have indirect fission generators, but have spent most of their effort on fission weapons."

"That can affect dimensional travel in this system," John slowly said. "That could be a problem."

"There are only a few governments that are capable, and their easily read secure systems will inform us if a test explosion is about to take place," Sam assured the Ambassador.

"Anything else of interest?" Tem asked.

"Well," Sam answered, "quite a few Faulid craft have been shot down, over many countries. Some of their craft have been recovered by the humanoids down there."

"Have they reversed engineered anything?" John sounded anxious.

"Yes, they have," Sam replied. "They have almost understood basic propulsion systems and anti-gravity systems."

"Dimensional travel?" John sounded even more anxious.

"They have no clue about that, sir," Sam assured him. "None of the Faulid craft shot down so far have that system."

"Are they using short range reconnaissance craft, piloted by biological drones?" John asked.

"Yes, so far."

"Configure our environmental suits for us," John ordered.

"At least I'm one of the boys this time," Tem added.

....

"This isn't a military base?" John asked.

Their ship, Sam, had transported the Ambassador and his Science Officer to a deserted area of a park; Riverside Community Park, just off Northcliff Drive. It was nine in the morning, the local date was April 19th, 1954. A slight scattering of clouds occasionally hid the bright morning sun. A light breeze from the south made the sixty one degree temperature feel a little cooler. Spring had begun; flowers were blooming and the trees had a fresh coat of new green leaves hanging in the morning light.

"I know, sir." Tem replied. "A General does not simply walk onto a military base."

"Do you have a plan?"

"I do, sir," Tem answered. "If you will notice, there's a car waiting for us on that street."

"It has a flag on the front of it, with two stars," John observed. "I distinctly remember telling Sam I wanted to be a one star general."

"It has to do with who can and who cannot get into the places you want to go, sir," Tem answered.

"I have more and more questions that need answering," John sounded impatient. "And, I have the uneasy feeling that you have more answers that I do."

"I am sorry, sir," Tem spoke in a calm voice.

"Why are you sorry?" John asked.

"I can hear your thoughts, sir, just ask me."

"When Sam tapped into the electronic data containing Army records, I did a small search of my own, right before we transported down here," John began.

"I know."

"And, I looked for the man I knew when we were last here, in 1924," John said. "You remember, Dr. Steve Hopkins, the man who helped us find the place Sam had crashed?"

"Yes, I remember him well."

"Well, I found out he joined the Army as a physician during the recent global war, but before that he married a woman named Elizabeth Winslow," John sounded impatient again. "Wasn't that your name when we were here last?"

"It was," Tem replied. "You made me assume a female role that time."

"When we normalized the time line for this planet upon leaving the last time, I assumed that Dr. Steve Hopkins would

199

probably no longer exist, let alone marry a woman with your old name," John slowly said. "I think that might be too much of a coincidence, don't you?"

"Just ask me the question that's bursting to get out of your conscious thought," Tem sighed.

"Who are you?" John asked. "You aren't Tempatt Groonghin, are you?"

"In a way, I am Tem," he responded. "But, in reality, I am not."

"You're a Time Keeper, aren't you?"

"I am."

"Why?"

"The why will become obvious in a short time, but for now, please treat me and this mission as if I were Tem, your Science Officer."

"How can I?" John pondered.

"Do you remember our mission to Ultym, three years ago?" Tem asked. "That mission turned violent quickly."

"I remember that incident," John answered. "My Science Officer and I became separated; then I heard a burst of weapon fire from the Office of Diplomatic Affairs conference room. I then observed you rolling out of the office on the floor, then diving towards me calling for Sam to transport us both back up."

"We had happened on a coup in progress, quite unexpected," Tem added.

"You saved my life that day, I do appreciate it still," John said.

"What actually was supposed to happen was that Tem, your Science Officer, was killed and you were seriously wounded." Tem outlined the alternative time line.

So." John paused more than a moment, "you, or my real Science Officer, is really dead and I am supposed to be still wounded?"

"Tem is really dead, but you would have been well recovered by now, and on this very mission with a different Science Officer."

"For some reason, the Time Keepers felt they needed to be on this mission with me?" John asked, trying to fathom the real reason this was happening.

"I should say no more," Tem answered. "We both need to continue this mission as if you knew nothing about our involvement in it."

"Does it have to do with this planet?" John asked. "Earth?"

"Not directly," Tem replied. "Please, will you get into your car and continue this mission?"

Ambassador Crackstone stared at who he thought was his Science Officer for a long time. Gentle morning sunlight, filtered by light green foliage, lit both their faces as they stared at each other in silence. Only the chatter of birds and rustling of foraging squirrels filled the morning silence.

John turned and slowly walked to the car, followed by Tem.

....

Everybody will salute you, sir," Tem instructed. "Just remember to return the salute each time, with your right hand."

"I know," John acknowledged.

The two remained silent as the car drove up to the main gate by the silent driver. As the car paused beside the guard, who saluted the General in the back seat, the driver handed him three identification cards. The guard read them quickly, handed them back to the driver, then motioned the car through.

"Who is that driver?" John asked.

"In simple terms, he's a figment of everyone's imagination." Tem smiled. "No real driver is up there."

"And, the car?"

"The same thing."

"Remarkable," John said as he shook his head.

The driver handed two identification cards back to Tem. Tem took one and passed the other to Ambassador Crackstone.

"Are these real?" John asked.

"These cards are quite real, and you are the real General Arthur G. Trudeau, at least for now you are," Tem answered.

"How did you do that?"

Ignoring the question, Tem replied, "This hangar is where you want to go."

"Why?"

"The growing skirmishes between the Confederation and the Faulid have resulted in many Faulid craft falling from the skies on this world. This government has made a concerted effort to collect as many of the crashed craft, as well as the pilots, as they can; many of them are here," Tem replied.

"That's why I came here." John nodded. "Okay, let's go see."

In front of the main entrance to a large freshly painted hangar stood two huge soldiers, each carrying an M-14. Both soldiers snapped to attention and crisply saluted the approaching two star general. John returned their salute, then handed one of them his ID card.

"We need to speak to Colonel Jarvis, now," Tem spoke for the General.

"Yes sir," The guard holding the General's ID card spoke loudly. "Wait here, sir, I will fetch the Colonel now, sir."

In less than a minute, the guard reappeared with a Lieutenant Colonel in tow.

"Sir, we were not expecting you," Colonel Jarvis said as he saluted the General.

"The General is aware of your latest find, and needs to see it with his own eyes," Tem interrupted.

"I'm sorry," Ambassador Crackstone said, "This is my aide, Colonel Bevins."

Colonel Jarvis nodded towards Tem, appearing as Colonel Bevins in his environmental suit.

"Sir, I wish you had waited until I can gather more information about this latest discovery," Colonel Jarvis spoke directly to the General. "I know the President wants an action paper soon, but we simply do not know what this new twist may mean for us."

"Just take me to it, please," John demanded.

. . . .

"As you can see, sir." Colonel Jarvis pointed into what looked like a crude operating room, "we have just begun to understand the gray creatures, but now, this."

Ambassador Crackstone and his Science Officer stared through a glass partition into the ten by fifteen meter room, portions of which were lit by high intensity lamps. Six small gray bodies lay on six operating beds in various locations around the room. A team of scientists hovered above one of the small bodies, carefully disassembling it with surgical tools.

"As you know, we have to protect every room housing one of the EBEs with a strong magnetic field, or their friends will transport them away from us," Colonel Jarvis spoke as if he were conducting a group of tourists.

"EBEs?" John whispered to Tem.

"Extraterrestrial Biological Entities, sir," Tem whispered back.

"And, in this room down the hall is our newly discovered creature." Jarvis pointed the way.

"It's just a Faulid without an environmental suit," John whispered.

"And, it's alive," Colonel Jarvis proudly announced.

"I can see," John said as he turned to face Colonel Jarvis. "I want to be in the room alone with him."

"Sir, that's highly inadvisable," Jarvis retorted.

"But." John glared at the lesser ranking officer. "I'm the General, and you aren't."

"Sir." Jarvis snapped to attention.

"I will accompany the General," Tem spoke up. "I will have my sidearm drawn the whole time."

"We've discovered that doesn't much matter," Jarvis snidely said. "In fact, you will have to leave the side arm out here with us."

"Very well," Tem replied "the General and I shall go in there together."

"May I ask, what do you hope to accomplish?" Colonel Jarvis asked.

"On two other occasions the entities have spoken English to me, and I am hopeful that will occur again," John noted.

"They have communicated both verbally and mentally with various members of our staff as well, but this one only grunts at us," Jarvis observed.

"I will try, but I need to be left alone with him, only my aide will accompany me," John insisted.

"Very well," Colonel Jarvis conceded. "I will have two armed guards outside, ready to defend you if needed."

"Please, turn off the cameras and the microphones," John insisted. "I have found they know when we are recording them and will not communicate with me unless we are truly alone."

"Very well, sir," Jarvis agreed.

As John and Tem entered the holding area, only low grumbling noises were audible; that noise was emanating from the three meter tall reptilian creature pacing the holding cell. John, through the universal translator in his environmental suit could understand the grumblings of the annoyed Faulid officer.

"Damn, I ask to be taken to their leader, and this is all I get? A damned General?" The Faulid muttered aloud to himself.

"You are right," Tem observed. "the Faulid do have a unique sense of humor."

"What?" The Faulid stopped in his tracks and stared at Tem. "Who are you, you certainly aren't Human!"

"I am a Confederation Ambassador, John Crackstone," John said.

"No way in hell," The Faulid insisted. "You've been dead for quite a while!"

"Why does everybody know my name three thousand years in the future?" John whispered to Tem.

"Later, sir," Tem whispered back to him.

"What's your name?" John asked the glowering Faulid.

"I am Captain Tguddoth, Fleet Captain Tguddoth!"

"Well, Fleet Captain Tguddoth," John said, "I have time jumped to investigate this conflict between my government and your empire."

"Why did the Time Keepers allow you to do so?" Tguddoth demanded.

"Why don't you ask them?" John said with a grin.

"Since I know that a Confederation Ambassador does not have a sense of humor, what are you talking about?"

"What I thought was my Science Officer seems to have been a Time Keeper all along." John nodded towards Tem.

"Is this true?" Tguddoth Asked in a calmer voice. "We are right then."

"Right about what?" John asked.

"They are convinced this race of humanoids are a future Time Keeper race, and since they are incapable of defending themselves, they are ripe for massive genetic experimentation by the Faulid and their allies," Tem answered the question.

"If you are a Time Keeper, it must be true," Tguddoth repeated.

"I think we need to be truly alone." Tem held her palm up as if to ask for a time-out. "This Earth humanoid race is not a Time Keeper race, they will be extinct in a hundred thousand years; it is a dead end for you."

Tem paused all activity outside the holding room; all the humans froze in place.

"What happened?" John asked as he looked through the glass partition into the hall, full of frozen humans.

"I stopped time," Tem replied. "They were becoming somewhat suspicious at our behavior; it appeared to them as if we were conversing with the Faulid in a series of grunts."

"You are speaking to me in a series of their grunts," Tguddoth smiled.

"Not to worry," Tem interrupted. "I will move us back in time to when we first entered the room; we will all stare at each other, the Faulid will grunt and we will look confused, then the Ambassador and I will leave, unable to converse with you."

"It must be nice to be immortal and omniscient," Tguddoth said.

"It is, and your race will never know just how it feels," Tem insisted.

"We are on the right path here," Tguddoth said slowly.

"If you were, don't you think the Time Keepers would simply make your race cease to exist?" John observed.

"He is smarter than you are." Tem smiled at the Faulid Captain. "Perhaps you should listen to him."

"We shall see," Tguddoth snorted.

"How long have the Gremlat been your allies?" John asked.

"You know that my telling you that would violate your Confederation laws," Tguddoth said with a smile. "Besides, the Time Keepers might not like me telling you."

"Almost two millennia and a half," Tem answered.

"I guess the Time Keepers don't care that much about me knowing stuff," John sarcastically spoke to Tguddoth.

"The burning questions the Ambassador wants to ask you are how you got to this galaxy, why you want this system, and who else became your allies," Tem said.

"We developed advanced folded space travel with the help of our Gremlat friends, we became convinced that the survival of our empire depended on us morphing into a Time Keeper race, and many old Confederation systems have joined our empire in that quest."

"Who?" John insisted.

"Many," Tguddoth replied

"Most of them were Time Keeper hunters, some of whom took over governance of their home systems just before leaving the Confederation." Tem fleshed out Tguddoth's answer.

John turned to face Tem and spoke calmly, "I have all the information I need, can we leave now?"

"Yes, sir," Tem answered.

In an instance, the whole scene returned to the moment when John and Tem entered the holding room. Captain Tguddoth was unaware of the previous conversations, but John was. Tguddoth repeated his joke about taking him to their leader, but this time John and Tem just stared at him. After a few minutes of silence on John and Tem's part, they indicated they wanted out of the room, and were escorted back into the hallway.

"Did it communicate with you, sir?" Colonel Jarvis eagerly asked.

"No, it did not," John replied. "Was the craft different from the ones piloted by the gray creatures?"

"It was similar, but our teams speculate that all the systems are much more advanced," Jarvis answered. "The anti-gravity system acts the same, but not much else does."

"As soon as you have anything, please forward it to my office," John said. "We need to return to Washington now."

"Yes, sir."

. . . .

After transporting back aboard Sam and returning to their natural form, Tem and John stared at each other.

"Not now, sir, especially in front of Sam." Tem broke the silence.

"All I want to know is, exactly why am I here?" John asked.

"What went on down there?" Sam asked. "Can you download your logs, sir?"

"We need to talk, sir," Tem said.

"Where is Sam?"

"I have paused time again, sir."

"Why do you insist on calling me sir?"

"I am your Science Officer," Tem replied. "As much as I'm anything else, I am your Science Officer."

"I find that hard to believe," John sounded incredulous.

"It's true, at least for now and the past three years it has been true."

"What about my logs?"

"They recorded exactly what happened down there, including what the Faulid Captain said," Tem replied. "The only thing missing is any reference to my being a Time Keeper."

"That will do, then," John conceded. "What happens on this blue planet?"

"Do you know the Jmabura?" Tem asked.

"The water based life form that has just begun space travel?" John replied.

207

"What do you know about them?"

"They are very aggressive and self absorbed," John replied. "They are almost an early type one civilization in this quadrant of this galaxy."

"By this time, they have not developed dimensional travel, nor do they have a clue as to how it works; they are limited to light speed," Tem said. "In a little more than fifty years they will be in this sub-sector in search of new territory to conquer."

"So?" John said. "They are very far behind the Faulid, they will be destroyed if they approach this system."

"While they haven't mastered dimensional travel, they have mastered a singularity weapon."

"They what?" John sounded amazed.

The technology to create a singularity weapon was not that complicated, it was, however, quite difficult for even a high level type three civilization to control. The weapon created a black hole large enough to not be quickly dissipated. The nascent black hole was immediately fed a massive infusion of gravitons, then hurled at great velocity towards a target; it then consumed the target, accelerated to the speed of light and meandered off into the universe, guided only by natural gravitational fields.

No self respecting advance civilization would build or use such a weapon because the resulting out of control rapidly growing singularity might, in all likelihood, destroy whole systems, some belonging to those who created it in the first place.

"The Jmabura are even crazier in this time period," Tem said. "They not only possess the singularity weapon, they have used it."

"Why don't you stop them?" John asked.

"They are part of the flow of this time line," Tem answered. "So, although we want to stop them, we will not."

"I can't understand that logic," John insisted.

"And, I cannot explain it to you, at least not now," Tem replied.

"Then," John asked, "why bring it up at all?"

"The Jmabura attempt to conquer this system, and, in the process drive the Faulid away," Tem answered.

"And, this affects our time line, how?" John quizzed.

"I cannot say at this time, sir," Tem replied. "We need to return to our mission at hand now."

. . . .

"Where are your mission logs from your trip down there," Sam inquired again.

"I'm sorry," John sounded flustered. "Here, enter them, and, as soon as we return to our time, transmit them to the Commissioner."

"Yes, sir," Sam confirmed. "I take it you want to return to our time?"

"Yes, please," John said.

"It is plotted, and in about thirty minutes of our time, we shall be back in the Brem system," Sam said. "But, sir, I must tell you that I will be at fifty percent power when we fold back into the Brem system."

"I understand," John acknowledged. "How long before you can get back to one hundred percent?"

"If I use every shortcut I know, I can be back to full power in about an hour."

"I hope we have the time."

13
What's love got to do with it?

"Sir," Tem asked carefully, "What do we do now?"

"We go back to the cloaked planet," John replied to Tem and the other Confederation craft in the Brem system.

"Why?" Tem asked.

"I want to see the Museum of Heretics again," John replied with a small grin.

"The what?" Ambassador Zillway interrupted.

"The Brem on the fourth, invisible, planet have several crashed craft in a museum, and two of them are Faulid," John answered.

"What can you possibly learn from that?" Zillway asked. "And, why did you go to G3 on a time mission?"

"The time mission was for the same reasons I need to go back to the Brem planet," John replied. "Ask the Commissioner to view my logs for that mission, then you will understand."

"I shall," Zillway said. "Why the Brem planet, and why now?"

"Perhaps a reason, perhaps a weakness, or perhaps nothing," John answered. "I do need to do it though."

"We shall wait here for your return," Ambassador Zillway replied. "But, don't be too long, I have the feeling that the Faulid are not through with this just yet."

"Have you sent my mission log from our time travel?" John asked Sam.

"Yes, sir," Sam replied. "I did notice some irregularities, though."

"What did you notice?" John inquired.

"They seemed." Sam hesitated in his reply, "choppy; as if parts were missing."

"How could that be possible?" John asked as he glanced at Tem.

210

"How would I know," Sam sounded irritated. "I wasn't there."

"Science Officer." John quickly changed the subject, "Please gather what we need to perform an in depth scan of the two Faulid ships."

"Yes, sir."

"Sam," John said, "Please take us back down there, and transport the Science Officer and me into the Museum of Heretics."

"Sir," Sam replied, "Although I can traverse the planetary shield quite easily now, I still lose the ability to collect power while in the energy shield or below it. I need to recover my loss from the inter galactic fold, so I hope you can conduct your business quickly."

"If not, you will leave us down there and return to open space to recharge yourself," John said.

. . . .

It was less than two days since Ambassador Crackstone had left for his original first contact mission and crashed on Brem. In that time, the Brem Wizard, Tamora, had revised the history of the moment and spread the story of two heretical outcasts from Grendela who tried to hide among the Brem. The strangers were discovered, and with Tamora's magical help, forced to return to Grendela to face the wrath of the gods. No mention was made of the third intruder, a lizard the size of two Brem guards.

"Just as we left it, sir," Tem said, as he looked around the large hall. The seven wrecked space ships seemed small in the cavernous space.

"You do know that you can make this a very short trip if you will only tell me what I want to know about these craft," John said.

"I told you, I am your Science Officer only," Tem insisted. "What you may, or may not know about me is irrelevant to this mission now; I am only Tempatt Groonghin, your Science Officer."

"Very well, then, let's try to be in and out of here as quickly as possible," John said.

Both the Ambassador and his Science Officer hurried to the first of the Faulid craft and began scanning it.

Initially, Tem used his portable utility pad to scan the craft. That piece of equipment, while quite sophisticated, was incapable of providing detailed information on the complete technology contained within the ship. Science Officer Tem now had a piece of equipment to construct a complete schematic of the broken craft. Another piece of scanning equipment could provide a map of what areas of space this craft had been in the year before it had crashed. Also, they would know how many times, and how far the craft had traveled in folded space. John used one of the devices, while Tem ran the other.

"Sir," Sam broke in. "You have company."

"Who?" John looked away from his device.

"It is the middle of the day at the palace of magicians, so it's quite busy," Sam began. "There are fifteen guards, and your old friend, the head mistress of the palace about five minutes from your present location."

"Science Officer," John ordered, "get your weapon out and prepare to stun everybody except Tamora."

"Sir," Sam interrupted, "Tamora's boyfriend is rushing into the fray."

"Keep Damnen awake too," John said.

"I hate to be a pest, sir," Sam interrupted again. "I need to recharge now, especially if we might be in a fight soon."

"Don't take more than an hour, please," John replied.

"I will recharge your suits before I leave," Sam responded., "Which will be in ten seconds."

"I'm not through with my scan," John quickly said. "Are you?"

"No, sir, not yet."

"We have to deal with our company now."

"Sam, could you wait a minute or two before heading back to open space?" John requested.

"Yes, sir."

John looked at his utility pad, noticing the location of all the Brem in the palace and beyond.

"I can stun every one of them in a five kilometer radius, sir." Tem informed the Ambassador.

"We don't have time for pleasantries," John acknowledged. "Do it, but leave Tamora and Damnen awake."

"Why?"

"Just do it," John insisted.

Tem followed the Ambassador's order and put every Brem in the palace, and in the nearby city asleep, except Tamora and Damnen. He then set his utility pad to give an alarm if any Brem were to come within a five hundred meter distance of them in the Museum of Heresy inside the palace.

Tamora stopped in her tracks as the guards ahead of her and behind her fell into a pile on the floor. She stooped down, checked the nearest guard, then rose to her full height.

"Damnen?"

"Yes, my love," Damnen replied as he rounded the corner, carefully stepping around and over the sleeping guards.

"It must be them, but why have they returned?" Tamora asked.

"Should we confront them again?" Damnen asked. "What if that giant lizard is with them?"

"I shall cast a protection spell over both of us," Tamora said. "We shall confront them, and drive them away again."

Tamora brushed her left hand in the air just above her head, causing a door to appear in the wall in front of then, then slowly open. She then raised her right hand, lowered her head slightly and concentrated on the protection spell. A pale blue cast enveloped both Tamora and her consort.

As Tamora and Damnen passed through the doorway, with Tamora leading, both Ambassador Crackstone and Tem looked up from the first Faulid wreck and stared at the two Brem, then looked back at the wrecked space ship.

"*I have finished my scan, sir,*" Tem reported to his boss. "*I shall move on to the next Faulid craft.*"

"*I'm almost through,*" John answered.

"*I'll leave the two lovers for you to handle,*" Tem said with a bit of relief.

"*I guess that's why I have the fancy title,*" John chuckled.

"Why are you back?" Tamora demanded,

"*I have completed my scan as well,*" John said. "*I shall join you as soon as I say something to these two Brem.*"

"I do apologize, but we had to return to look at three of your displays in this museum," John replied to Tamora.

"*Sir, do you still need me?*" Sam interrupted. "*Perhaps I could get back to recharging myself?*"

"*Perhaps you could,*" John replied. "*Do you sense any army of angry villagers massing for an attack?*"

"*I think not, sir.*"

"*Then, off you go,*" John ordered.

"Why?" Damnen meekly asked.

"Because the creatures who made this craft." John pointed to the first Faulid craft, "are intent on conquering your planet."

"How?" Tamora commanded an answer. "Our magic has obviously worked well against them before."

"You must believe me," John began, "we mean you no harm, and we are here to protect your world from those who seek to conquer you."

John moved to the second Faulid ship and began scanning it.

"Why should I believe you?" Tamora asked, the edge was off her voice now.

"I could take you up in my craft," John said. "You would be in orbit around your world, and soon you would see the fleet of craft intent on your subjugation."

"*Sir, that would not be a good idea,*" Tem interrupted the Ambassador.

"You can do this?" Tamora asked.

"*I wasn't planning on it,*" John answered his Science Officer.

"I could, but you might be safer in your palace," John answered Tamora.

"I would not like you to go with him, my dear," Damnen insisted.

"Why are you so insistent on the Brem not visiting our craft?" John inquired.

"I shall do as I please," Tamora sounded resolute.

"I'll explain later, sir," Tem replied to the Ambassador.

"Why are the off worlder's craft so interesting to you?" Damnen asked John, more to change the subject than pure curiosity.

"I will be honest with you," John began, "two of these craft are from the Faulid Empire, the race who intends to conquer your planet, and this one is from a planet that may be in league with the Faulid Empire."

"Are you fighting these Faulid creatures so you can conquer us instead?" Tamora asked.

"We hope never to fight," John replied.

"How?" Damnen quickly asked.

"We hope to avoid battle," John answered.

"Sir, perhaps you should scan the second Faulid craft now," Tem interrupted.

"Do you hope to find a weakness in their magic, so you can use trickery?" Tamora smiled as she asked.

"I may be much older than you, but I can still multitask," John replied to Tem. *"I am scanning the second Faulid craft."*

"You are perceptive, Tamora, that is our plan," John responded. "If we can trick the Faulid Empire, there will be no battle, and they will leave your world alone, and we too can leave you alone, hopefully forever."

"I have finished my scan, sir," Tem said to John. *"I am moving on to the Gremlat craft."*

"How can I believe any of what you tell me, unless I can witness it myself with my own eyes?" Tamora sounded quite sincere.

"Darling, no!" Damnen shouted.

"I'm almost finished with this scan," John answered Tem.

"I must see for myself if our people are in danger," Tamora replied to Damnen.

"But, it may be a trick played by these two creatures." Damnen pointed to Tem, then to John.

"I am the greatest wizard on this planet," Tamora insisted. "If trickery is your game, I shall see it!"

"You do have the strongest magic on in this world, my love," Damnen agreed. "But, neither you nor you and your guards could stun or destroy these two creatures."

Tamora became enraged; her cheeks flushed and her expression became dreadfully grim. She raised both her hands, palms facing Ambassador Crackstone. Pulses of red energy shot from both palms toward the Ambassador. The energy was easily dissipated around John and Tem; they felt almost nothing.

"*I have finished my scan,*" John said to his Science Officer. "*I'll join you at the Gremlat craft.*"

John walked slowly to the wrecked craft where Tem was performing a scan. The Ambassador carefully applied three sensors to the skin of the Gremlat wreck, then began his scan. All this while the red energy pulses continued to flow from Tamora's palms and surround John and his equipment.

"Darling," Damnen interrupted Tamora's concentration, "I see no ill effect from your killing spell."

"Curse them both." Tamora ceased her attack.

"*I'm glad she stopped,*" Tem said. "*She might have caused some of our readings to be off eventually.*"

"If we are strong enough to not be killed by your magic, perhaps we are telling the truth," John observed.

"I don't see the connection," Tamora still sounded upset. "If your magic is strong, so is your ability to deceive us."

"If our magic is stronger than yours, why wouldn't we overpower all of you and take this place by force?" John quizzed.

"It appears to me that you have," Tamora forcefully replied. "You have cast a sleeping spell on my entire staff and guards, and you move about in my palace as if you now own it."

"I could have as easily killed all of them, and I could have taken this palace and this entire planet as my own, if I wanted to," John sounded a bit harsher. "But, I didn't, and I won't"

"He may be speaking the truth," Damnen added.

"You just want them to leave," Tamora shot back.

"We will leave, and most likely you will see no more off world creatures until you want to," John said in a more calm tone.

"You told us that the last time you were here, and a day later, here you are, back among us," Tamora replied.

"*Sir, my scan is complete,*" Tem reported.

"Circumstances change," John abruptly retorted.

"What circumstances?" Tamora asked.

"*I too have completed my scan, Science Officer,*" John spoke to Tem. "*What do you suggest we do now?*"

"When we left, we didn't know the Faulid Empire wanted to claim this planet," John curtly replied.

"Perhaps our hosts could show us the bodies of the creatures that occupied these craft," Tem said.

"There should have been pilots to some of these craft," John thought out loud. "They might have even survived their crash."

"There are no such things here," Tamora insisted.

"Should we look in that smaller room to our left?" Tem pointed to a blank wall.

"Open for the magnificent Tem." John manipulated his pad.

A door appeared in the wall just before John opened it and ushered himself and his Science Officer through it. Tamora and Damnen quickly followed them through the door into a much smaller room with three long stone slabs supported by blocks of plain wood.

John and Tem paused beside the first stone slab. A mangled body of a Gremlat Science Officer was almost unrecognizable. The Brem had preformed a death cleansing and mummification ritual on the remains. Tem began scanning the body.

One stone slab was empty, the other had only bits and pieces of a body on it; the sum of parts on the slab gave no clue as to what the creature looked like in life. John began scanning that body.

"This one is Faulid," John spoke up.

"The Gremlat does not have the Allu virus," Tem announced.

"Nor does the Faulid," John added.

"This creature was from one of the worlds that wants to conquer us?" Damned asked.

"Yes, she was," John answered.

"What do they look like?" Tamora asked.

"Do you remember the emissary from Grendela who visited us in the caverns?" John replied.

"Yes, the one who appeared at first as a large Xenthia lizard?" Damnen answered.

"That's what they look like, very tall lizards who walk on their hind legs, and communicate by making noises you cannot hear; their thoughts are silent to you, as are the thoughts of your Drylaque and Kralok," John replied.

"Our magic is strong against them," Tamora proudly announced. "As you can see, they did not live long enough to even stand on my world."

"As soon as they figure out how to fly their craft in your atmosphere, they can kill all of your people in seconds," John said.

"I do not believe you," Tamora stammered.

"You do not have to believe me," John answered her. "We have more to prepare for in order to save your world."

"*I suggest we cloak ourselves in the fourth, no, the fifth dimension until Sam returns for us,*" Tem spoke to the Ambassador. "*Under no circumstances should we transport the Brem to our craft.*"

"*I like your suggestion,*" John answered.

"We have what we came for," John said to Tamora and Damnen, "now we will leave you, and I do hope we never see you again."

"*Cloak now,*" John ordered.

. . . .

Most Confederation craft can cloak themselves electromagnetically, some, from the more advanced societies, can cloak themselves by projecting themselves into another dimension. Almost all species perceived the universe as a three

218

dimensional construct. Mathematically, most advanced civilizations knew the existence of spatial dimensions above three, many Confederation species could use dimensional travel for moving through immense three dimensional distances. But, less than half of Confederation systems could project three dimensional mass into higher spatial dimensions for extended periods of time with no deleterious effects. The most effective method of cloaking was dimensional shifting; ambassador Crackstone's species were the Confederation's leading experts in this technology, a technology not easily shared.

When John and Tem's environmental suits shifted into a higher dimension, it masked anything contained within them from three dimensional observation. What a person saw from within an environmental suit in a higher dimension could be controlled so that the person wearing it could see three dimensional, as well as higher dimensional matter.

Although they were, through their environmental suits, in a higher dimension, they were also bound to three dimensional constraints; they stayed on the same plane as the three dimensional ground beneath their feet, although they could walk through walls.

Most sentient beings existed naturally in three spatial dimensions, however, some existed in the fourth, fifth and seventh dimension. The Confederation had diplomatic relations with all two hundred and eleven species found in the seven known galaxies who were native in dimensions other than three.

. . . .

"How long before our ship comes for us?" John asked his Science Officer.

"By your orders, he should be here in about twenty minutes," Tem replied. "However, he will require at least a half hour more to fully recharge."

"So, we have some time to kill?"

"I would bet on that, sir."

"Shall we make our way back to the chamber under the vortex?" John asked.

Tem agreed as he began walking towards the Temple of Grendela.

"The Brem legends of the gods and their home, Grendela," John mused. "I wonder where that came from?"

"Are you choosing between the Demela and some other source?" Tem inquired.

"That would be my first guess," John replied. "The Demela did create the Brem; in a narrow sense, they were the 'gods' who created this race."

"I actually think the gods of the Brem are in fact the Gremlat," Tem flatly stated.

"Are you speaking as Tem or a Time Keeper?" John asked.

"The Demela created a race of slaves, deaf and with no voice." Tem ignored John's comment. "They probably treated the new race of slaves quite poorly, so why would the Brem revere them?"

"I see some logic in that," John sounded thoughtful.

"The Gremlat and the Demela are both humanoid creatures, and look quite similar," Tem added.

"That's also true."

"The Gremlat killed all the Demela, the oppressors of the Brem, so the Brem would naturally think kindly of the Gremlat," Tem continued, "The Gremlat only stayed a year or so studying this system, then they all left; that also fits the legends."

"If this is Tem speaking, your thinking is quite good," John said. "You are showing great improvement, Science Officer."

"Enough to become an Ambassador soon?" Tem teased.

"Perhaps not soon, but eventually," John chuckled.

"Sir," Tem quickly said, "Tamora and Damnen are headed towards us."

"Can they sense us?" John asked, somewhat confused.

"I would think not, as long as we stay well cloaked."

"Well, we're here, at the Grendela Shrine," John observed. "So, maybe they are coming here to pray for our capture."

"Very funny, Science Officer," John sighed.

"Speaking of the lovely couple, Tamora and Damnen." Tem began a new topic. "I have another insight."

"And, what is that?"

"Before our last mission, I studied a lengthy report on time pirates," Tem said

"What?"

"Oh, I'm sorry, that's my name for the cultures who are obsessed with locating a Time Keeper home world." Tem corrected himself. "You call them Time Keeper Hunters."

"Right." John wondered where this was leading. "How does this fit in?"

"The list of traits that these people look for in a system's DNA includes innate abilities in non-linear thinking, decentralized neural systems, and unconditional affection that goes beyond procreation rituals," Tem replied.

"And?"

"And," Tem added, "think about the relationship between Tamora and Damnen."

"I see your point, but it's kind of a stretch," John sounded puzzled.

"There are factions in the Faulid Empire, and in the Gremlat Collective that are active DNA collectors, all hoping to hybridize their way into being Time Keepers." Tem proudly finished his thesis.

"But," John asked, "the Brem?"

"From the collector's point of view, the Brem may be ten million years from developing into Time Keepers, but that doesn't matter to them," Tem replied. "What matters is the possibility of becoming omnipotent and immortal."

"I never did understand the motivation of the cults that hunt for Time Keeper home planets," John said. "It can't just be a question of DNA, and if it's more then that, what purpose is there in harvesting DNA and cloning hybrids?"

"I can't really say, sir," Tem replied.

"Of course you can, you're a Time Keeper," John insisted.

"As a Time Keeper, I can say that DNA does play a role, so does social development, and so does technological development," Tem replied.

"That's kind of a non-answer."

"Well, it's my answer," Tem added.

"What about the Brem?" John asked. "Are they destined to be Time Keepers?"

"That's a good question," Tem acknowledged.

"You already know the answer to that question," John observed. "Can you tell me the answer?"

"Can you keep my answer to yourself?" Tem asked.

"For how long?"

"Forever."

"I can."

"Yes, the Brem will become Time Keepers."

"Could this be what's behind the Faulid interest in this system?" John sounded surprised.

"If I were a time pirate, I might also wonder about the Demela; they are from the same system and genetically related to the Brem," Tem mused. "The Gremlat may also be interested in both races."

"What I wonder more about is what you haven't told me, and why a Time Keeper has been by my side for three years," John observed.

"We have had a keen interest in you for longer than that," Tem answered. "For longer than you have been alive."

"What does that mean?" John asked.

"I really cannot tell you more right now," Tem insisted. "Please respect me in this."

"How long must I wait?"

"Soon, it will be over soon, and I will answer all your questions," Tem assured him.

"I will trust you," John spoke slowly, "partially because I have no choice, and partially because I actually do trust you."

"You must treat me as if I was just your Science Officer for now," Tem added.

"If what you have told me about the Faulid, Gremlat, Brem and Demela is all true, this makes a complicated problem even more difficult," John pondered out loud. "If the Gremlat are involved, it may not be for territory, but for DNA samples. The Confederation is more tolerant of such adventures in primitive systems, but there is a limit to their understanding."

"Will this change your operations in this system?" Tem asked.

"I think not." John thought for a second, "The Faulid Empire must abide by their treaty. If they choose not to, we must deliver the consequences or they will jeopardize the stability of this whole quadrant and billions may die from the resulting wars."

"The dynamic lovers are right outside the chamber, sir," Tem announced.

"And, I am right above it, sir," Sam announced.

"Please, transport us back aboard," John ordered.

"Once you are, you may wish you remained here," Sam said.

14

Was it something I said?

Sam quickly placed himself in formation with the other Confederation craft between the fifth and sixth planets in the Brem system.

"Analyze this data quickly, Sam," John said urgently.

"I'm working on it now, sir," Sam replied.

"Please check the DNA samples left in the Gremlat craft," Tem added.

"Easy," Sam quickly replied. "It's Brem; Brem from the fifth, uncloaked, planet."

"Now," John took a long pause, "that tells us a lot."

"What does it tell us?" Ambassador Zillway asked.

"It tells us that a group from the Gremlat Collective is out collecting DNA samples from primitive planets," John replied.

"They're hunting Time Keepers?" Zillway sounded shocked. "I wouldn't have guessed."

"Not so quickly, Ambassador Zillway," Sam interrupted. "I am sending the rest of the information to all of you now."

"What?" John demanded.

"The Faulid craft had Brem DNA samples in it as well," Sam said. "The Faulid craft also had been deep within Gremlat space for an extended time prior to crashing on the Brem planet."

"What were they doing around the cloaked planet?" John asked.

"Of course, I can't be sure, but they knew the existence of that planet. Remember the partial mapping of that planet in the Faulid navigation system," Sam replied.

"Did the Gremlat craft also know of the cloaked planet?" Ambassador Zillway asked.

"There is no evidence either way, ma'am," Sam answered.

"The Gremlat have had unofficial contact with the Faulid for some time," John mused out loud. "I wonder how high their contacts were?"

"Perhaps we should ask the Gremlat," Zillway mused. "But for now, what do we do?"

"Sam, send the Commissioner all this information. Immediately." John ordered.

"I have been monitoring," Commissioner Ythantrium interrupted. His image flickered on in front of Ambassador Crackstone and his Science Officer.

"Do you see connections?" John asked the Commissioner.

"I see how this relates to your last transmission to me," Ythantrium replied.

"What transmission?" Ambassador Zillway interjected.

"When this is completed, I will conduct an extended briefing with all of my Ambassadors involved in this new mission," Commissioner Ythantrium said. "But, for now, you all need to pay attention to more pressing business."

"Sir," Sam interrupted. "We have company."

"That's an understatement," Tem added.

"Over five hundred Faulid ships are exiting into this system," Ambassador Zillway announced.

"I see them," John replied. "I suggest we all maximize our shielding."

"I only have class twelve shielding." Ambassador Kundergton quickly entered the conversation.

"I suggest you return immediately to the nearest Confederation planet," John replied.

"He has left, sir," Tem announced.

"Sam, coordinate targets with the other two Confederation ships," John commanded.

"We already have, sir," Sam replied. "It will take one minute and forty seconds to destroy them all, sir."

"What are they doing?" Zillway interrupted.

"They are arranging all the ships in some sort of a three dimensional formation," Tem observed.

"We're waiting for your order to fire," Ambassador Zillway nervously said.

"Should I fire first?" John looked at Tem.

"Perhaps we should position ourselves first," Tem replied.

"I think the two of you should move to flank their formation while our ship stays in front," John, relaying the order to the small Confederation fleet. "We will draw fire while the others start destroying Faulid craft."

"This in an act of war," John communicated to the Faulid fleet. "Leave immediately, or we shall begin firing on you."

"This is Fleet Admiral Xntu of the Faulid Empire, and we demand your surrender," the lead ship replied.

"Why?" John asked.

"This is our territory, and you have destroyed our ships and killed our citizens," Admiral Xntu answered. "We are defending our empire, you are the aggressors."

"Begin firing," John ordered.

Sam's first volley did not destroy the intended target; it seemed to be absorbed by a field encompassing the entire five hundred and twenty Faulid ships. The weapons of the other two Confederation craft did begin to destroy Faulid craft, just not as easily as they should have.

"Sir, we have a problem," Tem shouted.

"My power is only sixty percent, sir," Sam reported.

The Faulid ships coordinated their weapons fire, combining the anti-matter packets into one concentrated stream which paused for a fraction of a second before slamming into Sam's shields. Impact caused a bright flash of photons to stream from the shields in the direction of the weapons fire.

"We have sustained damage," Sam reported.

"What's going on?" John insisted.

"Sir, I don't have enough power to maintain class fifteen shielding any more," Sam quickly replied. "Plus, I never regained all the power I lost in our time mission to Earth."

"Sir," Tem hurriedly interrupted. "They have somehow combined their shielding to convert their individual class six shielding to a class thirteen."

"What about the weapon that just hit us?" John demanded.

"It too is an aggregate technology," Tem replied.

"Fold into another system immediately," John ordered.

"I cannot, sir," Sam replied. "My propulsion systems are damaged."

"Shielding?" John asked.

"Down to class twelve, sir," Sam replied.

"Move us somewhere!" John shouted.

"I cannot, sir," Sam replied. "If I am to maintain any shielding at all, I must not shift any power to propulsion."

"Sir," Tem interrupted. "Ambassador Zillway and Ambassador Hynk have destroyed almost half of the Faulid fleet."

"Can the Faulid formation still maintain their class thirteen shielding?" John asked.

"No," Sam replied. "It's down to class ten, sir."

"Fire on the lead ship only, with every system we have," John commanded.

"Sir!" Tem shouted, then fell silent.

What was left of the formation of Faulid craft slammed them with a huge amount of anti-matter at a high acceleration. As the ship's shields collapsed, a small amount of anti-matter leaked out, enough to annihilate the entire left side of Ambassador Crackstone's craft. Sam's higher functions disappeared, leaving no usable atmosphere anywhere on board.

15

What went wrong, or, what went right?

"Tem?" John Crackstone sounded nervous, slightly lonely. "Sam?"

There was no reply.

"Ambassador Zillway?"

John looked around, then down at himself. He wore an environmental suit as a humanoid, a species that felt familiar. His surroundings were unclear; a background yellowish light bathed the entire scene, leaving details further than a few meters fuzzy at best.

He was reclining on a medical chair; an oversized soft upholstered light brown chair reclining at a thirty degree angle. He thought he could hear some monitoring devices behind him, but when he turned around, nothing was there.

"Is anyone here?" John asked aloud.

No one replied. John thought he could hear some background noise, as if from a busy office, or perhaps a medical facility just out of sight. But, he couldn't make out any visual detail beyond a radius of a few meters. Everything beyond a few meters faded to a blurred, yellow-white light.

All of a sudden, John felt a wave of exhaustion. He melted back into the large, soft chair and fell asleep.

....

"Who are you?"

John rose up, propping himself up on his elbows. To his left, John stared at a male a little less than two meters high, humanoid, two legs, two arms and from a somewhat familiar race.

228

"I don't recognize you," John observed. "What species are you?"

"My name is Matt," The person standing replied, "Matt Johnson."

"Do I know you?" John asked.

"Well, sort of," Matt replied. "For the last few years in your time line, I was Sam, your craft."

"Sam?" John sounded confused. "How is that possible?" He hesitated a beat. "What happened? Where is Tem?"

"I'm here, my friend." A soft female voice appeared on the opposite side of John's chair.

"Tem?" John sounded more confused.

John focused on a female humanoid, the same species as Matt. She was shorter than Matt, and she had much longer hair.

"Why are you in that environmental suit, why am I?" John asked.

"For the last few years in your time line I was Tem, but my real name is Sylvia Johnson," she answered.

"I remember, you told me that you were a Time Keeper on our time travel mission to Earth," John said. The others waited silently, watching John absorb what he had just said.

"You do remember," Sylvia replied in a calm voice.

"What happened?" John asked. "Am I dead?"

"No," Matt replied. "Well, not really dead, but not really alive as you think of it."

"What the hell does that mean?" John demanded.

"The Faulid fleet was completely destroyed by the Confederation, as was the Faulid's ability to wage war for the foreseeable future," Matt answered. "The Brem system is off limits to all other civilizations. The Demela are now confined to their system. Only a small secretive group from the Gremlat Collective were currently involved in the Demela plot, and only to collect DNA samples."

"All right," John asked. "what happened to me?"

"You, your crew and your ship were destroyed by the Faulid fleet," Sylvia answered.

"The Faulid discovered a way to combine shielding and weaponry so that in formations of two to five hundred ships they could muster enough energy to destroy any ship, even the best of the Confederation fleet," Matt said.

"The flaw in their plan was that they could only target one ship at a time," Sylvia said. "And, it took over ten minutes to re-target another ship."

"They were able to kill you, but the other two Confederation ships were able to destroy all of the Faulid fleet before they could resume firing." Matt said.

"So, am I dead?"

"As I said," Matt replied. "Sort of dead."

"I thought dead was one of those dualities," John mused. "Either I am or I'm not."

"In that black or white construct," Sylvia said, "you are not dead."

"I'll cling to that." John smiled. "Why am I humanoid?"

"Because we are," Sylvia answered.

"Could you explain that?" John sounded baffled.

"Matt and I can be anything, anyplace, at any time," Sylvia replied.

"You are both Time Keepers, I assume?"

"We call ourselves the Civilized Universe, but, yes, to you we are Time Keepers," Matt answered.

"What are you?" John quickly asked. "I mean, what species, and where are you from?"

"The Civilized Universe are many different advanced races that are now one race," Sylvia answered. "Matt and I are Humans, from Galaxy G-3, Quadrant C."

"I was there on my last mission, then again just a moment ago on that time travel mission." John looked carefully at Matt, then Sylvia. "That race is not even industrialized in our current time, how could what you say be true?"

"If time were not linear, the end result is all that matters," Matt replied.

"Is your whole race Time Keepers now?" John asked.

"No, just the two of us," Sylvia replied. "In most cases, a race that enters the Civilized Universe has from a few thousand to a few billion individuals, but for our species, only Matt and myself."

"What's even more mind expanding," Matt added, "is that once we become Time Keepers, we all become one being."

"How?" John asked.

"We need to focus on the problem at hand." Matt steered the conversation in another direction. "In your time line, you are dead. Your ship was destroyed, your Science Officer went missing and presumed dead."

"But." John insisted gently, "you say I am not dead."

"In your time line, you are dead, but in a wider reality, you are not," Sylvia replied.

"Within the exclusion zone is the home planet of a Civilized culture in its infancy. That culture is a very important part of us, and we cannot risk the Faulid Empire attacking them and conquering the system," Matt said.

"More importantly, this new species becomes allies with the Brem as their society emerges into a technological species with the capability of traveling to other star systems," Sylvia added.

"How is that possible?" John stuttered. "The Brem are tied to their planet by the fusion power plants."

"Species change," Sylvia assured him. "The Brem slowly lose their perceived magical abilities and cope by developing technology that sustains and improves their lives."

"So, a temporal abnormality didn't exist?" John asked.

"No," Sylvia replied. "A sequence of possible temporal events occurred that would lead to the destruction of half the universe."

"What?" John sounded confused.

"Before you sacrificed yourself in the battle with the Faulid Empire," Matt replied, "the time line eventually included the Faulid's occupation of the area of space we had set aside, plus the Brem system."

"If the Faulid had conquered the Brem and the exclusion area, those two races would never develop into Time Keepers, with dire consequences for this cluster of galaxies, all seventeen of them," Sylvia added.

"Was there a time line where I didn't die?" John asked.

"Yes," Matt replied.

"In that time line, you simply went to the Demela home world, made first contact, then went on to other assignments," Sylvia added.

"So," John asked, "why did you change things?"

"The real problem wasn't the time pirates' DNA plundering, it was the seemingly inconsequential discovery of the Brem's past interaction with the fusion power plants. All that combined with Faulid folded spatial theory," Sylvia added.

"As you already know, the Faulid theory of folded space is incorrect, but it does intersect in a very negative way with the Brem neurological discovery the Faulid were to make after sixty years of Brem occupation," Matt said.

"What discovery is that?" John asked.

"You will discover that for yourself, all in good time," Sylvia replied.

"This is why I died?" John asked.

"Your sacrifice in your time line was necessary for the desired time line to unfold, and in the greater view of the universe, the survival of all of us." Matt said. "And, we saved your life as payment for your sacrifice."

"I may be slightly unclear on all this because I may be dead," John began, "but, what did you say?"

"As members of the Civilized Universe, we can see all possible time lines," Sylvia answered. "The only time line that would fix this anomaly, unfortunately, resulted in your death."

"Can I return home?" John asked.

"In your sense of that request, no," Sylvia answered.

"What does that mean?" John asked.

"Think of a place and of a time that you would like to live out your life," Matt began. "It cannot be the place and time you just left."

"What if that's where I belong, and where I want to be?" John quizzed.

"How can you?" Sylvia asked. "You're dead there."

"We made the assumption that you might like our home planet," Matt interrupted. "You did take an Earth name, and you seemed to like it there."

"Is that why I'm in an Earth environmental suit?"

"This is no environmental suit, you are a human now," Matt answered. "You are as human as us."

"What if I like being a Zizthanthe?"

"That's possible, but you would have to live in the distant past on your home planet," Sylvia replied.

"Does my race become Time Keepers?" John asked.

"Sadly, no," Matt answered. "It's the luck of genetics alone that determines which race has a potential to enter the Civilized Universe."

"But, Tem, or Sylvia, told me it was only partially DNA," John said.

"I had to tell you that partial lie at that particular moment in your time," Sylvia replied.

"Do you mean to tell me that the time hunters are correct?" John sounded surprised.

"Only in that DNA of a race determines if they can become a Time Keeper," Matt answered. "Combining potential Time Keeper DNA with their own DNA will never work."

"In order to evolve into a Time Keeper, a race must also survive long enough," Sylvia added. "Most do not."

"Can I exist among your advanced race?" John requested.

"I am sorry, John," Sylvia said. "Not as a Zizthanthe."

"Can I think about it?" John asked, stalling for time.

"In a non-linear universe, time isn't a factor." Sylvia smiled at John. "Take as long as you want."

"We too can read minds, and escaping isn't an option," Matt added. "This construct that appears to surround us exists entirely within your own mind. Your physical body doesn't exist yet, so you can get off your medical chair and run around all you want, but it will get you nowhere."

"I hear people out there," John sounded weary. "Am I in a hospital?"

233

"What you hear reflects how you perceive the non-linear existence," Sylvia replied. "What you perceive as voices is actually the trillions of individual consciousnesses comprising the Civilized Universe."

"Trillions?" John slowly asked. "I thought you said there was only one Time Keeper being now?"

"That's right," Matt replied with a grin. "One being with trillions of individual consciousnesses."

"Blows your mind," Sylvia chuckled. "In a manner of speaking."

"We all care a great deal about your welfare, and are willing to do everything possible within the constraints of the situation to make your life as enjoyable as possible," Matt added.

"What are the constraints?"

"You cannot exist as yourself in your old time line, where everyone thinks you are dead," Matt answered.

"Why not?" John asked. "All you have to do is appear as Time Keepers and tell Confederation officials that you have restored my life."

"Over the next million years, if your last mission in your past time line had failed, you would have lived a full life, but the interaction of the Confederation, Faulid, Brem, humans and Demela would then result in the destruction of all life in this half of this universe," Sylvia replied.

"You are the linchpin of the entire chain of events leading to this disaster, so you cannot be allowed to exist in your time line any more," Matt said.

"What gives you the right to interfere?" John sounded angry.

"What gave you the right to kill all those Faulid?" Matt asked calmly.

"The Confederation," John flatly replied. "To keep the greater peace."

"We have a far greater view of the universe than the Confederation," Sylvia replied.

"This is becoming a useless argument," John said.

"Right now, what do you want?" Sylvia asked.

"My old life back," John quickly answered.

"As an Ambassador?" Sylvia asked.

"For the Confederation," John insisted.

"When?" Matt asked.

"When I lived."

"By strict definition, you're alive in a nonlinear state, so all time is your time," Sylvia chuckled.

"You're just trying to confuse the issue," John insisted.

"No," Sylvia replied. "To clarify it."

"The only way we could assure that your time line worked out the way it did was to influence you to make the decisions you made, leading up to your death. But, your decisions and related events also led to the confinement of the Faulid Empire," Matt said.

"Now." John smiled. "that is somewhat confusing."

"How?" Sylvia asked.

"I went three thousand years into my future, and two galaxies away," John answered. "I saw not only the Faulid, but several other high level Faulid allies battling the Confederation for a apparently useless planet."

"You did," Sylvia admitted.

"So, how are the Faulid contained if they will be hundreds of millions of light years from their home system fighting over an insignificant star system three thousand years from now?" John asked.

"With the destruction of the Faulid attack fleet and especially the death of their most valuable Senior Ambassador, the Confederation pursues a restrictive policy on the Faulid Empire," Matt answered.

"With that policy in place, the Faulid Empire never makes it to galaxy G3," Sylvia added.

"What about the Time Keeper hunters?" John asked.

"Some of them do make it to G-3, and they do interferer in what would have been Earth's natural course, but that is a harmless part of the natural flow of time," Sylvia replied.

"Does your race interfere all the time in the natural flow of time, or do you alone decide what the natural flow will be?" John asked.

"As a race, we have only interfered four times in the natural flow of time, and those four times were to reset errors introduced by mistakes by non-enlightened cultures, plus one mistake by our civilization," Sylvia answered.

"I find that hard to believe," John quizzed. "You have reset my time travel errors twice."

"We change millions of time travel errors in any time line," Matt responded. "Those are simple resets, we are talking about major mistakes which could lead to the destruction of a large part, if not all of the universe."

"Four times?" John asked. "Over what period of time?"

"In a linear sense, infinity," Sylvia answered with a grin.

"If you people are omniscient and immortal, why did you need me?" John asked.

"The chain of events, that lead to the containment of the Faulid Empire, we could not do ourselves; only you, in your own time line, had that influence," Sylvia replied.

"As with your actions in the Brem system, your future life is entirely your decision," Matt added. "Within the conditions we must adhere to."

A long silence hung in the air as John considered all he had heard up to that point.

"All you know about are five galaxies, we can show you all of them." Sylvia broke the silence. "Perhaps you could choose a place and a time you've never seen before."

"That might be interesting," John asked, "how long will that take?"

"Time is irrelevant, remember?" Sylvia said.

"This is amazing," John sounded bemused. "How did you do this?"

"The how is less important than the result," Matt said. "Where and when?"

"Earth, beginning of the twenty first century, New York," John replied.

"We understand." Sylvia smiled.

"You are quite intelligent, Ambassador," Matt also grinned.

Author's post script
All's well that never ends

Mary Jensen and Adam Zeller married; Sylvia Johnson was a bride's maid at the wedding. Adam stayed at CNN for three years, then moved to New York to work as a print reporter. Mary and Adam had three children, two boys and a girl, The last boy was born five years after their daughter. Their youngest son was named John, a suggestion from their good friend Sylvia. John Zeller didn't look exactly like either one of his parents, but he was a genius, graduating from college at fourteen and receiving a PhD in astrophysics from Berkeley at nineteen. Matt and Sylvia kept in touch with the Zellers, especially with their son as he grew older; John began to call them Aunt Sylvia and Uncle Matt.

Ambassador John Crackstone chose a human form because he was familiar with the culture, and because humans had the genetic predisposition to become members of the Civilized Universe, or Time Keepers as he knew them. Although this race of humans went extinct before they developed into Time Keepers, they did have the genetic predisposition to become Civilized. Sylvia and Matt had told Ambassador Crackstone that the Civilized Universe was indebted to him for his actions in the Brem system; he wondered how indebted they might be.

Matt and Sylvia did prepare John for ascension to a nonlinear existence his entire life, up to his thirtieth birthday; after that, there were three humans in the Civilized Universe. John then changed his last name to Crackstone.

As a Zizthanthe, John's best friends were Tem and his craft, Sam. In his final reality those two were Sylvia and Matt, so life has a way of working out in the end.

I am John Crackstone's older brother; at least I was before he transformed. My grandfather was a doctor in the early part of the Twentieth Century; the doctor who remembered another linear time line where he was a friend of John

Crackstone; my father didn't remember any of this narrative. For reasons unknown, I remember every minute detail of this entire version of reality. My younger brother, Matt and Sylvia have recently visited me, I suppose to see the anomaly first hand. The Civilized People decided this was just an unexpected consequence of their actions; a benign consequence which they would not correct. My knowledge of these events stops here, so I have presented them to you for whatever good they may do for humanity.

The Author

Bob Henneberger has been writing for the past decade, working mostly in Science Fiction and Mystery, He has also written short stories, plays, television scripts and articles for professional journals. He lives in Vermont, close to Lake Champlain with his wife and several cats; not that that's an indication of anything unusual.

www.ingramcontent.com/pod-product-compliance
Lightning Source LLC
Chambersburg PA
CBHW070745180626
46818CB00007B/2991